THE FORGETTING

NICOLE MAGGI

Published by Sourcebooks Fire, an imprint of Sourcebooks, Inc.
P.O. Box 4410, Naperville, Illinois 60567-4410
(630) 961-3900
Fax: (630) 961-2168
www.sourcebooks.com

Library of Congress Cataloging-in-Publication data is on file with the publisher.

Printed and bound in Canada.
MBP 10 9 8 7 6 5 4 3 2 1

To Chris and Emilia, for teaching me the art of love.

But the beating of my own heart
Was all the sound I heard.

—Richard Monckton Milnes, Lord Houghton

PROLOGUE

The last thing I remember is a push. Two strong hands, fighting for their own life, pushing me out of mine. The world went white all around me and then I was gone, forced out of the darkness that had always surrounded me and into the light.

But part of me got left behind.

CHAPTER ONE

The first thing I remembered was a great big push. Air rushed up from my lungs and out of my mouth. My spine tingled from the imaginary touch where the two invisible hands had been, pushing me back into consciousness. Whose were they?

I pulled at my memory. Somewhere nearby, a machine beeped. My eyes would not open; it was like they were nailed shut. The thing nearby beeped again, echoing the drum of my heartbeat. Deep inside I felt a shift, a change within the fabric of my inner being. What had changed? What had gone wrong? My fingers grappled at something, anything, to hold on to… My oboe, where was my oboe? It was never more than an arm's length away from me.

The thing beeped again. In its wake other sounds grew clearer. Voices. Footsteps. My fingers found nothing but air. I balled my hands into fists. Another beep, loud and insistent, right next to my ear, and my eyes flew open.

Spots pricked painfully at my vision. Everything around me was white. The gauze taped across my chest, the hospital gown I was dressed in, the sheets and pillows, even the wires running from my body to the machines next to my bed were white. Nearby, a voice said, "She's awake."

"Baby? Baby, can you hear me?" My mother's face bloomed in front of my own, her mouth and nose covered by a white paper mask. I tried to answer and couldn't. With a little squirm of panic, I realized there was a tube running out of my mouth to a ventilator just behind me. I put my hand on the tube, but my mother gently took my hand in hers. "It's okay, baby. They're going to take that out soon." Her voice was thick behind the mask.

"Her vitals are good," said the other voice. "I'll let Dr. Harrison know she's awake." Footsteps echoed away.

Dr. Harrison. The name was a familiar piece among all the strange bits flying around my brain. I clicked it into place in my memory. The holidays…no, the holidays were over. I'd gone back to school after winter break, but then Mom kept me home because I had a fever. It didn't go away. I furrowed my brow; wading through the memories was like cross-country skiing through deep, powdery snow. I'd gone to the doctor I'd seen since I was a baby. He'd admitted me to the hospital for pneumonia. Was that right? I looked at my mother for confirmation, as though she could understand what I was thinking.

She nodded. "What do you remember, baby?"

It felt like a fever dream. Tests, the prick of an IV going into my arm. Not being able to breathe. The tube down my throat. The machine next to my bed beeping erratically. Alarms going off. Footsteps running. Getting hooked up to even more machines. Something *had* gone wrong… A calm, kind voice explaining to my parents—not me—that my heart was failing and I needed a new one. *"And luckily, there's a match right down the hall…"*

My hands scrabbled at the air again and came up empty. Mom grasped my shoulders, murmuring something that was supposed to be soothing. I shook my head. The motion made my whole body ache. I let Mom ease me backward and raised my hand to my chest, splaying my palm flat over the gauze.

That was the change. The rhythm—*my* rhythm—was different.

My heart was gone.

Someone else's heart had taken its place.

I curled my fingers into claws, as though I could reach through my skin and touch that strange, foreign thing. Mom grabbed my hand, softening my fingers into hers. She was wearing thin surgical gloves. "You're doing amazing. Better than even the doctors hoped." She stroked the back of my hand the way she used to when I was a kid. "Dad's just outside. They only let one of us in at a time. And Colt's here too. He's been dying..."—she swallowed—"waiting to see you, but they won't let him until you get moved to a nonsterile room. I told him to go to school, but he refused."

Mom babbled on but her voice grew dim. All I could hear was the beat of my new heart, a Frankenstein body part that didn't belong. The rhythm of it sounded wrong, like a timpanist slightly off the beat. I dug my nails into my palms. Would my own rhythm be different now? What if this new heart changed the music that had always played inside me?

The door swished open and the nurse came back with a tall, dark-haired woman in tow. I recognized her as the doctor who'd done the surgery. "It's good to see you awake, Georgie," Dr. Harrison said. "Let's see about getting you off this ventilator." She unwound the stethoscope from her neck and plugged it into her ears, then slid the metal disk under the gauze.

"Don't you have machines to do that?" Mom asked.

Dr. Harrison smiled, still focused on my chest as she listened. "Nothing can replace a good old-fashioned stethoscope." She nodded once and slung the stethoscope back around her neck. "Sounds good. Let's look at the printout."

"Right here." The nurse handed her a sheet of paper, leaning over me slightly. She smelled like vanilla and spices. I saw now that the little name tag on her shirt read *Maureen*. A bracelet of yoga beads bulged beneath her surgical gloves. As she pulled back, she caught me looking at her and winked. "Glad you're back with us," she said and tucked a stray hair behind my ear. The gesture made my throat grow hot.

Dr. Harrison flipped through the papers. "Her other organs are responding beautifully to the new heart." She glanced at Mom. "She's definitely at the top end of recipients' recovery. It helps to be young," she added with a little laugh.

"That's wonderful." Tears gathered at the corners of Mom's eyes. "That's—you have no idea—" She leaned her elbows on the side of my bed and buried her face in her hands.

Dr. Harrison looked back at me, as if my mother's display of emotion was happening in another room. "Well, Georgie, I think we can get you off that ventilator. We'll keep you in this room for another day or so and then move you to a regular room where you can have more visitors. Not too many, though. You need to build your strength. You'll be here for at least another ten days—"

Ten days? I might as well have shouted it. Dr. Harrison could see the alarm on my face. "We need be sure that your body doesn't reject your new heart. And give you time to rest too, of course. You'll have a whole new regimen you'll need to get acclimated to." She stopped, maybe sensing that my eyes were about to pop out of my skull. Mom had gathered herself together too. "But first things first. Maureen?"

Having the tube pulled out of my mouth felt like having the *Alien* creature pulled out of my throat instead of bursting out of my stomach. I gulped in air, letting the sweetness of it fill my mouth and lungs. "Long, slow breaths," Maureen told me. I counted in and out, in and out, until I could breathe normally again.

"Good girl," Dr. Harrison said. "I'll check back on you a little later." She turned to go.

"Wait." It came out raspy and hoarse. I took a deep breath. Pain seared across my chest. I pressed my hand there. "Are you sure—everything's alright?"

Beside me, Mom tensed. Dr. Harrison stepped over to the machine that I was still hooked up to by the white wires. Maureen picked up my wrist and placed two fingers over my pulse. For several minutes, the beeping and whirring of the machine were the only sounds in the room. But I could hear my heartbeat as loud as though it was outside my body. It sounded out of tune with the rest of my body.

Finally, Dr. Harrison looked up, and Maureen laid my arm on the bed. "Her pulse is fine," she said. "Strong."

"And I see nothing unusual on the machine."

Mom relaxed with a sigh. Dr. Harrison gave me a tight smile. "It's normal for transplant recipients to feel a little off for a while after the surgery," she said. "I'm sure you'll feel like your old self in no time." She looked at my mom. "Would you like me to update your husband on Georgie's condition?"

"Yes, of course." Mom got up. She patted my leg. "I'll be right back, baby."

The two of them left the room. "Let me arrange those pillows so you're more comfortable," Maureen said.

As she moved around the back of the bed, I looked up at her. "Do you know—who it was? Whose heart, I mean?"

She paused for a moment in her work. "I'm sorry, Georgie. All organ donors are kept anonymous."

"Oh. Of course." I knew that. But as I watched her tuck one pillow behind another, I knew that she knew. It was completely unfair that she knew and I didn't. This person's heart was now living inside me. Didn't I deserve to know their name, at the very least?

Maureen told me to get some rest and dimmed the lights as she left. I lay back on the pillows and stared at the ceiling. What did Anonymous die of? Was it a kid like me? Was there another set of parents in another room grieving over their child? Bile rose in my throat. I took a deep, sharp breath in through my nose.

Don't think about it, I told myself. *Think about Juilliard.* I forced myself to hear the Poulenc Oboe Sonata in my head, tapping out the fingerings on my thigh. But the sound of my new heart interfered, knocking me off the beat. A deep distrust stole through me. Nothing was safe anymore, not even my own heart.

I squeezed my eyes shut. Dr. Harrison said that I would feel like my old self in no time. I curled my fingers into a fist. Was that even possible now that I had someone else's heart? Was I still the same old Georgie?

And as if in answer, I heard the thing that was knocking my new heart off my old rhythm. A pause. A hiccup. A *catch*. Like my heart was thinking about something other than its next beat in that infinitesimal span of time.

Like my heart wasn't beating for me.

It was still beating for its old owner.

CHAPTER TWO

That night I slept badly. In my dreams, I stood on a lonely street corner, waiting for someone to come pick me up. But when a car finally pulled up to the curb, I turned and ran, shadows at my back as I fled across rooftops and fire escapes.

When I woke up, I couldn't shake that feeling of being chased. Maybe it was my new heart, trying to keep up with the rest of my body. That little catch echoed in between my heartbeats. I tried to ignore it as I lay in bed, counting the ceiling tiles. The more I pretended it wasn't there, the louder it became.

Dr. Harrison had glossed over it, but I knew enough about organ transplants to know that rejection was very possible. Was that what the catch meant? Was my body rejecting my new heart? I couldn't go back to sleep. Every breath felt fragile as blown glass. My hands ached for my oboe. It was the one thing that would tether me to my old self.

Another nurse came in the morning to take my vitals and announced that I could move to a regular room. I sunk low onto my pillows while they wheeled my bed down the hall, onto the elevator, and up one floor. My new room was beige instead of white, and no one wore masks.

Mom showed up less than an hour later. She looked a lot better; the circles under her eyes weren't quite so dark. "Dad and Colt are coming later this morning," she said after she'd kissed my cheek and settled herself into the chair next to the bed. She reached for a canvas bag at her feet. "I thought you'd like to see all the cards you got."

I raised the bed so that I sat upright. Mom set the bag gently in my lap. Cards in every shape and color spilled out onto the blanket. "Who sent all these?"

"Everyone." Mom tucked an imaginary stray hair behind my ear. "Everyone was so worried."

I thumbed through the cards from all my friends and teachers, my aunt and uncle and cousins, my grandparents, even the secretaries at school. "People wanted to send flowers, but they're not allowed in the ICU," Mom told me. "So everyone sent flowers and gifts to the house. You'll get them when you come home."

"Did Dr. Harrison tell you when that will be?"

"I haven't seen her this morning, but I'm sure she'll be by soon."

As if on cue, the door opened. It wasn't Dr. Harrison, though. It was the orderly with my breakfast. "Liquids and soft foods for the next twenty-four hours," he told me. "Got to get your system back on track."

I made a face at the mushy food on the tray. "Is any of this actually healthy?"

The orderly laughed. "Sadly, 'healthy' doesn't always mean appetizing." He leaned in conspiratorially. "Tell you what—if you eat one thing on this tray, I'll get you a milk shake."

Mom looked up from the card she was reading. "I really don't think—"

"Oh come on, Mom." I pointed at the orderly. "He says it's okay and he works here." I picked up the least disgusting-looking dish and dug in while the orderly watched. When I was done, I looked up at him, eyebrows raised.

He nodded his approval. "One milk shake coming up. What flavor?"

"Ooh, do you have strawberry? That's my favorite."

"Georgie." Mom shook her head. "She's kidding, of course."

"No, I'm not," I said. "It's always been my favorite flavor."

Mom narrowed her eyes at me. "What kind of meds is she on?"

The orderly reached for my chart at the end of the bed. I looked from him back to Mom. "What does that have to do with anything?"

"Because you can't eat strawberries and you know it," Mom said. Her gaze was hard on me, like she was trying to see into my brain. "You've been allergic to them your whole life." She spoke to the orderly but didn't take her eyes off me. "I fed her strawberry-banana yogurt when she was nine months old, and she went into anaphylactic shock. It was the scariest day of my life…until…"

The orderly held up my chart. "It says right here. Strawberry allergy." He peered down at me. "You have a weird sense of humor."

I forced a laugh. "Yeah. So I've been told." The relief was palpable as he and Mom laughed, and I changed my order to vanilla. As he turned to go, I asked in as casual a tone as I could muster, "So, um, the meds I'm on—*are* they, like, really strong?"

He peeked at my chart again. "Pretty strong. Why? Are you in pain?"

"No, but I—" I made myself shrug. "I feel a little fuzzy. That's all."

"You should talk to your nurse about lowering the meds. That might help."

"Okay."

He smiled at me. "One vanilla milk shake coming up."

"Thanks." I turned my head to Mom. She was still watching me like I might explode at any moment. "I'm pretty tired, actually. I didn't get a lot of sleep last night."

Her face softened and she reached for my hand. "Maybe I should leave you alone to nap. Rest is the most important thing for you right now."

"Okay." I leaned back on the pillows but my whole body was tense. The minute the door closed behind Mom, I sat straight up and wrapped my fingers around my head, pressing into my skull like I could touch my thoughts.

How could I simply forget a lifelong allergy? And it wasn't just that. I distinctly remembered strawberry being my favorite flavor of anything—ice cream, Jell-O, Pop-Tarts. I knew the taste of strawberry, could even recall the feeling of strawberry seeds in between my teeth. How could I know that if I'd never eaten them?

It was the meds. That had to be it. Drugs did things to your brain. My parents had been drilling that into me ever since I could understand the phrase "peer pressure." I eased back onto the pillows. Without effort, a memory surfaced—not of an allergy, but of a cake. *Three layers of shortcake dripping with strawberries...a big number FIVE candle flickering at the top. I lean over to blow it out, a voice whispering in my ear. "Happy birthday, baby..."*

I blinked. The memory was so vivid that I could smell the whipped cream on that cake. But if I'd been allergic to strawberries since I was nine months old, that could not have been my fifth birthday cake. It couldn't be my memory. There was no way.

And in the quiet of the room, that little catch in my heart swelled like a symphony.

I spent the entire time I should have been napping trying to ignore the sound of that catch and racking my brain for any memory of an allergy. It wasn't there. It was just—gone. Was Vicodin really that strong? A little squirmy something inside me told me it wasn't. But that *had* to be the reason. There was no other logical explanation.

Mom returned after "naptime" with Dad and Colt in tow. "Nice hair," my little brother said when he saw me.

Considering that it hadn't been washed since I'd been admitted to the hospital, I could only imagine how my hair looked. "I almost *died* and all you can come up with is 'nice hair'? You're slipping."

Colt sat on the edge of my bed and pinched my leg. "Can you feel that?"

"I'm not paralyzed, you moron."

"Okay, stop it, you two," Dad said. He kissed my forehead. "How are you feeling today, sweetie?"

"Like someone cracked my chest open, ripped my heart out, and put in a new one."

He winced. "Not funny, Georgie."

"I thought it was hilarious," Colt said. He was still pinching my leg. I kicked him. It was a nice distraction. Maybe the strawberry shortcake was at a birthday party that I'd been to when I was five. Memories faded after a while... I had to be remembering it wrong. Except I could remember biting into that cake...could still remember the sweet taste and the feel of the strawberry juice dribbling down my chin. I kicked Colt again and pulled my mind into the present.

The door pushed open and Dr. Harrison bustled in. "How's your new room, Georgie?"

"Great. Thanks."

She read the printout on the monitor next to the bed. "Everything's looking good, really good."

"You're sure?" I regretted the words the instant they were out of my mouth. Mom and Dad looked terrified, and Colt leaned in closer to me like I might sprout wings at any moment and *how cool would that be*? Dr. Harrison lowered the printout, her eyes narrowed.

"I mean, I just wondered, because I feel..." I trailed off. Dr. Harrison looked like she was about to wheel me back into surgery.

"Yes? You feel?" she prompted.

I cleared my throat. "Nothing. I mean, I feel fine. Physically. I just feel…I don't know. Off."

Dr. Harrison half smiled. "It's natural to feel that way. Your body has been through a major trauma. But according to this"—she waved the printout—"everything is absolutely on track."

Mom and Dad relaxed, and Colt pulled back, disappointed.

"Okay," I said, eager to get off this train of thought. "So when can I go home?"

Dr. Harrison pulled a pen out of her coat pocket, wrote something on the chart attached to the monitor, and tucked the pen back into her pocket. "At least another week." I groaned and she gave me a sympathetic smile. "I know, I know. But we need to make sure all your other organs are cooperating with your new heart. And we have to get you used to your new regimen."

"Regimen?"

"Well, you'll be on medication for the rest of your life—"

"The rest of my life?" I clamped my lips together. I hadn't meant for my voice to go up that high.

"To ensure that your body doesn't reject your heart." She made it sound so matter-of-fact but that word—*reject*—was a punch in the gut. "You'll need to learn the signs of rejection—fever and chills, kind of like the flu—and come in immediately if anything like that happens. Most of the time it's just a matter of adjusting your medication."

Most of the time. My face must have registered my anxiety because Dr. Harrison gave my shoulder a little pat. "Don't worry, pretty soon you won't even think twice about it. People who have heart transplants can have healthy, normal lives."

"Yeah, but what's normal now?" Everything seemed to have a new definition. Would I graduate on time? Ace my Juilliard audition and start there in the fall?

"Kelly Perkins climbed Mount Everest several years after receiving a heart transplant," Colt said. We all stared at him. He shrugged. "I looked up how long people live after getting a new heart and she came up."

"How long?" I took a deep breath. "How long *can* I live?"

"A long time," Dr. Harrison said firmly. "And your brother is right; some heart transplant survivors have gone on to do extraordinary things."

"She also climbed Mount Fuji, Mount Kilimanjaro, and the Matterhorn," Colt said. He dug a piece of gum out of his pocket and popped it into his mouth. "Dwight Kroening competed in Ironman competitions after getting his. And Erik Compton qualified for the PGA tour after getting his *second* heart transplant." He chewed loudly.

"Thanks, Wikipedia." I rolled my eyes at him but I'd never been so grateful for his obsessive web-searching tendencies. Still, I wondered if Kelly Perkins heard a little catch in between her heartbeats. "So I'm assuming that if I can climb Mount Everest, I can play my oboe, right?"

"Your oboe?" Dr. Harrison raised an eyebrow.

"My Juilliard audition is in six weeks," I said. "I can still do it, right?"

"Let's just take things one day at a time," Dr. Harrison said. "Your prognosis is excellent. I see no reason why you can't eventually return to your normal activities."

Eventually? What the hell did *eventually* mean? "But the audition—"

"You shouldn't be worrying about that now," Dr. Harrison said. "You need to be focused on your recovery."

My entire family snorted in unison. Dr. Harrison raised her eyebrows. "Georgie has been focused on Juilliard since she was ten," Dad explained. "It would take nothing less than a heart transplant to make her think about anything else."

"Well, she'll have to," Dr. Harrison said. She looked down at me, and her impassive face cracked a smile. "But I anticipate a full recovery. You're doing better than most heart patients I've had. That is one strong heart you have in there now."

My insides shuddered. I didn't want a strong heart inside me. I wanted my old heart, no matter how weak it was. And as if in answer to my thoughts, I heard *IT*. That Catch. I was starting to think of it with a capital *C*. I sucked in air and looked up at Dr. Harrison, but she was talking medical jargon to my parents. If nothing showed up on the monitor, then it was all in my head. Great. Now, on top of everything, I was crazy. The last thing I wanted was for them to wheel me right into the psych ward. That would definitely cancel out Juilliard.

Before they all left, Mom gave me my phone so I could slog through all the get-well emails and Facebook messages. The minute my family was out the door, I did what Colt would do and looked up "pneumonia and side effects" on the Internet. Maybe the fever I'd had with the pneumonia caused memory loss. I searched that too but came up with the answer that memory loss caused by a fever usually equaled a brain tumor. I clicked out of that right away and went to my Facebook page.

That, at least, I could make sense of. All my friends had posted well wishes, and now that I was in a regular room, some of them were planning to visit and there was a back-and-forth conversation about what worked for everyone. As I read through it, I realized how much I had missed. Days of music lessons and orchestra practice, an audition for a community orchestra that my best friend, Ella, had gotten accepted to, classes and tests that I'd have to make up, Sydney's birthday party that had apparently spawned a dozen inside jokes I wasn't privy to, and a class trip to the Isabella Stewart Gardner Museum that I'd been looking forward to for weeks.

I tossed my phone to the foot of the bed and lay back. The big sci-fi machine had followed me to the new room, and I was still hooked up to it for monitoring. But I was allowed to get up and go for a walk. I buzzed the nurse and she helped me to the elevator.

It was hard to go more than a few steps without having to rest. I sat in front of a huge plate-glass window that looked out over the Healing Garden in the middle of the hospital complex. Sunlight sparkled on a rock fountain. The garden looked warm and inviting, but the bare branches that clacked together in the wind told the truth. Boston was freezing in January, and no matter how badly I wanted a breath of fresh air, the nurses would never let me outside.

An old woman in a hospital gown shuffled slowly past me, using her portable IV like a crutch. I shivered and sat on my hands. I wanted out of this place. I needed to be home in my room filled with my own stuff, living my normal life. Maybe then I would stop feeling the Catch. Maybe the reason my heart was out of step with everything was because I was out of step with my old life.

A nurse bustled by, her shoes squeaking on the linoleum. I drew my hands out from underneath me and looked at my fingers. It had been days since I'd held my oboe, the longest I'd ever gone without it. Even when we went on family vacations, I took it with me. My fingers tingled with the desire to play again. Yes...that was the answer. Everything that made me Georgie was at home, and once I got back there I would be myself again.

On the afternoon of my fourth day out of the ICU, my sulking routine was interrupted by a knock on the door. "Georgie? Are you decent?"

I recognized Ella's voice and sat up in bed. "Yes! Come in!"

Ella entered with my other bestie, Toni, on her heels. They both squealed when they saw me and crushed me into the bed in a bone-crunching hug. Literally bone-crunching—my chest incision felt like it was going to split open. "Ow! Open-heart-surgery survivor here!"

"Sorry, sorry!" As Toni pulled back, I saw tears glinting in her brown eyes. "Oh my God, Georgie. You have no idea. We were so worried."

Ella nodded and climbed right up into the bed next to me. She tucked her arm in mine. "It's been *awful*," she said. "Life really sucks without you in it, you know that?"

I leaned my head on her shoulder. "Thanks, El."

"She's right." Toni sat at the foot of the bed and folded her legs up underneath her. "We all miss you."

"I miss you guys too," I said, trying not to sound glum but failing. "It sucks in here."

Ella grinned. "Well, this oughta cheer you up." She hoisted her backpack onto the bed and slid out a familiar square, black case.

"My oboe!" I snatched it from her hands and held it tight against me. All was right with the world again. "How did you—"

"We have our ways," Ella said, tossing her hair back.

"We snuck into your room when we were dropping off flowers," Toni said.

"Toni!" Ella punched her arm. "I wanted her to think there had been plans and blueprints and secret meetings."

I laughed. "Thanks, you guys. You have no idea…" I stroked the brass rivets on the corners of the case. "I don't feel like me without it."

"Well, you can't afford to lose the practice time," Ella said. "I am *not* rooming with some random stranger at Juilliard." Ella played flute. We'd been concocting our Juilliard plan since the fifth grade.

I bumped my knee against hers. "Hey, congrats on getting into the Roslindale Symphony."

"Thanks. I bet I can get you in too."

"Really? But I missed the auditions."

Ella tossed her hair. "So what? They know how good you are. You'll have to go in and play a little something for them, but that's no big deal."

"It might be a big deal getting past my parents, though." I flopped back onto my pillows. "You guys won't believe what they're pulling."

"What?" asked Toni.

"They said they're keeping me out of school for at least *a month* after I get home."

"Are you freaking kidding?" Ella shrieked. "*Why?*"

I blew a hard breath out through my lips. The discussion had gone down that morning, with me being overruled by several variations on *We're the adults and we know what's best*. "My doctor doesn't think it's a good idea for me to go back right away. 'It's too stressful,'" I said in a high-pitched mimic of Dr. Harrison's holier-than-thou tone. "And of course they're following her advice to the letter. My dad's getting one of his professors to tutor me."

Toni's eyes widened. "Seriously? That's amazing."

"*Amazing?* Uh, no."

"Georgie! You're going to have a Harvard professor tutoring you. What kid at our school wouldn't kill for that?"

I scrunched up my face. "Not me. I'd rather be in classes with all of you." It wasn't just that I wanted to go to school; I *needed* to. School was my second home. I fit in there. It was part of who I was. How could I return to my old self without it?

"Will you still get to graduate with us?" Ella asked.

"I freaking hope so." I shook my head. "I can't believe this happened and screwed everything up."

"Georgie, everything's going to be fine." Toni put her hand on my knee. "I know this wasn't part of the plan—"

"The plan, the plan!" Ella said, laughing. "God forbid anything gets in the way of Georgie and her plans!"

I gave her an evil look. "Shut up. You'd be the same way if it happened to you."

She put her hand over her mouth in mock offense. "I like to think I'm a little more devil-may-care than you."

"I can be devil-may-care," I said. Ella and Toni exchanged a look and burst out laughing. I kicked at them halfheartedly. "Fine, whatever. So I like to plan everything out. Big deal." I laid my hand flat on the pebbled surface of my oboe case. "As long as it doesn't affect my Juilliard audition. That's all the matters."

Ella squeezed my arm. "You have nothing to worry about. You're as good as in."

Sitting on my hospital bed, chatting about normal things, I started to feel better. Maybe the reason I'd survived was because I was meant to be a great oboe player like Richard Woodhams. As soon as Ella and Toni left, I flicked open the latches on the case and looked at the three pieces of gleaming rosewood that lay nestled in their blue velvet bed. I fitted them together, dug out a reed from the little case I kept strapped to the inside lid, and stuck it in my mouth to wet it. When it was ready, I slid it into the top hole.

I closed my eyes and breathed out into the instrument. My fingers moved on pure instinct; I had been playing the oboe since I was ten and there was not a fingering I didn't know. It was like an extension of myself, and whenever I wasn't playing, I always felt a little incomplete.

The music swirled around me like a tangible thing. It drowned everything out, and the sudden touch of a hand on my shoulder jolted me so hard, the reed banged against my teeth. "Ow." I looked up to see Maureen smiling at me.

"You're pretty good." She wheeled the blood pressure machine up to the bed. "What was that, Mozart?"

"No, Vivaldi. He was earlier than Mozart." Most people used Mozart as their first guess when it came to classical music. And, to be fair, sixty percent of the time, they were right.

Maureen wound the blood pressure band around my arm. "You must be pretty serious about it. I mean, you did just have a heart transplant." She leaned in and winked. "It's okay to take a break."

I shook my head. "No. I can't. My Juilliard audition is in March."

"I'm sure you could postpone it. You do have extenuating circumstances."

"You can't postpone Juilliard. It doesn't work like that."

The machine beeped. Maureen squinted at it. "Maybe we shouldn't talk about Juilliard. Your blood pressure just shot through the roof."

I picked up my oboe and started to play again. Maureen half

smiled and started the machine again. I was so lost in the music that I barely felt the band squeeze my arm. After the beep, I laid my oboe across my lap. Maureen nodded. "Normal."

"See?" My hands curled around the instrument like a beloved pet. "It's helping me heal."

She ripped the band off my arm, chuckling. "Okay, okay. Just don't let Dr. Harrison see it. She's not as into alternative medicine as I am."

I played well into the night, the sky darkening outside my window. It wasn't just that the oboe kept me calm. As long as I was playing, I couldn't hear the Catch.

CHAPTER THREE

Finally, eight days after waking up from surgery, I got the okay from Dr. Harrison to check out. Maureen gave me my last vitals check before Mom and Dad arrived to pick me up. The thermometer slipped out of my mouth twice as I clenched my jaw up and down. "Stay still," she admonished.

"Sorry."

The blood pressure machine beeped. "Whoa. Maybe we need to get your oboe out."

"That high?"

"Yeah." Maureen adjusted the band around my arm. "Take a few deep breaths."

I concentrated on inhaling and exhaling. In, out…*catch*…in, out…*catch*. There it was. In between every breath, every heart-beat. It was so obvious to me. How could no one else hear it?

Maureen ripped the band off my arm. "What's going on?"

"What do you mean?"

"Well, you're definitely anxious about something." She waved the band in the air. "This doesn't lie."

I squirmed. "It's nothing."

"Georgie, I'm going to have to tell Dr. Harrison and she's probably going to want to keep you here another day for observation."

"No!" I bit my lip and looked down at my lap. The sooner I got home, the sooner I could surround myself with the noise of my life and drown out the sound of the Catch. I couldn't stay in the hospital another minute or I'd lose myself.

"Then tell me what's up."

"Okay." I toyed with a loose thread in my sheets. "I keep feeling this...thing. It's sort of in between my heartbeats. Like a...a catch or something." She didn't say anything so I shook my head. "Forget it. It's probably just in my head."

"Let me take your pulse." Maureen picked up my wrist and counted my pulse against her watch. Her yoga beads brushed my skin. A gentle, calming heat emanated from them. After a minute, she set my hand down. "Your pulse is good. Strong. Steady."

"I'm sure I'm just imagining it."

Maureen tapped her finger on the side rail of my bed. "Maybe. Or...maybe not."

I furrowed my brow. "What does that mean?"

She pressed her mouth into a thin line. When she spoke, it was deliberate, like she was thinking a lot about what she was saying. "Some transplant recipients say they can feel the organ of their donor, that it feels...different. Like it's slightly out of step with the rest of their body."

I sat up a little straighter. "Exactly like that! Does that mean something's wrong?"

"No," Maureen said firmly. "But you do have someone else's heart in place of yours now." She sat down in the chair closest to the bed and rested her forearms on the rail. "The human body is a marvelous piece of machinery. It's designed to work beautifully together. And it does, when everything is working right. Then something goes wrong with one part, and the machine fails.

"You can replace that one part and the machine will work again. That's science, and it's amazing what science can do." Her lips curved into a half-smile. "But there's something beyond science. Call it God or mystery or whatever you want. It's the metaphysical. And I think that's what happens after an organ transplant. Some part of your donor was imprinted on her heart, and now that's inside of you."

I shivered. So I *was* a different person now. "Who was she?" I whispered.

Maureen shook her head. "I can't tell you that."

"If part of her is imprinted inside of me, I have a right to know."

"Georgie, there are rules—"

"Please."

Her features softened. "I'm so sorry, but I can't tell you." She looked over her shoulder and leaned in closer to me. "I really can't," she said, her voice so quiet it was barely there, "because she was a Jane Doe."

My breath froze somewhere between my throat and my mouth. A Jane Doe? As in, unidentified? What kind of person was so alone in this world that no one claimed her, even in death? *A lost girl…*

Maureen rose from the chair and perched herself on the side of the bed. "Listen, I need to take your blood pressure again, and it needs to be in the realm of normal before I can let you leave.

You can't reach for your oboe every time you feel anxious, so let's try this." She put both her hands over her heart and moved them in small circles. "There's a word in Sanskrit—*sukha*. It means sweetness. Close your eyes and just imagine sweetness flowing in and out of your heart."

I rolled my eyes. "Is this some yoga thing?"

"Yes, and it's been known to work. Just try it."

With an exaggerated sigh, I closed my eyes and put my hands over my heart. The warmth of my palms seemed to sink through the layers of skin and bone that separated them from the heart within. After a minute, I felt Maureen gently wrap the band around my arm. I kept up the motion until the machine beeped. I opened my eyes. "One-thirty over eighty-five," she said. "I'll take it."

She rolled the machine toward the door and paused. "It doesn't matter who she was, Georgie," she said. "The heart is yours now. It's what you do with it that matters."

I shook my head as she left the room. How could that be? If part of Jane Doe was imprinted on her heart, how could I ever be myself again? As long as I heard the Catch, as long as I could still feel her echo there, the heart would never be mine.

Our house had never looked as inviting as when we pulled into the drive. The Christmas lights twinkled merrily in the falling dusk. "You guys still haven't taken the lights down?" My parents procrastinated about this every year, but this was a little late even for them.

Mom twisted her head back to glance at me. "We've been a little preoccupied."

"Besides, we thought it would be festive for your homecoming," Dad said.

Festive was an understatement when we walked into the house. A huge banner proclaiming *WELCOME HOME, GEORGIE* hung across the archway leading to the living room. Candles covered every surface, alongside dozens of vases filled with flowers. Colt and half a dozen of my friends stood clustered under the banner, cheering and clapping as I entered. Our closest family friends were there too, along with—

"Grandma!" I lurched forward and buried my face in my grandmother's hair. I breathed in her Shalimar scent, the smell I'd forever associate with her. "I didn't know you were coming!"

"I wanted it to be a surprise," she said, giving me a kiss that I was sure left a perfect imprint of red lipstick on my cheek. "Though your mother wanted to tell you because she was worried about the shock to your heart." She winked. "I told her you could handle it."

"I'm so happy to see you." My throat was tight and the edges of my vision blurred a little. I swallowed hard several times and eased out of her arms. I didn't want my friends to think I was a complete sap who cried over a visit from Grandma. She seemed to understand and gave my arm a little squeeze before disappearing back toward the kitchen.

My friends dragged me into the living room and started the party. They sat me in the oversized armchair and piled presents on my lap. Tray after tray of heart-healthy food came out of the kitchen (the avocadoes must've cost a fortune this time of year), music was turned up, and at one point I looked up to see my parents kissing in the corner. The relief and happiness on their faces mended something inside me, that piece of guilt for the dark circles under my mother's eyes, for the fact they hadn't had time to take the Christmas lights down, that my mother worried about the shock a surprise as lovely as my grandmother might give me. I was home, and we were whole again.

It was very late before everyone left, and even though I begged to have Ella stay over, Mom put her foot down. "You need your rest and I know you'd stay up all night talking," she said. "It's your first night back. You can have a sleepover next weekend."

"I'll call you in the morning," Ella promised. Face half-hidden in a thick woolen scarf, she galloped down the front steps to Toni's waiting car by the curb.

I shut the door and leaned back against it. The house was quiet now, with just the soft whoosh of the central heat and the murmur of voices from the kitchen. Without the pulse of music and the loud chatter of my friends, I heard it again. The Catch. I pressed my hand to my chest. No. Not here. I was home, I was safe. It was just my imagination…

I pushed away from the door and walked back to the kitchen. Grandma stood at the sink, working through the massive pile of dishes. "Need some help?"

"No, sweetie. You sit down."

I sank into one of the chairs at the kitchen table without arguing. I *was* tired. Being in the hospital was boring, which was exhausting in its own way, but being home took energy too. I set my elbow on the table and rested my chin in my hand. "When did you fly in?"

"This afternoon. I was going to come last week, but Liv thought it would be more helpful to have me here after you got home."

"You'll be here a while, right?"

Grandma stacked the last bowl in the dishwasher and smiled at me. "As long as you want, sweetie. I have an open-ended ticket."

I smiled back. Having Grandma in the house always made it seem more lively. Most of my other friends had cozy grandmas, ones who knitted and baked and had short hair. My Grandma was, well, *cool.* She lived in an off-the-grid house just outside of Santa Fe that was covered in solar panels and overrun with rescued animals. She practiced yoga and attended meditation workshops. She didn't knit but she made her own candles, and almost everything she baked had ingredients like sprouted wheat and sunflowers. And she wore her hair in long braids that she spiraled up at the crown of her head.

Mom and Dad sauntered into the kitchen, each with an almost-empty glass of red wine in their hands. "Thanks for cleaning up, Mom," my mother said.

"I'm here to help." Grandma wiped her hands on the dishcloth and tossed it lightly onto the counter. "Anyone up for a game of Hearts?"

"I am!" Colt appeared behind my parents and pushed into the kitchen past them. "Hey, that's appropriate, isn't it? *Hearts*!" He poked me in the arm. I slapped at his hand while my parents groaned at his obvious joke. Grandma, though, looked a little stricken.

"I didn't mean anything by it. I didn't even think—"

"Oh please," I said. "'Heart' is not a dirty word. We can talk about it. Right?" I looked at each of them in turn, at their faces. *Could* I talk about it? Could I tell them about the Catch? Right off, I knew I couldn't talk to my mom. There was still a shadow around her face, the shadow of almost losing her daughter. It was too raw. My dad would pull something like Shelley or Dante or Kipling off the shelf and flip open a page that he thought explained exactly what I was going through. It was like he didn't trust his own words to relate something to me.

Colt would get excited and start looking up all the sci-fi blogs he read and probably tell me that what I was experiencing was most definitely an alien invasion.

But Grandma… I watched her watching me, her bright blue eyes so inquisitive and curious. She hadn't spent Christmas with us because she'd been at an ashram in India. Yes, she was a possibility.

The thing was, I wasn't sure there was anything to tell. It could be the meds or my own overactive imagination. Or I could just be crazy.

I looked at all of them and suddenly wanted nothing more than to be alone. Faking a huge yawn, I got to my feet. Immediately, my parents were at my side, helping me to my feet. "I'm fine," I said. "Just tired."

"Of course, sweetie—"

"You need your sleep—"

I hugged Grandma on my way out of the kitchen. "We'll play Hearts tomorrow for sure. Okay, Grandma?"

"Of course." She kissed my temple. "Sweet dreams, love."

I climbed the stairs and paused at the top to catch my breath. Dr. Harrison had said it would feel like an anvil on my chest for a while, and she wasn't kidding. I pushed myself away from the wall and headed to my room. The dim hall light cast shadows along the walls, and the ancient floorboards creaked under my feet. It was strange, but my gut twisted and my palms tingled as I approached my room, like I wasn't quite sure what I'd find when I opened the door.

Inside, everything seemed to be in its right place. The paisley bedspread, the clothes that I had thrown on the floor the day before I went into the hospital…it was all still there. My music stand and the tall stack of music at its base, just waiting for me. Everything was the same.

But it all felt completely different, like a place I'd never been and had no memory of. Why was my room so *pink*? I hated that vile color. I walked in circles around the room, touching things here and there, trying to relearn them. I stopped in front of my dresser and fingered the jewelry tree with its jumble of necklaces and earrings. I slipped on a big cocktail ring. It rubbed against my skin, like I was borrowing it without asking.

I pulled open the top drawer and fished out a pair of sweats and a tank top to sleep in. A good night's sleep in my own bed... That would fix everything. I turned off the light and crawled under the covers.

I jerked awake after what felt like only a minute. Darkness cloaked every inch of the room. I sat up. Panic snaked through me. This wasn't my room. This room smelled sweet and clean, and moonlight spilled in through a window. I had never slept in a room with a window.

I never know what time it is in my room because no light squeezes in. Even the door reaches all the way to the floor. Dankness clings to the walls and I can't breathe deeply in here, not without getting a mouthful of mold. The air is too close, like there's not enough of it. I grope for the flashlight I keep next to my bed so I won't have to step onto the concrete floor to flip the switch by the door...

But the flashlight wasn't there.

Pain seized my chest. My hand collided with the ornate lamp on the nightstand and I clicked it on. A soft circle of light pooled on the wall. I blinked. I was in my own room, with its plush carpeted floors and large bay window and lamps on each side of the bed. Why would I think I was in a room barely bigger than a closet, sleeping on a cot that was too small for me? Where had that memory come from? I closed my eyes and let the picture form. Clear and vivid, I saw that room. I knew every nook and cranny of that room. But as far as *I* could remember, I had never been there. How could I remember someplace I had never been?

The middle-of-the-night hush closed in on me and the only

sound was the Catch, breathing in between my heartbeats like it was its own being. I moved my hand in slow circles over my heart but there was no sweetness to be found. In the stillness of the sleeping house, I let myself think the unthinkable. The memory of that room didn't belong to me, and neither did the memory of that strawberry shortcake.

Those memories belonged to the previous owner of my heart.

CHAPTER FOUR

I eased back on my pillow and stared at the ceiling. Slivers of moonlight slit the dark, illuminating things in pieces. A shard of my closet door, a fragment of the dollhouse in the corner that I hadn't played with in years. It was crazy. How could I have memories that didn't belong to me? But they were there, as crystal clear as other memories I knew were mine. My heart donor had slept in that room. I *knew* it. Just as I knew she had loved strawberries and hated pink.

I rolled onto my side and stared at the shadow the lamplight made on the wall. This was insane. Was it, though? Reports I'd found online often said that transplant recipients retained something from their donor, like a sudden sweet tooth. Was it that far of a leap from a sugar craving to a memory?

Well, yes. It was a pretty big freaking leap. I stared at the old-fashioned alarm clock on my nightstand. The hands pointed to four thirty-three. Now fully awake, I could easily think that it had been a dream.

But it wasn't. I knew the difference between a dream and a memory. And I hadn't taken a Vicodin since the strawberry incident. Despite the whir from the heating vents, cold swept over my bare arms. I pulled the covers up to my chin but I was wide awake now and there was no way I could get back to sleep. Even under the heavy comforter I was cold, cold down into my bones.

I leaned over and opened my nightstand drawer. The scent of lavender wafted into the air from the potpourri sachet Mom had given me for all my drawers for Christmas. I pulled out scarves and trinkets and funny cards that Ella had given me over the years and laid them all in a careful semi-circle on my bed.

Each item represented something special: a birthday, making the National Honor Society, the summers I spent at Interlochen. This was who I was, not some stupid memory of a bedroom belonging to a girl I'd never met. What mattered was where I went from here, and where I was going was Juilliard.

I picked up the music-note pin I'd worn to my very first recital. What mattered was the future—*my* future—and no one could take that away from me.

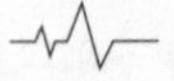

When I turned up in the kitchen the next morning for breakfast, Grandma handed me a bowl of oatmeal. "Heart-healthy and delicious," she told me after I made a face at the mush.

"I guess I have to learn to like it, huh?"

"I put brown sugar in it to sweeten it up." She sat down across the table from me, a steaming mug of coffee wrapped in her hands. "How are you feeling today, sweetheart?"

I dug my spoon into the thick oatmeal, not meeting her eyes. "Okay, I guess. My chest still hurts a lot."

Grandma grimaced. "Didn't they give you something for that?"

"Yeah, but I hate taking it. It makes my head feel weird." That was true. But I knew the drugs weren't to blame for the memories.

"Well, better that than being in pain, right?"

I shrugged and swallowed a spoonful of oatmeal. It was actually pretty good, and I couldn't really remember why I hated it so much. Great. Another thing I couldn't remember.

Grandma took a sip of her coffee, looking at me over the rim of her mug. "What's wrong, sweetie? You don't seem like yourself."

"I'm not." I stared down into the bowl, swirling the brown sugar into an endless spiral. "I have someone else's heart inside me. I'm not me anymore."

"Oh, Georgie." Grandma put her cup down and came around the table. She cupped my cheek. "Of course you are."

I leaned my face into her palm and looked up at her. "But what makes a person? Isn't it their heart? If mine is gone, who am I now?"

Grandma pulled one of the other chairs next to mine and sat in front of me, our knees touching. "You are still the same person, Georgie. The heart is just an organ. It's what you do with it that matters. Your thoughts and dreams and memories make you who you are."

Memories. I took a deep breath. "But what if—I'm remembering things that aren't my memories?"

Grandma pulled back a little, her hand dropping to her lap. "What do you mean, sweetheart?"

I chewed at my lip. "I forgot I was allergic to strawberries."

"Your mom told me about that." Grandma tilted her head and

smiled. "You'd just had major surgery, sweetie. You were still groggy. That's all it was." She reached out and took my hand in hers. "I know you're scared, Georgie. You just went through a trauma. But you survived and you are going to be *just fine*."

She sounded like she was saying it to reassure herself more than me. I stared into her overbright eyes and tried to imagine what it must've been like, waiting by the phone to get updates from my mom while I was in the hospital. They were all so worried about me. I couldn't tell her about this. I'd just have to figure it out on my own.

I squeezed her hand. "I'm so glad you're here," I whispered and picked up my spoon again. It took a few swallows of oatmeal to get the lump out of my throat.

Grandma pushed back from her chair and stood up. "I have something for you, actually." She bustled out to the hall and came back a minute later with something wrapped in tissue paper. "I thought this might help you heal. Give you sweet dreams."

"You didn't have to get me anything." I unwrapped the tissue paper to reveal a dream catcher. Spidery threads stretched across the hoop, and long, fluffy feathers hung down the sides. "It's beautiful. Did you get it at that store we love in Santa Fe?"

Grandma blinked at me. "No, sweetie. It's from your bedroom at my house. You always said you sleep better there than anywhere else, so I wanted to bring a bit of that room to you here."

I traced the intricate web with a shaking forefinger. "It's from my...bedroom?"

"Don't you recognize it?"

No, I didn't recognize it. Not only that, but I had no memory of my room or her house at all. I squeezed my eyes shut, fighting to pull up a picture, an image, even just a fragment of her New Mexico house. I knew it existed, I knew I'd been there, but I could not see it in my mind. It had disappeared.

I sucked in a hard breath and opened my eyes. "Of course I do," I told her. "It was so sweet of you to bring it here to me."

Grandma examined my face. "Are you okay, sweetheart?"

"Yes. I'm just…tired. I think I'll go lie down." I stood and cradled the dream catcher in my hands. "Maybe this will help me rest," I added with a forced smile. "Thanks for the oatmeal."

Once in my room, I closed the door and leaned against it, breathing hard. The dream catcher fell to the floor and sat there, mocking me with its gentle swoops and curves. How could I not remember my grandmother's house? I'd been there dozens of times since I was a little girl. I could even remember riding horses through craggy valleys along desert trails. But the memory of the house was gone, like a puzzle missing that last important piece.

And in its place was the memory of a dank basement room where I had never been.

If she was going to hijack my memories, I *had* to know who she was. That thought permeated my brain as I sunk myself into my music all that day and the next, practicing the Poulenc Sonata—my audition piece—over and over. There was one phrase that I just couldn't get in the Scherzo section, that my fingers just couldn't grasp, and I attacked it like a war general, battering at it until Mom knocked on my door. "Georgie, we have to leave for your checkup."

I sighed and put my oboe away. I was barely out of the hospital and yet I had to go back for a follow-up. All the way to the hospital I heard the Catch, drowning out the notes of the Poulenc. What else was Jane Doe going to take away? And what about the memories I didn't yet know I'd forgotten? My heart started to pound. I could've forgotten a whole lifetime already and not even know it.

As Mom checked us in, I shifted my weight from one foot to the other and counted off the memories I'd lost. My allergy. Grandma's house. Then I counted the ones I'd gained. Strawberries. A dank, dark basement bedroom. I'd lost two...and gained two. I froze in mid-shift, balanced on my right foot. I was losing a memory for each one I gained.

I set my foot down and stared at the Van Gogh print over the Admissions desk. The colors swirled. I dragged my mind back over the last several days. Yes, two whole complete memories had been placed into my brain and two had been taken out. A fair trade. Maybe the brain could only hold so much information, and when Jane Doe forced herself in, she forced something out.

In a daze, I followed Mom to the waiting chairs and sat down. I picked up a magazine and pretended to read an interview with a plastic surgeon to the stars. Had it happened the moment they removed my own heart from my body and put Jane Doe's in?

But what did the heart have to do with memory? Were memories contained in the human heart? If that was true, then what Grandma and Maureen had said was a lie. It wasn't just an organ. It made me who I was, like my soul.

I pressed my fingers to my forehead. I wasn't a philosopher, for crap's sake. These were big questions; how was I supposed to know the answers? All I knew was that I now had two memories in my head that weren't my own, and I wanted to know whose they were.

Mom nudged me. I looked up. The nurse was calling me into the office. I dropped the magazine on the empty chair next to me. As Mom stood, her phone buzzed. "Shoot… It's my editor. Do you mind if I take this, honey? I'll meet you in there."

"Okay." I followed the nurse into a small beige room with an oversized chair. I sat in the chair and she hooked me up to the same kind of heart monitor I'd been on in the hospital.

"Dr. Harrison will be in soon," she said and whisked out the door.

The machine beeped, bringing me back to the moment when I'd first woken up in the hospital. Everything had felt different the instant I'd become conscious. I'd known that something was *off*. The machine's beeps grew distant as I turned inward and listened hard to the Catch. Was Jane Doe trying to tell me something?

The door opened and Dr. Harrison bustled in, Mom on her heels. "Hi, Georgie. How are you feeling?"

"Okay, I guess."

"Good, good." She went straight to the machine and checked it without looking at me. Mom hovered over me, alternately sitting on the arm of the chair and pacing in front of it. I wished her editor would call her again.

Dr. Harrison marked something off on the machine's print-out and finally looked up. "So how is it being home? You taking it easy?"

"Yes."

"Good." She peered over my head at Mom. "I don't want her to start with her tutor for at least a few more days. Absolutely no stress." She perched herself on the arm of the chair and arranged her features into her "bedside manner" expression. "I know we spoke a little bit about rejection but I want to be sure you understand the symptoms."

"Fever, chills, flu-like symptoms," I recited.

She nodded approvingly. "That's right." She switched the machine off and removed the pads from my chest.

As she turned to go, I reached out and touched the sleeve of her crisp white coat, just enough to make her pause. "Does it really have to be anonymous?" I said, so low that if the machine had still been on, she wouldn't have been able to hear me. "Why can't I know who she was?"

Her head turned so sharply I thought it would snap. She raised an eyebrow at me. "You shouldn't even know that she's a she."

"Oh. No..." I shrank into the chair. That nurse, Maureen, had been so nice to me and I didn't want to get her in trouble. "I just guessed. I mean, can you give a male heart to a female recipient?"

"Yes, you can." Dr. Harrison folded her arms across her chest.

"Your curiosity is only natural, Georgie. But donors have to be kept anonymous to respect their family's privacy. It's the law. After a length of time, you can contact the United Network for Organ Sharing, and it's up to the family to release any information about the donor. Now," she said with forced casualness, "I need to run some lab work. Just wait here and a nurse will be in to take some blood."

But I couldn't wait for that; I was losing my memories *now*. Besides, if she was a Jane Doe, then she didn't have any family. UNOS wouldn't have any information to release. I squirmed in the chair, trying not to let my desperation show on my face.

The door opened and the front-desk nurse peeked her head in. "I'm sorry, but I have a question about your insurance, Mrs. Kendrick."

Mom sighed and went out into the hall, muttering, "They never get it right," under her breath. Dr. Harrison followed her out, leaving me alone again. I squirmed against the chair. I understood why they had to keep organ donors anonymous. But my case was different. I mean, I was remembering things from her life, for crap's sake. Didn't that entitle me to some information?

Several minutes later, the nurse still hadn't come to take my blood, and Mom was still MIA. I slid off the chair and poked my head into the hall. "Hello?" No answer. Voices murmured from a couple of doors down. I tiptoed to the open door and was about to reach around to knock when the conversation inside stopped me.

"...said nothing to her. It must've been one of the other nurses."

"Well, I'd like to find out who. That's a serious lapse." It was Dr. Harrison's voice.

"It doesn't seem like she knows any more than the gender of the donor. That's not so bad."

A loud sigh. "I suppose not. As long as she doesn't find out more. Do *not* tell her anything if she asks."

"Of course I won't. Can you imagine if she knew?"

Knew what? I inched as close to the door as I dared. *Say it, say it, say it…*

"Well, I would think that she'd still feel lucky to be alive. It doesn't matter how the donor died."

"Still…*suicide*… It's so sad."

I stumbled back, thankful for the carpeted hallway to hide my footsteps. My ears buzzed. Somehow I made it back to my chair and collapsed into it a moment before the door swung open and a nurse entered, carrying a tray with a needle and four vials.

"Hi, Georgie," she said, and I recognized the same voice that had just uttered the word "suicide." I stared dumbly as she inserted the needle into my arm. My blood flowed into the vials, one after another, its dark red stain proof that I was alive. *Suicide.* I had life because Jane Doe had taken hers.

From the research I had done, I knew that a transplanted heart had to be the same size as the recipient's. That meant that my donor had been my age, or close to. She had been young. And she had been so hopeless as to take her own life. Tears leaked out of the corner of my eyes. I blinked fast to keep them from falling on my face.

"Almost done," the nurse said cheerily as she swapped the third vial for the fourth. I wanted to slap her. When she was done, she taped a piece of gauze to the needle-prick site and folded my arm up. "Just sit still for a minute before you leave."

"Okay." It came out a little strangled. I kept my head turned from her as she left. As soon as the door closed, I wrestled my phone from my jeans pocket and brought up Google. I typed in "Boston suicide teenage Jane Doe" and waited for the page to load.

How could no one know who she was? What kind of life had she led that no one had come forward to identify her? Where were her parents? A pang thrummed inside me. Were there really people on this planet that no one cared about?

The page finished loading a number of random, unrelated pages. But at the top, there was a link to a Boston police precinct website, dated the week before I'd gone into the hospital. I tapped it. A short paragraph popped up.

> Police are investigating an apparent suicide attempt by an eighteen-year-old female on the night of January 17. Authorities say she jumped off a fifth-story balcony at 826 Emiline Way and lay for several hours before being discovered by a man walking his dog early the next morning. The girl is in critical condition at Massachusetts General Hospital and not expected to live. Police have been unable to identify her. Anyone with any information is asked to call the BPD Hotline at 617-481-5162.

I pressed my palms against the chair to keep my hands from shaking. That had to be her. Same time frame, same hospital. They must have tried to identify her for several days before declaring her brain-dead. I went into the hospital on January 22. My heart failed a day later, and I was bumped to the top of the UNOS list. How lucky that there was a perfectly matching heart just down the hall from me.

Still, I didn't get it. If she committed suicide—if she had wanted to die—why was she still holding on to life? *My* life? Why were her memories still present? Shouldn't she—and her memories—be off floating in some afterlife-y fourth dimension or something?

Mom popped her head in the room, a harassed look on her face. "I think I finally got that straightened out," she said. "Ready to go?"

"Yeah." I slid off the vinyl chair and followed her out of the office, out of the hospital, down to the parking garage, and into the car. Night was falling as we emerged onto the street, the lights of the Boston skyline twinkling against the dusky gray sky. Was Jane Doe haunting me? I pressed my hand to my chest. Was I possessed?

Beneath my palm, my heartbeat alternated with the Catch. Somehow that didn't seem right. I didn't think I was possessed. But Jane Doe *was* in there, her memories imprinted on her heart that now beat in my chest. And maybe the Catch was an echo of her, a reminder that this lost girl who had killed herself, all alone, had existed.

I curled my hand into a fist against my heart. All I wanted was to get on with my life. Play my oboe, go to school, and be normal again. But it seemed like Jane Doe had other plans for me.

And if that was the case, then I needed to know who the hell she was. Because no one but me controlled my life. No one.

CHAPTER FIVE

How did one find a lost girl? I wasn't even sure she wanted to be found. I was working purely on guesswork in a territory I had never known existed. But I had to do something before I lost another memory. And I did have one solid piece of information.

I had an address.

826 Emiline Way. As soon as we got home, I went up to my room, closed the door, and sat on my bed. I pulled up the police website on my phone again and tapped the blue-highlighted address. Google Maps launched and clocked 826 Emiline Way at five miles away. So close.

But in a city like Boston, with its twisty streets, you could never just go from Point A to Point B. You had to go to Points C, D, and E first. I would have to take two buses and then the T to travel the five miles from my house to 826 Emiline Way. I couldn't drive; that wasn't allowed until my chest was fully healed. Two buses and a T ride wasn't a hop, skip, and a jump. It was like a long and winding hike over two valleys and a river. I couldn't climb the stairs without my chest hurting, so I wasn't sure I could travel that far without serious pain.

Not to mention I'd have to come up with a really good excuse for why I was leaving the house at all. Also, there was no way my parents would ever let me go to Mattapan without an armed escort. There was a reason its local nickname was Murderpan.

My brain clicked and whirred all through dinner and the Hearts tournament that Colt insisted on playing afterward. I lost spectacularly, finally calling it a night after Colt had shot the moon for the third time.

"I've got nothing more to teach you," I said, slamming my cards down. "The pupil has become the master."

Colt punched the air with his fist. I laughed and headed upstairs, my smile disappearing the moment I was out of sight of the kitchen. I closed my bedroom door and leaned on it for a moment, taking shallow breaths until the ache in my sternum eased.

I could ask one of my friends to drive me to 826 Emiline Way, I thought as I changed into my pajamas. But if I told them why, they'd think I was crazy. This was so far out of the realm of things I could trust them with. As I pulled my shirt off, I caught sight of my bare chest in the mirror, the ugly red scar bisecting my body. That scar was like a wall between me and everything that made me who I was. The instant they'd removed my old heart, they'd disconnected me from my life.

I tugged my tank top over my head, the scar just peeking out from the neckline. Maybe my friends could still be useful, even if I didn't tell them what was going on. As I crawled into bed, I began to formulate a plan to get me across those five miles to 826 Emiline Way.

"You're sure Ella can drive you home?" Mom asked as she steered the car to the curb in front of the Roslindale Community Center.

"Yes." I unbuckled my seat belt and leaned over to kiss her cheek. "Don't be such a worrywart."

"Fat chance." She peered over my shoulder at the building. "Are you sure about this? You should be at home resting—"

"Going out of my mind is more like it," I said. "I'm just going to sit and listen. Nothing strenuous."

"And what time does the rehearsal end?"

"Nine."

Mom pressed her lips together. "I don't know—"

"If I start to feel tired, I'll call you to come pick me up. Okay?"

It was the right thing to say. She settled back into her seat. "Okay."

I slid out of the car and shut the door. Conscious that she was watching me, I climbed the steps to the hall very slowly. When I reached the top, I turned and waved, backing toward the entrance. She waved back and drove off. For a moment, I stood on the threshold to the community center, listening through the open door.

The orchestra was warming up, a violinist practicing scales, a cello sighing out the thematic through line of Tchaikovsky's Fourth Symphony. I could just forget this whole thing and go inside. That was where I belonged, not tracking down some unknown girl at some godforsaken address in a bad neighborhood. A bassoon joined the cello, their voices in perfect synchronicity. I should be with them. I should be playing my oboe right now. That was my life.

A gust of wind blew the door shut, cutting me off from the orchestral sounds inside. I hugged myself. I couldn't go back to that life until I figured out what was happening to me. What if the next memory I lost was of my oboe? I dug out my cell phone and dialed the number of the car service I'd stored in my contacts earlier.

"Are you sure this is the right address, honey?" the driver asked fifteen minutes later, twisting around in the front seat.

"Yes," I said, but looking out the back window, I wasn't so sure. The street was desolate, lit only by a dim street lamp that flickered on and off. The building at 826 Emiline Way was dingy, with a crumbling facade and a couple of boarded-up windows.

"You want me to wait?"

"No, that's okay." I handed him the fare through the window and opened the door. The cold wrapped itself around me like an icy blanket. I walked away from the car without looking back, but he didn't pull away until I was at the stoop.

There wasn't one light on in the whole building. I tilted my head back, counting floors. At the fifth-floor level, a bright piece of yellow tape caught my eye. It dangled from a small wrought-iron balcony, flapping in the wind. With an inward punch, my breath left me. That was where she'd jumped.

I stumbled backward, my feet tripping over each other on the ground where she must have landed. And lain for several hours, her life bleeding out of her, until someone found her. Bile rose in my throat. I doubled over, retching on the sparse patch of weeds next to the stoop. Pain arced across my chest until I heaved out everything that had been inside me.

Panting, I dropped down to sit on the stoop and fished in my bag for the bottle of water I always had on me. I rinsed my mouth out, then swallowed half the water in the bottle. Closing my eyes, I forced myself to take long, even breaths.

I wasn't cut out for this. I should've stayed at the community center. The streets I existed on were leafy and clean, well lit and full of people. I had never been in a place that felt lonelier. I placed my hands over my heart and circled them. *Sweetness*, I thought. *Sweetness*. No warmth came this time. The cold concrete seeped under my skin, chilling me to the bone. I should just go home. Did I really need to know who this girl was?

The answer shattered through me so hard my eyes flew open. *Yes*. I had to know. I didn't care what Maureen or Grandma or anyone said. I couldn't move forward until I knew whose heart this had been. The Catch whispered in my ears, like Jane Doe's voice guiding me. *If you want me to belong to you*, it seemed to say, *you have to know who I used to be*.

I picked myself up and stood for a moment, hugging myself against the cold. I wanted my life back. And if I had to visit the loneliest corner of the city to get it, then that's what I'd do.

Outside the door was a row of mailboxes and an intercom. I buzzed next to the stuck-on label reading "Landlord," but there was no answer. I glanced up at the windows again. I didn't want to buzz anyone else. Who knew what would come to the door?

I dug through my bag until I found a pen and a piece of paper. I scribbled a vague note asking about vacancies in the building, signed my name and cell number, and shoved it in the landlord's mailbox. I checked my watch. I still had two hours before I was expected home. Shivering, I glanced up and down the street. If Jane Doe had come here to die, it made sense that this was a neighborhood where she hung out. Maybe a little exploration would yield a clue.

At the curb where the cab had dropped me, I looked left and right. Taking a guess, I turned left. The Catch got louder. I turned right at the next corner, then left again. Cold wind blew down the empty sidewalks, skittering a candy wrapper across my path. My footsteps echoed on the pavement. I glanced over my shoulder, but the street here was as lonely as back at 826 Emiline.

My incision started to ache. This was *weird*, knowing exactly where to go in a place I'd never been, moving without thinking. My steps were usually so deliberate and measured, and now my unconscious mind propelled me forward. I rounded the corner onto a long stretch of dark road. Shabby brownstones, practically built on top of each other, lined one side of the street while a tall, wrought-iron fence ran along the other. I peered into the expanse beyond the fence. Rows and rows of uneven headstones dotted the hill that sloped away from the street. I took a step toward the cemetery.

The memory came so strong and fast that the wind was knocked out of me. *A full moon rises above the cemetery gate, lightening the iron from black to gray. Headlights sweep the potholed street, pooling on the pavement as the car pulls to a stop. The door opens. It's dark in the car, so dark that I can't see who or how many people are in there.*

No one speaks, but I know that I have to get in. I know I have to… but I don't want to… I don't want to…

Air returned to my lungs. I gulped it in and straightened. My mind spun, trying to wrap around why Jane Doe was here, why the car had come for her. I crossed to the cemetery and pulled at the gate. A chain looped through the iron bars rattled, breaking the stillness of the street. An instant later, light swept across the length of the fence.

I whirled around. A silver sports car had turned onto the street. It slowed as it approached, just like the car in Jane Doe's memory. I pressed myself into the wedge between the gate and the concrete base of the fence. But when the car reached me, it flicked its high beams on and I was blinded by white-hot light.

I threw my hand up to shield my eyes and blinked, trying to see. The driver's window rolled down. I gripped one of the bars behind me, my heart thudding in my chest. I had nothing to protect myself; the sharpest thing I had in my bag was a lip pencil.

Over the soft hum of the car's engine, a disembodied voice floated into the night. "Hey, baby, it's my birthday."

"What?" Confused, I let go of the gate and took a step toward the car. Out of the bright light, I could see the speaker clearly as he leaned out his open window. Gray hair framed an over-tanned face, his skin the orangey shade that you got from a cheap bottle. The absurd thought that if he drove a car that nice, he should be able to afford a better fake tan flashed through my head. "What did you say?"

The man squinted at me and pulled back a little. "I thought you were someone else. Where's—"

"Yo, birthday boy, wanna surprise?"

I stumbled back, the new voice brash against the dark, still night. High heels clicked on the pavement toward the car and a girl, no older than me, emerged from the shadows across the street. Her tight minidress impeded her strides as she teetered over to us.

Throwing me a malevolent look, she tossed her long, black hair back and bent to lean on the car window. "Hey, sugar."

The man glanced from the girl to me. "Where's the other one? The blond? I always meet her here."

The girl spoke in a purr. "She's old news. I'm here for you now."

His eyes flicked back to me and then fixed themselves on the girl's cleavage. "How much for both of you?"

She straightened, her hip thrust out as she turned to me. "Two-fifty an hour. *Each*."

My voice finally found itself. "What? I'm not—I don't—*no way*." I backed away from the car, my hands in front of me like a shield.

The girl arched her back. "Guess you get me all to yourself," she told the man in the car.

"I want both. It's my birthday."

"I thought it was *always* your birthday," the girl said, giving him a slow wink.

"Well, today it actually is, and I want both of you."

The girl looked at me, her eyes narrowed. "Come *on*."

"No!" It came out as a shriek and echoed over the empty street. Nearby, a dog barked.

"Hey, I don't need any drama." The guy glanced up and down the deserted street. "I'll go somewhere else then." The car revved to life. Just as he peeled away from the curb, I remembered what he'd said. *Where's the other one?*

"Wait!" I called. "What did you mean—" But it was too late. His tires squealed as he took the corner without slowing down and disappeared.

The girl rounded on me, her dark eyes flashing. "What the fuck was that?"

"I—"

"That guy serves himself up on a silver platter and you say *no*?"

"I'm not—"

"Jules is gonna tear you a new asshole when he hears about this."

"I don't even know who Jules—"

"And Jules told me this was *my* meeting place now." She stepped right up to me, her nose inches from mine. "It woulda been nice if he'd given me a heads-up about the company."

I took a step back. "Look," I said, "I'm really sorry. But there's been a misunderstanding. I'm not—not a—" I stopped. The girl's face pinched up and she put her hands on her hips, daring me to say the word. I swallowed hard. "What did he mean," I said, jerking my head in the direction the car had sped off, "about the other girl who used to hang out here? The blond?"

The girl surveyed me for a long moment. I forced myself not to look away. Despite her tight skirt and heels, she looked like she could beat me up inside a minute. She planted her hand on her hip. Her nails were bitten down to the quick.

"Why do you want to know?" she said.

"I'm looking for her. That's why." I mirrored her stance—chest thrust out, hands on my hips.

She smirked at my lame attempt at bravado. "Well, you'll be looking a long time. Jules told me she's dead."

"Jules is your—um—handler?"

"Yeah." She snorted. "My *handler*." She tossed her head and her dark hair slithered around her shoulders. "Look, all I know is a few weeks ago, he told me I should take this spot, and it's a better shithole than the shithole I was in, so I took it."

"Did he say what happened to her?"

"No, and I didn't ask." She stared over the fence at the gravestones beyond. "I know when to shut up and do what I'm told."

Footsteps reverberated from around the corner. The girl squared her shoulders and perched at the curb. "You better go. I don't want you fucking up another one of my deals."

"But—"

"*Go.*"

I didn't want to tell her I had nowhere to go. A figure appeared across the street and she backed up. "Oh, great. Here comes the knight in shining armor." She jabbed her finger at me. "This is *your* fault. He probably heard you yelling your head off."

I backed up into the shadows of the gate. The "knight in shining armor" crossed the street. "Everything okay, Char?"

"It *was* before you got here."

"Thought I heard someone yell."

"It was nothing."

I shifted against the cold iron. From my new position, the dirty yellow light of the street lamp fell over the newcomer. My breath caught. *Blond hair, blue eyes*...the memory was instant. Before I could stop myself, I moved out from the shadows. "Nate?"

The boy turned, confusion written on his face. "Yeah?"

"What—are you—doing here?"

He squinted at me. "I'm sorry. Do I know you?"

I stumbled back a step. "Ye—no," I corrected myself. My insides twisted and turned with something other than pain, other than the Catch; something I had never felt before. Something I had read about in books and dreamed of but never experienced.

He didn't know me. And I—*Georgie*—didn't know him. But Jane Doe did. She knew everything about him, and now I did too. I could feel it all around the heart, the knowledge of him imprinted there.

She didn't just know him. She loved him.

Love shook my heart
Like the wind on the mountain
Rushing over the oak trees.

—*Sappho*

CHAPTER SIX

The boy, Nate—*how did I know his name?*—turned to Char. "Who's your friend?"

She shrugged. "No one. Never seen her before." She whipped around to face me, hands on her hips. "And I hope I never see her again."

"I–I'm sorry…" Shaking my head, I edged away from them along the iron fence. I had to get away from them, from *him*. I had to get someplace where I could feel myself and not *her*.

Nate stepped closer to me, light from the street lamp bisecting his face. "Are you okay? Do you need some help?"

"No, I'm fine."

He blocked my path, his eyes narrowed at me. "Are you sure? Because I can help."

Char snorted. We both glanced at her. She was facing away from us, looking down the empty street. "You two are really cramping my style. Why don't you take your little Batman-and-Robin routine someplace else?"

"I just wanted to check in with you, Char."

"Yeah?" Char spread her arms wide. "Well, here I am. There, you've checked."

Nate cocked his head to the side, staring at her for a moment. "What'd you take tonight, Char?"

Her face tightened and she jerked her shoulders back. "*Go. Away.*"

That sounded like a good idea. I stepped around Nate, but as I passed him, he grabbed my wrist. I pulled away with such violence that he stumbled backward. He threw his hands up and said, "Hey, I'm sorry. I didn't mean—"

"No, it's okay. I have to go." Jane Doe was everywhere inside me, pounding my heart into my ribs, my throat, my brain, filling me with her emotions. The other memories had been vivid; I'd experienced them with all of my senses, but this one was stronger by far, brimming with some kind of exquisite pain that I felt in every corner of my being. *Go away*, I told her, echoing Char to Nate. *Please just go away.* I stepped off the curb, my body shaking.

The low thrum of a heavy beat-box shattered the silent street. I turned just as headlights shone over the sidewalk and a black Escalade rolled around the corner.

"Shit," Char said. "You're in for it now." Her voice was still tough, but even in the darkness I saw the fear plain on her face.

"Dammit," Nate breathed, his eyes fixed on the SUV.

I moved toward the opposite side of the street, hoping to get around the block before whoever was in the Escalade saw me, but pain seared my scar—my own pain, not Jane Doe's. I doubled over in the middle of the street, my breath coming in shallow gasps. The Escalade's headlights caught me in their glare. I tried to straighten. My chest felt ready to crack open. I bent over again and felt an arm come around me.

"Hey," Nate said, "are you okay?"

"I...just...need...to...catch...my...breath." Red spots popped in front of my eyes. I heard the car door open and I felt Jane Doe's fear in my heart, the same fear I'd felt in her memory of this place. She was afraid of whoever was going to step out of that SUV.

"What the fuck is this?" The voice, deep and ruggedly male, rang out over the street. Footsteps smacked the pavement, measured and confident, as he made his way closer to us. "You. Are you fucking with my girls again?"

Nate kept his hand on my shoulder as he straightened. "I'm not fucking with anyone, Jules."

The footsteps stopped. From my bent-over vantage point, I could see black boots with silver steel toes and heels. "You think I was kidding around when I said if I ever saw you near my girls again, I'd fuck you up? Do you?" His tone was even and calm, like this was a threat he made every day. It probably was.

I forced air past the fear in my rib cage and took a couple of deep breaths. "It was my fault," I said, drawing myself up. "He's with me."

The light from the street lamp flickered so that the whole of Jules came to me in pieces. His tight designer jeans, ripped in all the right places. His long, manicured fingers, tensed at his side, each knuckle adorned with a silver ring. His bright white teeth, just visible behind the grimace of his lips. I took in his face—the strong slant of his cheekbones, the perfectly trimmed sideburns—before I had the guts to meet his eyes. From a distance, I would've thought he was hot. But his eyes were a bottomless nothing. Like any soul in there had disappeared long ago.

Jules took in every inch of me, moving his gaze very deliberately up and down my body. The pink tip of his tongue darted in and out of his lips. "And who are you?" he asked. He smiled. The way a cat smiles when it has trapped a mouse beneath its paw.

I took a step back. Beside me, Nate tensed, and I immediately knew that I shouldn't have moved. "I'm nobody," I said, the words trembling in my mouth. The fear was tangible, my own and Jane Doe's. But there, entwined with Jane Doe's memories of this man, was her disgust for him. I fixed on that and pulled it to the surface. Planting my feet and squaring my shoulders, I never took my eyes off Jules's face. "Nobody to you, I mean."

Jules raised an eyebrow. "You better be nobody. Because I don't like somebodies who *get in my way*." His gaze flickered to Nate. "And *you* have gotten in my way one too many times."

The passenger-side door of the Escalade opened and a hulking figure with a mop of white-blond hair stepped out. He just stood next to the car, but the bulge of a gun was clear through his suit jacket. Nate shifted so that he was in front of me.

Jules laughed. "Yeah, real brave, man. You know what they say about the brave, right?" He stepped toward us. "They die young."

The blond guy reached into his jacket. I grabbed Nate's arm.

"It wasn't him," I said before I could think. "I told him to bring me here. I wanted to help him." I walked backward, dragging Nate with me. "I'm sorry. It was a really bad idea. We'll just leave now, okay?"

"Not okay." For every step back we took, Jules took one forward. He pointed at Char without looking at her. "She wouldn't be standing here if it was okay. She'd be off making me money." He swung his arm so that his finger pointed directly at me. "You're costing me money, bitch. That is definitely *not okay*."

The air around all of us froze, tension thick as ice. I tried to swallow but my throat was stuck. The silence stretched on and on as Jules and I stared at each other. Finally, he broke the world's longest minute with a cold laugh.

"Hey," he said, shrugging his shoulders, "I'm a reasonable guy. You get one get-out-of-jail-free card. But…" He stepped in close, so close that his breath was cool on my face. I was right; there was no soul heating his insides. I willed myself to not look away as his eyes stabbed into me. "If I ever see you again," he went on, like honey dripping with poison, "I will hurt you. I will hurt your little boyfriend here, and I will hurt whichever of my girls you are trying to help. Got that?"

I tasted blood in my mouth as I bit the inside of my cheek. He held my gaze until I nodded once, short and quick. His lips curved into a smile. "You know, you're kinda cute," he said. "Let me know if you wanna make some extra cash."

Nate's hand tightened on my arm as I shuddered. The big blond guy ducked back into the Escalade. On his way back to the car, Jules said something in Char's ear and slapped her hard on the ass.

The Escalade revved its engine as he climbed in. Nate pushed me out of the way as the SUV zoomed by us, and the three of us stood frozen until the sound of the car faded. Nate cleared his throat. "Char, you know where to find me if you need help."

Without waiting for an answer, which she didn't seem inclined to give anyway, he propelled me across the street. "He'll be back to check that we're gone," he told me. "Let's make sure we are."

"You think?" I said. My whole body shook. The reality of this street, of the place it had held in Jane Doe's life, crashed through me. *She'd been a prostitute.* I felt like I might throw up. I pulled my arm out of Nate's grip and backed up against the nearest wall. "I…need a minute." I slid down until my butt hit the ground and dropped my head onto my knees.

Nate squatted in front of me. "Take deep breaths."

I concentrated on counting my inhales and exhales. With each breath, I felt Jane Doe subside. I was becoming Georgie again. Whoever the hell Georgie was now. The old Georgie would be at home, practicing her oboe until she sounded better than a recording. I pinched my forehead together. What the hell was happening to me?

"Feeling better?"

I looked up. I'd almost forgotten Nate was there. "Yeah," I lied and pushed myself up to stand. The instant my legs straightened, I fell back against the wall, dizzy. "Whoa."

"'Whoa' is right." Nate took my elbow. I didn't have the strength to shake him off. "Let me get you someplace warm."

A chill ran through me, from the inside out. Chills, dizziness… *rejection.* With shaking fingers, I touched my forehead. My skin was cool and dry. No fever. *Still…* "I have to get home."

He helped me along the sidewalk. "Is it nearby? I'll walk you."

I shook my head. The motion made me stumble. "I need a cab."

Nate looked sideways at me. "Yeah, you don't really seem like you're from around here." He raised an eyebrow. "What were you doing out here?"

"Looking for—never mind." I tugged away from him and stopped at the curb, looking up and down the street. It was deserted except for the flickering pools of light given off by the street lamps. I reached into the front pocket of my bag and pulled out my phone. I could feel Nate's eyes on me as I found the number of the cab company I'd used to get to this corner of hell in the first place. I edged away from him as the line picked up.

"Forty-five minutes?" I repeated in a high-pitched voice when the receptionist told me how long it would be. "Seriously?"

"Sorry, hon. All of our drivers are out. Where are you, exactly?"

"I'm—" I turned a half-circle and stopped when the movement made me dizzy again. "In the middle of nowhere. I don't know. Somewhere in Mattapan."

"I need an address, hon."

"Tell them All Saints on the corner of Almont and Nashua," Nate said. "It's nearby."

I kept my eyes on him as I spoke into the phone. The receptionist confirmed it. "Keep your phone on you. We'll call you when they're out front."

"Okay. Thanks." I hit End, my eyes still locked on Nate's face. He returned my gaze, but his eyes were full of questions and suspicions. Questions I couldn't answer and suspicions that were probably nowhere near the truth. "Um, so where's this All Saints?"

"It's just around the corner."

He walked slowly for my benefit. I ignored the way he kept glancing at me out of the corner of his eye. Everything about him was familiar. What the hell was Jane Doe doing to me? I had never been in love before, but I could feel the knowledge of that emotion in the blood that Jane Doe's heart was pumping through my veins. I turned my head away from Nate so my hair fell over my shoulder and shielded my face from him. It wasn't fair. I wanted to fall in love in my own way, not have it thrust upon me. She was taking over everything. She owned not just my physical heart but my emotional one too.

"Here we are."

I looked up at an old stone church, towering over the block like a giant gargoyle. I started up the steps but Nate touched my arm. "Not that way." I followed him around the side of the building and down a short flight of stairs to a little red door. Nate dug into his pocket and pulled out a set of keys. I glanced up at the eave that hung over us as he unlocked the door. This felt familiar too. Had Jane Doe also come to this place?

He swung open the door, reached to his left, and flicked a switch. The fluorescent lights illuminated the green linoleum floor and the mismatched tables and chairs. The Catch echoed inside me. Yes, Jane Doe had come here.

"Do you want some tea?" Nate didn't wait for an answer and headed over to the little kitchen on the other side of the room.

"Yeah. Tea would be great. Thanks." I followed slowly, running my fingers over the edges of the furniture I passed. With each touch, a new memory of this place blossomed. *Laughter. Warmth. Safety.* This had been Jane Doe's refuge.

Nate pulled two mugs down from the cabinet and filled them with water from the water cooler against the wall. "Black or herbal?"

"Herbal, please." I perched on the table closest to the kitchen. "Do you, like, work here?"

"Sort of." He put the mugs in the microwave and set it for a minute. "I volunteer for FAIR Girls. They run a chapter out of here."

"What's fair girls?"

"It's an organization that helps trafficked kids." He pointed to a poster on the wall. "TRAFFICKED CHILDREN ARE HIDING IN PLAIN SIGHT," it read beneath a picture of a young girl surrounded by shadowy adults. "FAIR GIRLS" was emblazoned in yellow across the top.

"Trafficked? Like—"

"Sex trafficking? Yes."

The microwave dinged. I watched him take the mugs out and dunk a tea bag into each. When he turned and held a mug out to me, I took it and our fingertips grazed. My heart jumped a little, but who the hell knew if it was my own reaction or Jane Doe's?

"I, um, didn't realize that happened here in Boston."

"A lot of people don't." Nate half smiled. "That's a lot of what FAIR Girls does. Educate the public." He narrowed his eyes at me. "I'd like a little education here. You still haven't told me your name."

It seemed odd that he didn't know when I knew everything about him. I took a sip of tea and let its heat burn through me. "I'm Georgie."

"Okay, Georgie." He was watching me over the rim of his mug but I kept my eyes trained on the floating tea bag in my own cup. "What the hell is a Beacon Hill girl like you doing on this side of town?"

I lowered my mug. "I'm from *Brookline*, not Beacon Hill."

Nate shrugged. "Same difference. What are you doing here?"

I swallowed. I wasn't about to tell him the whole truth, but I wanted whatever clues he had about Jane Doe's life and death. "I was looking for…the other girl. The one who used to work that corner before Char."

A shadow darkened Nate's face. "Why?"

"I just wanted to…find out about her." I swallowed hard under his intense gaze.

"What for?"

My hands tightened around my mug. "Why are you getting so defensive?"

"Why are you so interested?" Nate shot back. "FAIR Girls is here to protect these girls."

"Well, you certainly failed in her case," I said, banging my mug down on the counter. My tea had gone cold.

"What's that supposed to mean?"

I froze, looking at him. Did he not know? I stood there, unable to move or even breathe. Nate's brow furrowed. "Georgie? Are you okay?"

The sound of him saying my name softened something in me. I sank into the closest chair and raised my face to him. "You don't know, do you?"

"Know what?"

I tasted tears in my mouth. "Nate, I'm so sorry. She...she's dead."

CHAPTER SEVEN

Nate fell back against the kitchen counter. "What? When? How?"

"A few weeks ago. She…fell. From a balcony not far from here." I had to look away from him to say the next words. "They say it was suicide."

Nate's body seemed to crumple. He turned away from me and bent over the counter, his face buried in his hands. I kept my eyes averted and picked up my cold tea. I barely knew him; it seemed way too personal to watch him cry.

After a few minutes, I heard him clear his throat. He moved closer to me and dropped into the chair closest to me. His eyes were red-rimmed but dry and clear. "Suicide. *God.*"

I watched his jaw work up and down; he was still fighting tears. "Does that happen…a lot? With…girls like her?" I asked.

"Girls like her…" he murmured. "There were no girls like Annabel."

I gasped and almost dropped my mug to the floor. The name uncoiled a dozen memories inside me, snatches of images: Annabel on the street, here at All Saints, in her dank little bedroom. *Annabel.* "That was her name."

"Yes." I started at Nate's response; I hadn't realized I had spoken out loud. "But not her real one," Nate went on, his eyes unfocused. "That was just the name she used on the street. I never knew her real name."

My shoulders deflated a little. But at least I'd gotten something. And now at least I could stop thinking of her as Jane Doe. *Annabel.* "What did you know about her?"

Nate's eyes slid back into focus and his expression tightened. "Why?" He leaned forward, his body knife-like. "And why were you looking for her if you knew she was dead?"

"I wasn't looking for *her*. I was looking for information *about* her." I squirmed in my chair.

"And again I ask, *why*?" His voice rose. I flinched. Nate softened a little. "Sorry. I didn't mean to yell."

"I wasn't doing anything wrong." I got up and went to the microwave under the pretense of reheating my tea, but really I was covering. I hadn't thought this far ahead. How was I supposed to know that I'd run into the boy that Jane Doe—Annabel—had loved? I pressed my hand to my heart as the tea rotated inside the lighted microwave. What other secrets were contained in this vessel she'd given me?

The microwave dinged. I took a long time getting my mug out and turned around to face Nate. "I've been working on a piece for my school paper," I said. "About teen suicide. And I stumbled across a mention of a Jane Doe suicide on the police precinct website. It had the address of where she'd jumped, so I came over here to see if I could find out anything more about her. That's when I bumped into Char, and she mentioned the other girl who used to hang out there."

"How'd you know that was Annabel?" Nate demanded.

"I didn't," I stammered. "It was just a hunch. Char said the other girl was dead, which seemed a pretty big coincidence, so I was asking her about it, and then you showed up, and then Jules showed up and…now we're here."

"Uh-huh." Nate's eyes searched my face. I tried to keep my face as guileless as possible. I wasn't skilled in the art of lying; I'd never had to be. "You're writing an article?"

"For my school paper."

"What school?"

"Hillcoate Prep."

He raised an eyebrow. "Really."

"So?"

"That's a nice school, from what I hear."

"Yeah, it is. Our paper competes for a national award every year."

As soon as it was out of my mouth, I knew it was the wrong thing to say. He stood up so fast his chair wobbled. "You want to use Annabel's death to *win an award*?" He flung his arm toward the door. "Get out. Get out *now*."

The darkness in his eyes chilled me to my veins. I grabbed my backpack off the table and clutched it to me. But I couldn't just leave. He was the only connection I had to Annabel. I could feel him everywhere in her heart. Even the timbre of his voice squeezed my insides. I looked up into his face.

"I'm sorry. I didn't know. When I went looking for her, she was just research. But after learning…what she was…and meeting you…she's not."

Heat constricted my throat. I swiped the tears at the corners of my eyes. It wasn't an act. She wasn't just a heart anymore. She wasn't just some inconvenient echo of a ghost who was stealing my memories. She had become a mystery I had to solve.

"That's what I want to write about now. About these lost girls no one ever finds."

Nate held my eyes with his own for so long that I could count the little gold flecks in each of his blue irises. "You shouldn't write about teen suicide," he said finally. His voice crackled. "You should write about FAIR Girls. About human trafficking. About how it's happening around the corner from your fancy private school. You could open people's eyes to that."

We stood there for a long moment, frozen in stillness, our eyes melded to each other's. In the silence that stretched between us, I heard the Catch so loudly that it bounced off the walls. Without breathing, I asked him, "Will you help me?"

Without hesitation, he answered, "Yes."

When I got home, all I wanted to do was head upstairs to the privacy of my room and think about everything I'd learned. But my family had other ideas.

Grandma blocked my path the instant I walked in the door. "Where have you been?" she demanded. "Do you have any idea what your parents have been through?"

"I—"

My mother emerged from the living room into the hallway, the phone in her hand. "Georgie!" She lifted the phone to her ear. "She just got home. Thanks, Bill."

Bill was Ella's father. Crap. I was in for it now.

Mom tossed the phone onto the bench in the hallway where all our hats and gloves and scarves seemed to congregate. "Where the hell have you been? Your father and I have been worried sick."

As if to reinforce this, Dad appeared behind Mom, his face a mask of concern. "Georgie, you nearly gave us a heart attack." He looked stricken. "Oh jeez, you know what I mean."

Grandma took my elbow and led me into the living room. "Explain yourself, young lady."

"We know you weren't at that rehearsal tonight," Mom said. "So if you weren't with Ella, what were you doing?" She sounded like she was fighting very hard to stay calm.

I looked from her to my dad to Grandma and started a little when I noticed Colt sprawled out in the armchair in the corner. He was scribbling in the margins of a thick textbook. "I told you she'd be home," he said without looking up.

Dad glanced at him and back at me. He folded his arms over his chest. "Look, we're not mad, Georgie. We just want to know what's going on with you."

I loved how adults said they weren't mad when they clearly were. I heaved a sigh. "I'm really tired. Can we just talk about this tomorrow?"

Dad looked inclined to allow this, but Mom crossed the room until she stood right in front of me. "No. We'll talk about this now." She stared at me for a moment, her jaw working hard. "Do you have *any* idea what it was like sitting in that hospital room? Watching you almost die? Do you?" Her voice had tipped over the edge into hysteria now. "And this is how you repay us? By running around God-knows-where with God-knows-who at all hours of the night?"

I looked at my watch. "It's nine-thirty."

Grandma threw her hands up. "Georgie! Just answer your mother."

"Fine. Can I sit down first? I did just have *a heart transplant*, you know."

From his corner nook, Colt laughed. No one else looked amused, but they waited until I had taken my coat off and settled myself comfortably on the couch. "Look, I'm really sorry I'm late," I said. "I didn't realize it would take so long."

"What would?" Mom asked.

I tucked my feet up underneath me and arranged my face into a beatific expression. "Sydney asked me to write an article for the paper. About human trafficking," I added, widening my eyes. Sydney was another close friend of mine. She edited the *Hillcoate Banner*.

"What? Why?"

I didn't know who to look at since they'd all said it at once. "I think she felt bad," I said, looking at Mom first. "That I can't go back to school with everyone else. So she asked me to write the article as a way of, you know, including me."

Mom sank down next to me on the couch. "Honey, we're not keeping you out of school to punish you. It's for your own good."

"I know that," I said in my best I-trust-you-because-you're-the-parent tone. "But I really want to do this article. If it's good enough, she's going to submit it for the National Student Journalist Award."

That got them. Dad perched on the edge of the coffee table across from me. "Honey, if it's for school, of course we support that. But you could've told us where you were going tonight."

"I'm so sorry," I said, furrowing my brow as I looked back and forth between him and Mom. "I just didn't think you'd let me go on my own, so soon after my surgery."

"Where did you go?" Grandma interjected.

"There's this organization called FAIR Girls," I said. "They have a chapter at a church in Jamaica Plain." There was no way I was telling them I'd been in Mattapan. I'd be grounded until my sixty-fifth birthday. "I went to meet one of the volunteers there. And I didn't think they'd talk as openly with an adult there."

Mom put her hand on my knee. "Honey, just tell us from now on. Okay?"

"Okay," I said. "I, uh, may have to go back. To do more research."

"Just try to go during the day," Dad said. "Deal?"

"Deal." I slid away from Mom and stood up. "Um, I'm really tired. Do you mind if I—"

"Yes, yes. Good night," Dad said.

I leaned over and pecked him on the cheek. But my face pinched together as I climbed the stairs. I loved my parents. I really did. I wasn't one of those ungrateful teenagers who was embarrassed to be seen with my mom. I'd been known to stay home on a

Saturday night for family movie night—and I'd enjoyed it. It felt inherently *wrong* to lie to them—and yet, I'd just done it as effortlessly as, well…as effortlessly as Annabel must have done it to sell herself on the street.

I tottered over to my bed and collapsed onto it. The ceiling seemed to swirl as I stared up at it. What had driven Annabel to the streets? And Nate…involuntarily, I pressed my hand to my chest. She had loved him. That I knew for sure. I could feel it inside me. It was the one thing that was quiet and still.

Well, I could see why, with his angled cheekbones and deep ocean-blue eyes. And the way he had looked at me, like he could see all the way into my mind. And the passion in his voice when he told me I should write a story about trafficking. I replayed that bit of the scene over and over in my mind. He *cared*. Not like most of the boys I went to school with, who didn't give a crap about anything other than which frat they were going to pledge when they got to their Ivy League college.

I sat up. Was that why Annabel had loved him? Because he was the only one to care about her? I wove my fingers into my hair and pulled my topknot down. My excursion to Mattapan had given me a few answers, but it had brought on even more questions.

And most terrifying among them was which memories I would lose for the ones I'd gained tonight.

I jerked awake the next morning, out of dreams full of windowless bedrooms and dark street corners, gated cemeteries and silver sports cars, church basements and bottomless blue eyes. Every single one of those things belonged to Annabel, not me. I looked around my pink bedroom, naming each thing in it that was mine and mine alone.

When I got to the stack of music in the corner, I slid out of bed and crossed to it. The taste of the wooden reed between my lips was delicious. Annabel had never held an oboe in her life—that I knew for sure. This was mine alone, and it was a place where Annabel couldn't come.

I started with scales and moved on to passages I knew from memory—Saint-Saën's *Samson and Delilah*, Tchaikovsky's Fourth Symphony, Dvorak's *New World*. Pieces of music I was sure Annabel had never heard. I slid into the Mozart Concerto in C, a piece I'd mastered as a freshman. Then Benjamin Britten's *Six Metamorphoses*, which I'd played at my last recital, and finally on to the Poulenc. Every note, every passage and phrase grounded me to who I was. She could take allergies and dream catchers away from me, but she couldn't have this. The oboe tied me to myself, and I would not let her undo that knot.

"You sounded good," Mom said when I came downstairs to the kitchen for breakfast. She sat at the table reading the paper, a half-drunk cup of coffee within reach.

"Thanks," I said. I poured myself a bowl of (heart-healthy!) cereal and added some blueberries from the fridge. "Sorry again about last night."

Mom waved her hand. “It’s forgiven. Do you want me to call Joel to set up a lesson?”

“Absolutely. The sooner, the better.” Joel was my private oboe teacher. I’d been studying with him for five years. I smiled as I spooned cereal into my mouth. Lessons with Joel always seemed to be outside of time and space. Surely they would push Annabel further out.

“You’re still on track to audition next month, yes?”

“I think so.” I frowned. “They won’t let me postpone, will they?”

Mom looked over the top of her paper. “Do you want me to call and find out? I’m sure once they understand the circumstances—”

“No. I want to do the audition in March. I don’t want them to think I’m making excuses.”

“Good girl.” Mom smiled. “You’ve been working for this for so long. I’m proud of you for not letting anything get in your way.” She folded her paper down. “And I think we’ll have Mr. Blount start on Monday. Sound good?”

“Mr. Blount?”

“The tutor your father hired,” she said. “We’re very lucky he could fit you in. He’ll come for three hours a day. Mostly in the mornings so you can have the afternoons to practice and study. And rest,” she added.

“Perfect,” I said. And it was. Nate had told me he was usually at All Saints every day after three. My hand tightened on my spoon. Except…I really would need the afternoons to practice. But what was more important—that or keeping my memories intact? I set my spoon down and pushed away my half-eaten cereal. These were the choices I had to make now. A month ago, the biggest decision I'd faced was what to wear to the winter formal. I plucked a dried flower from the vase in the center of the table and toyed with it.

"Hey, do you think it would be okay if Ella and Toni came over tonight? They said they'd bring over notes from school." I needed to surround myself with as much of my old life as possible.

"That's nice of them." Mom glanced up and smiled at me. "It's good to see you getting back to normal."

I slumped low in my chair. *Normal.* If she could see into my heart, she would know that I was anything but. As good as playing my oboe felt, as much as I looked forward to seeing my friends, something inside me still pulled me back to Annabel. To retrace her footsteps and learn what she had to tell me. To see Nate again. I balled my hands into fists and dug my nails into my palms. Nate…I couldn't get him out of my head, couldn't get him out of my heart. Those were *her* feelings, not mine…but the lines were blurred now. I didn't know where Annabel ended and I began.

And that scared the hell out of me.

CHAPTER EIGHT

Ella came to the front door bearing cupcakes. "I know you're not supposed to have chocolate," she said as she squeezed past me, the bright pink box balanced on her palm, "but I couldn't resist."

I kissed her cheek. "You're a goddess. My parents have interpreted 'heart-healthy' to mean 'totally bland and completely disgusting.'" We'd just finished a dinner of brown rice pasta with sauce devoid of flavor. I needed to have a conversation with Dr. Harrison the next time I saw her.

Toni followed Ella inside the house and closed the door behind her. "Hey, I paid for half," she said, tapping her finger on her cheek. I laughed and gave her a kiss too.

We smuggled the cupcakes up to my room and sat on the floor to eat them. Toni and Ella spread their notes out. I held a red velvet cupcake in one hand and flipped through the notes with the other. "You guys finished *Crime and Punishment*? I'm only halfway through," I muttered, glancing at my nightstand where the book lay. I hadn't opened it since I got back from the hospital.

"I don't know why you're stressing," Toni said. "Only a heartless monster would fail you."

"Ha-ha."

Ella licked frosting off her fingers and tapped my knee. "So, I have a surprise for you."

"Are you sure my heart can take it?"

She smirked. "The first oboist with the Roslindale group flaked. I told the conductor about you, and he wants you to come in next rehearsal." She clapped her hands together. "Isn't that awesome?"

"It is." I bit my lip and looked at Toni's calculus notes in my lap. "But I don't think I can do it."

"What? Why?"

I glanced up. Ella's eyes were narrowed at me, her face filled with questions I couldn't answer. My insides squirmed. "I'm just—so behind with everything. And I need to prep for Juilliard. That *has* to be my main focus. I don't think I'll have time."

Ella sighed, long and dramatic. "Crap. I went on and on about how amazing you are."

"I'm sorry, Ella!" I reached out and flipped her long hair behind her shoulder. "I'll talk to the conductor so you don't have to. I would love to do it, but I can't." I looked at the window and the reflection of my room on the glass. A month ago, I would've loved to do it. I would've pushed myself to do it. But now…I knew I should want to, but I didn't. I was torn in so many different directions that I'd lost my way. "I mean," I said, turning back to Ella, "I'm sure he'll understand once I explain the situation."

"What situation?"

I let the notes in my hand flutter to the ground. "Uh, just the fact that I had major heart surgery a couple of weeks ago?"

"Oh." Ella waved her hand. "Whatever. It's not like playing the oboe is stressful or anything."

"Ella, I get winded walking to the bathroom. It's hard for me to be out and about."

She crossed her arms over her chest. "Then why were you gallivanting all over Jamaica Plain?"

Toni shifted, her eyes fixed on the floor. I swallowed hard. "How did you—know about that?"

"Well, your mom called my house looking for you." Ella cocked her head. "Next time you use me as your alibi, let me in on the secret."

"I'm sorry." I nudged her with my toe but she didn't soften. "Look, I was working on something. An article that I'm writing for the *Banner*." The lie had become so comfortable that it was almost truth now. "I went there to do some research. I just knew that my parents would never let me go, so I told them I was hanging out with you."

"I don't mind covering for you," Ella said, "but you gotta tell me first. Deal?"

"Deal." I picked up the notes I'd dropped. "So what's after *Crime and Punishment* on the syllabus?"

"What's the article about?" Toni asked. I looked at her. Ella and I didn't fight often, but when we did, Toni usually disappeared. She stretched her legs out in front of her and flexed her feet.

"Oh, um..." The images of that lonely street corner, the silver sports car, Char...*Nate*...streamed across my mind. "I decided to do a report on human trafficking. There's an organization at a church in J.P. that helps trafficked girls. That's where I went."

Ella shuddered. "Ugh. That's so depressing."

I shoved the notes at her. "Just because it's depressing doesn't mean you should ignore it. And it's a real problem. Even right here in Boston."

"Look at you, all humanitarian." Ella shimmied her shoulders. "How's the air up on that high horse?"

"Did you find out anything useful?" Toni cut in before I could say anything. "At the church, I mean?"

"Oh." I drew in a long breath and decided to let Ella have that one. "Um, no. I'm gonna have to go back."

There was a knock on my bedroom door. Ella shoved the cupcake box behind her in the second before Mom peeked her head in. "You girls need anything?"

"No, we're good," I told her.

She opened the door wider. "Well, I have a surprise for you." We all looked up at her expectantly. She leaned on the door frame. "Your dad and I just booked the same house we stayed at last year on Nantucket. Not just a month this time, the whole summer. Won't that be wonderful right before you head off to Juilliard?" Her eyes danced as she smiled at me.

"I haven't even auditioned yet—"

"Oh, you'll get in. We're counting on it." She looked past me to Toni and Ella. "And you girls are welcome to come up for a few weeks again, like you did last year."

They both squealed and pounced on me. "Thank you, Mrs. Kendrick!" Ella yelled as she hugged me around the neck.

"This year will be even more epic than last year," Toni said in a rush.

Beneath their shrieks, I heard the Catch. The room was shrinking, the walls closing in. "Air, air," I mumbled, shoving them off me.

"Oooh, sorry," Ella said. She peered into my face. "Are you okay?"

"Yeah, I'm fine. Just heart surgery, remember?"

"Well, I figured you girls would be excited about it," Mom said. "Georgie talks all the time about how it was the best summer of her life. She deserves an even better one, after what she's been through."

"Definitely," Toni said.

Mom shot us one last smile and slipped out into the hall. Ella and Toni leaned in, their heads almost touching mine. "We'll all be eighteen by this summer," Ella said, "so we'll be able to get away with a lot more."

"I bet some of the bars might even serve us," Toni said.

Ella rolled her eyes. "Good luck with that."

"What? I—"

"I just hope that ice cream stand is still around," Ella said. "I've been craving their cookie dough all winter."

"I think I gained ten pounds from that place," Toni said. "We went there, like, three times a day."

"I wonder if your next-door neighbor will be back," Ella said, elbowing me hard.

"Ow! What next-door neighbor?" I asked without thinking as I rubbed my side.

Ella rolled her eyes. "'What next-door neighbor?' she asks." She tickled the spot she'd just elbowed. "Um, only the guy you were making out with all summer."

"Oh, yeah. Him," I said.

"*Him*," Toni laughed. "She doesn't even remember his name!"

"Sure I do—"

"*Evan!*" They both gave a loud sigh and mock-swooned into each other's arms.

I forced a laugh. "Evan. Yeah…he was…hot." I dropped my eyes from their shiny faces and pushed myself up to standing. "I gotta pee. Be right back."

"Georgie!"

I looked back at Ella from the door, my hand resting on the frame that my mom had just vacated. "Yeah?"

"You okay?" Her eyes searched my face, like she could see beneath its lie.

"Sure. I'm psyched. Last summer was epic, right?" I ducked out into the hall and hurried to the bathroom. I shut the door behind me and leaned over the sink, pressing my forehead against the cool tile.

Last summer had been the best summer of my life.

But I remembered none of it.

CHAPTER NINE

All Saints looked completely different in the light. At night, it had looked formidable and imposing. During the day, it looked sad and dingy. There were cracks in the stone steps and faded graffiti on the gray walls. I followed the little path around the side until I found the door that led to the basement.

Inside, I found a loud room full of life, totally different from the darkened, empty place I'd come to with Nate. Kids lounged on the couches, stretched out on the floor rugs, sat in chairs turned backward. There was a handful of adults too, but from the loud music that blared from an iPod docked on the long table near the kitchen, this was the kids' territory.

I stood in the doorway, scanning faces for the one I would recognize. I finally spotted him at the far end of the room. He was leaning over a chair in which a pretty black-haired girl sat. Her face was turned up to his and she was smiling. She tipped the chair backward, and he put his foot up on the edge of it to keep her falling over. She laughed.

Angry heat shot through me. I squared my shoulders and marched halfway across the room before I realized I had absolutely no reason to be jealous. Gritting my teeth, I turned away.

That jealousy was *hers*. Just like my memory of last summer. It belonged to her now. Everything belonged to her.

"Georgie?"

I whirled around. Nate had left the girl in the chair and stood a few feet from me. A ghost of a smile shadowed his face. "You came back."

I hunched my shoulders a little. "You didn't think I would?"

"Honestly? I wasn't sure." He stepped closer to me. "I figured you were probably pretty freaked out by what happened the other night."

"I was," I admitted. I started to unbutton my coat. "But that wasn't going to prevent me from coming back."

"Anything for a story, right?"

"Oh—right," I said, forcing a laugh. As if my life didn't depend on what I found out. *Or at least my memories*, I thought as Nate led me to the back of the room.

I had known the memory of Nate—of Annabel's feelings for him and all she knew about him—would not be free. It just seemed completely unfair that I didn't get to choose what memory I could exchange. Like, why couldn't she take the memory of the time I peed in my pants in the middle of the Aquarium on a second-grade field trip? Why did it have to be the memory of what was supposedly the best summer of my life?

Off to the side of the kitchen was a quiet corner with two unoccupied armchairs. Nate dropped into one and turned on the banker's lamp that sat on the end table between the chairs. I tossed my coat over the back of the other chair and sat, pulling my backpack up into my lap.

Out of the corner of my eye, I spied the girl Nate had been talking to. She was watching us from across the room. I nodded toward her. "Who's your girlfriend?"

Nate followed the line of my gaze and burst out laughing. "Um, Tommy is not my girlfriend."

"*Tommy?*" I squinted. Now that I was looking for it, I could see the angular shape of Tommy's jaw and, yep, an Adam's apple when she swallowed. My face grew hot. "Uh, my bad."

Nate winked. "Tommy's great, but not my type."

"I knew that."

"Oh?" Nate raised an eyebrow. "How?"

"I don't know...you just don't seem..." I chewed my lip. I had to be careful.

"You can't judge a book by its cover," Nate said. "You'd be surprised how many girls on the street are as clean-cut as you. There's a real misconception out there that trafficked kids are all from bad homes or runaways or drug addicts." Nate leaned toward me a little. "I'd even wager that at least one of your Hillcoate classmates is being trafficked."

My mouth went sour. I shook my head. "No way."

"How would you know?" Nate asked. "You wouldn't believe the double life some of these girls live. Most of the time when they finally get free, their family had no idea."

"That's awful," I whispered. I wanted to think that if Ella or Toni or one of my other Hillcoate friends was in real trouble, I'd know about it. But would I? Suddenly, I wasn't so sure.

But Annabel...Annabel couldn't have been from a good family

or have had close friends. If she had, someone would've claimed her. She wouldn't have been a Jane Doe. "But some of the girls are runaways, right?" I asked.

"Yeah," Nate said, "or foster kids. They just don't have anyone who cares enough to keep them off the streets."

I tried to imagine what that would be like, to not have a family who cared about me, and failed. The thought was like a foreign country I had never heard of. I pressed my lips together and swallowed hard. From the other side of the room, Tommy laughed again, long and loud. I nodded toward her. "Is Tommy a…prostitute?"

Nate smiled. "Not anymore. She's been off the street for almost a year now." He tilted his head to the side. "Her parents kicked her out when she told them she wanted to transition." At my quizzical look, he added, "From male to female. A lot of parents have a hard time accepting that. So she was on the streets, and a heroin dealer was nice enough to take her in."

"And get him—sorry, her—hooked," I finished. "Right?"

"Yeah. But she was lucky. She had friends who pulled her out of the abyss and brought her here."

I pointed to one of the banners that adorned the walls. A bright rainbow arced the length of it with the words "EMPOWERING LGBTQ" underneath it. "How do they," I jerked my chin up to indicate the church above us, "like having heathens and sinners hanging out in their basement?"

Nate laughed. "You didn't read the sign too closely out front, did you? This is a Universalist Unitarian church. They'll take anyone who walks in the front door. Which is the truly Christian thing to do anyway, right?" He nodded toward my backpack. "Don't you want to take notes or something?"

"Oh. Yes." I had actually come prepared. The sight of Nate's scruffy blond hair and blue eyes had just made me forget to play the part of the journalist. I pulled a pen, a notebook, and a little tape recorder from my bag.

"Do you mind?" I asked, holding up the tape recorder. Nate shrugged. I pressed the record button and set it down on the table in between us. "So did, um, Annabel come here a lot?"

Nate narrowed his eyes at me. "You just want to talk about Annabel?"

"No," I answered quickly. I flipped to a blank page in my notebook, not looking at him. "I wanted to use her as the, you know, cautionary side of the story. And then maybe we could—I don't know—use, um, Tommy as the hopeful side." I chewed on my pen and glanced at him. "What do you think?"

"I guess that makes sense." One corner of his mouth turned up. I couldn't stop looking at it. "You're the writer."

I snorted and turned it into throat clearing. "Uh, yeah, I guess. So, Annabel. She came here a lot?"

Nate looked down at his lap. "Often enough."

"But not enough to get her off the streets," I said softly.

"No," he said, his voice as hushed as mine. "No, I guess not."

"Tell me about her." I tucked my legs up underneath me. "Why was she special?"

Nate leaned his head on the back of the chair, his eyes fixed on the ceiling. "She was special because—because—she was *infuriating.*"

I jumped a little in my chair. "What?"

Nate straightened up and leaned over the arm of his chair toward me. "Ever since the other night, when you told me that she was..." He swallowed. I nodded so that he didn't have to say the word. "I keep thinking about the last time I saw her. It was in December, right before Christmas. FAIR Girls always has a holiday party here, and all the girls show up. It's catered," he explained. "Free food is a powerful attraction."

"I get that," I said. "I can't tell you how many times I've let my dad drag me to a boring work party just for the buffet."

He smiled at me, his eyes crinkled at the edge. I tore my gaze away and focused on a tear in the leather armchair, trying to ignore the warmth that spread through me.

"Anyway," he went on, "Annabel was there. We were talking, and she got a call. And I knew it was Jules, telling her to go to the cemetery to meet someone, and I just...I got angry with her." Nate's voice was hoarse. His head bent so that I couldn't see his eyes anymore. "I told her she didn't have to do this anymore, that I—we—would take care of her, get her some place safe. And she just looked at me and said, 'Nowhere is safe. Not for me.'"

"What did she mean?" I asked. I wanted to reach out and stroke his hair. Instead I clenched my hand into a fist.

"I don't know exactly. She wasn't talking about, you know, the world not being safe." He glanced up at me through his eyelashes. "I think she meant that she wasn't safe from *herself*."

"She wasn't..." I murmured, thinking of the cold pavement outside 826 Emiline Way.

"Anyway, I followed her," Nate said. I watched his face as he talked, noticing how he avoided direct eye contact with me. "I followed her out of here and toward the cemetery. And around the corner, there was a homeless woman huddled against a building. She greeted Annabel by name—they obviously knew each other from the area—and Annabel stopped and gave her a whole bag of food she'd gotten from the party."

"Wow," I said.

"And her coat." He met my eyes. "Annabel took off her coat and gave it to this woman. She was wearing this tight little sleeveless minidress, but she stood there in the cold like it was nothing and would not take the coat back even though the woman tried to refuse it. Then she walked off and met her—client—and I never saw her again."

I shifted in my chair so that I faced away from him and dug the heels of my hands into my eyes. Who *was* this Annabel? Why did she stay on the streets? What had driven her to jump off that balcony?

"That was the saddest thing about Annabel." Nate's voice floated to me. I looked back at him. His blue eyes were clear but faraway. "Everyone who knew her could see how beautiful and brave she was, but she couldn't see it herself. That's why she kept going back to Jules. It wasn't drugs. She was one of the few who never took drugs." He blinked and only then did I see the whisper of a tear. "It was because she didn't think she deserved any better."

I sat very still. Even my insides felt frozen. Pain clenched my heart, a strong, sweet pain that made me want to weep and scream and curl up in a ball. For all the memories I'd gotten of Nate, for all I knew about how she'd felt about him, there were no memories of how he'd felt about her. This was the closest he'd ever come to telling her, and I felt it deep inside me, deep inside *her*. I drew a shuddering breath. "Um—"

"Yeah. *Um*." Nate ran his hands over his face. "I'm sorry. I didn't mean to unload that all on you."

"That's okay." I slid my hands beneath my legs so that Nate wouldn't see them shaking. "I asked."

"You didn't ask for *that*." Nate shook his head. A lock of hair fell across his forehead, and he brushed it aside with an angry stroke. "It is really hard to come here day after day and see these girls… You want so bad to help them, but for every one that you help, there are ten more that you've failed—ten more that *disappear* or wash up on the banks of the river or overdose on heroin or…" Nate stopped and let the silence fill in what he'd left unsaid. *Or jump off a balcony*. He took a big breath and let it out. "But I've found that sitting around moaning about how sad it is gets no one anywhere. That's why I got involved."

"So, what do you do exactly?" I repositioned the tape recorder to make it look like I was actually doing some reporting. "Do you just come here after school?"

Nate shook his head. "I don't go to school."

"You don't? Did you graduate?" He didn't look much older than me.

He shrugged. "In a manner of speaking. I dropped out when I was sixteen and got my GED instead."

"But why?"

"Why?" He pressed his lips together. "I guess because I hated sitting in class every day when I knew it was all bullshit out in the real world."

"And you just...dropped out? Your parents let you?"

"Please." Nate rolled his eyes. "My parents didn't know what end was up back then. I put the paper in front of them and told them to sign and they did."

"So you just work here now?"

"Nah. I would, but unfortunately saving lives doesn't pay the rent." Nate tilted his head toward the door. "I work at the Starbucks a short walk from here. I work mostly mornings so I can come here in the afternoons."

"Oh." I toyed with the tape recorder. "That's...cool."

He narrowed his eyes at me. "You've never known anyone who dropped out of school, have you?"

I tossed my hair back. "I—what makes you say that?"

He laughed. "No offense, Georgie, but you look like a red button on a black coat in this place."

"What's that supposed to mean?" I grabbed my pen and uncapped it with unnecessary violence. The cap went flying straight into the air.

Nate pointed to the pin on my coat's lapel. "I highly doubt anyone drops out of Hillcoate."

I gritted my teeth. "So?"

"You know what?" Nate held up his hands. "I shouldn't be judgmental. It's not your fault that you were born into privilege."

I stared at him. Privilege? Was that what he thought of me? My life was *not*—I scrunched my forehead and thought about my old Victorian house on a leafy street in Brookline, about Hillcoate's gated drive and spotless hallways, about the trust fund that sat waiting for me in the brick-building bank in Harvard Square. *Huh.*

"I just..." I said slowly, "I never thought about it before."

Nate put his hand over mine. My heart jerked a little. His skin was smooth and warm against mine. "There is a whole world outside the walls of your fancy school that they don't teach you about in there."

My eyes met his and it was like I was looking at him through a stained glass window. He was so many different colors and shapes. He was the hot guy that Georgie saw and the beautiful person that Annabel had known. And all he saw of me was a spoiled little rich girl. I wanted him to see me differently. I wanted him to think I was beautiful and brave just like *she* was.

"Well, I'm here," I said. "Educate me."

Later, when he walked me out to my cab, I asked him, "You're here every afternoon?"

"Pretty much."

"I'll come back."

He raised an eyebrow. "You didn't get enough for your article?"

"No." I searched his face. "I need more."

We stared at each other for a long moment before he reached around me and opened the car door. "'Til next time then, Georgie."

As I sat in the cab on the way home—with the same driver I'd had on my first visit to Mattapan—I thought about Ella, how easily she'd dismissed the topic of trafficking as depressing. And it *was* so much easier to dismiss. Who wanted to think about teenage prostitutes? Especially when they could be your next-door neighbor? But I didn't want to run away from it. And I couldn't. Not with Annabel ruling my heart.

I'd only gotten a little more information on her, but whatever she wanted to tell me, I was on the track. I could feel it in the way the Catch shushed through me.

The house smelled like roasting chicken when I walked through the door. This time I didn't have to worry about being out. I'd told my parents exactly where I was going. Mom had even given me the cab fare. For once, I was grateful for the deadline that kept her hidden away in her office and unable to chauffeur me around town.

I found Grandma in the kitchen, bent over the oven and brushing olive oil onto the half-roasted bird. "Can I help?"

"Oh no, sweetie." She straightened and laid the brush on the counter. "Not with this anyway. Your mom wants to send out invitations for their Valentine's Day party, and I cannot for the life of me figure out that stupid Evite site."

I laughed. "I'll do it." I sat at the kitchen table and pulled Mom's laptop toward me. I stroked the silvery rim with the tip of my finger. Everyone in this house had their own laptop, plus the desk computer up in the office where Mom was locked away. I knew we had a lot, more than most people, but being in that basement at All Saints made me realize how truly blessed we really were.

I pulled up the invitation website and went into Mom's account to find the invitation for last year's Valentine's Day party. It was an annual event in our house. Mom and Dad said having a holiday party just made you compete against everyone else having a holiday party, so they'd searched around for a holiday that everyone celebrated but usually didn't have parties for. Colt was rooting for Groundhog's Day, but Mom and Dad had settled on Valentine's Day. And ten years later, it was a tradition.

I changed the invitation design and copied the guest list from previous years. "Are you sticking around for the party?" I asked Grandma.

"You know, I think I might." She carried a bowl of sweet potatoes to the counter and started cutting them up. "I've been hearing about this party for years and have always been curious."

"It's nothing special," I said and hit Send on the Evite. I looked up. "Actually, you know, it is. The whole neighborhood shows up."

Grandma dropped a handful of diced potatoes into a pan. "Do you want me to stay?"

I smiled at her. "Yeah. Yeah, I think it would be nice."

"Then I'll stay."

"You can help us decorate." I shut the laptop and stood up. "Colt always goes overboard with the paper hearts." I kissed her on the cheek. "I'll be upstairs. Call me if you need help."

Before I left the kitchen, I grabbed a box of trash bags from under the sink. When I got to my bedroom, I flicked on the light and stood in the doorway. My gaze swept over every surface and took in the excess of jewelry I never wore, my overstuffed closet, the shoes spilling out like a pool of black and brown sludge. Shelves full of books I'd already read, trinkets that I'd bought and forgotten about.

I didn't need any of this. The soft lamplight seemed to glare off the bright pink walls as I pulled piece after piece of clothing off their hangers and stuffed them into the trash bags. By the time I was done with the mountain of shoes, I could actually see the floor of my closet, something I'd never been able to achieve before. I shoved all the costume jewelry I'd worn once into a little velvet bag and flung it in after the shoes.

The books were next. I'd noticed a half-empty bookcase in the corner of the basement at All Saints. My own bookcase overflowed with glossy hardcovers that I'd already devoured and were now just taking up space. Maybe one of these books would keep one girl off the street for an afternoon.

I dumped the unwanted books into a cardboard box I'd found at the back of my closet and was dragging it across the room when the door opened. "Dinner's—Georgie! What—here, let me help you." Mom nudged me out of the way. I dropped to the floor and panted as I watched her pull the box into the hallway. My scar seared.

Mom came back into the room. I followed her gaze to my pared-down closet, the clutter-free dresser, and the half-empty bookshelf. Sweat ran down my forehead and my shirt clung to my skin. I pulled the neckline away from my throat and waved it a little to fan myself. Mom raised an eyebrow at me. "It's a little early for spring cleaning."

I shrugged and let my breathing slow to normal before answering. "I was just feeling a little claustrophobic in here."

Mom peered into one of the trash bags. "Are you sure you want to get rid of all this stuff?"

"I don't need it."

"What do you, uh, plan to do with all this?"

"Donate it." The pain in my chest had eased. I pushed myself up from the floor and sat on the edge of the bed. "I know a place."

Mom leaned against the door frame and crossed her arms. "Georgie, does this have something to do with this report you're working on?"

"No. I mean, maybe." I pulled my shirtsleeves down over my hands and clenched the fabric. "But so what? I don't need all this stuff, and it doesn't seem fair that I should have all of this when so many others have nothing."

"Well, I think it's very nice that you want to donate this," Mom said. "But, you know, it's not really about fairness. Your father and I have worked very hard to be where we are."

"Oh, come on, Mom." I rolled my eyes at her. "You and Dad both had trust funds. You had every advantage."

Mom's jaw tightened. "But we still worked very hard. Your father didn't become a Harvard dean because of his trust fund."

"That's true," I said calmly, my eyes still on her face. "But you never had to struggle. You always knew where your next meal was coming from. You never had to—I don't know—sell yourself on the street—"

"Georgie!" The blood drained from her face. "That's a horrible thing to say."

"Yeah, well, it's a horrible thing to have to do." I stood up. "And you'd be horrified to know how many girls do it every day, right here in Boston."

As I moved past her, she pulled me into a fierce, tight hug. "Thank God you don't have to do that," she muttered into my hair as she pressed her lips hard against my temple. I softened into her. It wasn't her fault we were privileged. She only wanted to give me every advantage she'd had. But that didn't mean there wasn't a whole world out there that I deserved—*and needed*—to know about.

CHAPTER TEN

I finally asked the cab driver's name when he picked me up for the third time. Manny helped me carry the trash bags of clothes and boxes of books to the basement of All Saints when he dropped me off the next afternoon. Nate stood by the door, eyebrows raised, as I deposited a bulging bag just inside. "What's all this?" he asked.

"I cleaned out my room," I said. I leaned on the door frame opposite him to catch my breath. My scar itched.

"All this was just in your *room*?" Nate whistled long and low. "That's a lot of stuff."

"A lot of stuff I don't need," I said. "Is it okay that I brought it here? I thought the girls could go through it and take whatever they wanted."

Manny squeezed in between us and dropped the last bag on the pile. I paid him a large tip on top of the regular fare and closed the door behind him. Nate was watching me, his blue eyes intense on my face as I turned around. "What?"

He gave a shake of his head, and the intensity broke. "Nothing. It's just really thoughtful of you to do this."

"Well..." I bit my lip. I had been about to say something smart and sarcastic, but somehow that seemed all wrong. "What you said the other day got to me."

"Oh." He cleared his throat. "Well…good." He bent down to pick up a box of books, but I could swear that I saw redness in his cheeks. It was gone when he straightened. "Let's get these on the shelves."

I bent down to pick up the other box. Pain ripped through my chest as I lifted it, and I dropped the box with a loud clunk. Panting, I crouched over, fingers pressed against my breastbone. I squeezed my eyes shut and tried to breathe through the pain. Why did this have to happen now, in front of him? My body had become such a traitor.

Hands gripped my shoulder. "Georgie? Are you okay?"

The pain eased a bit and I took a full breath. For an instant, it felt like my scar was breaking open. *Not possible*, I reminded myself. Dr. Harrison had told me at my last appointment that couldn't happen. I took another breath and looked up at Nate. "I'm fine." I took his offered hand and stood up. "Really."

"Are you sure?" He leaned in, his eyes searching my face. He was so close that I felt his breath, warm and sweet, on my nose. "Because you almost collapsed the other night too."

My eyes flew open. I swallowed. "It's nothing." I glanced around. "I was, um, really sick about a month ago and I'm still recovering from that."

Nate's forehead crinkled. "What kind of sick?"

"Oh…pneumonia. It was pretty bad. I was in the hospital." At the deeper wrinkling of his brow, I smiled. "But I'm fine now! Really."

"If you say so." He pressed his lips together like he didn't really believe me, but I kept smiling. "But I'll carry the books. You go sit on the couch."

"Okay." I settled myself into the couch next to the bookshelf and watched him bring the other box over. I touched my nose, still feeling the tickle of his breath there. Nate was concerned about me. He was—*literally*—carrying my books for me. *Stop it*, I told myself. These weren't my feelings. They were *hers*. I shook my head a little. Everything was mixed up inside me. I couldn't sort out what was mine and what was hers anymore.

Nate set the box down and straightened. "Are you sure you're okay? Do you want some water or something?"

"If I have to say 'I'm fine' one more time, I'm going throw this at you." I grabbed a book and shook it in the air. He threw his hands up in surrender, then settled on the floor next to the boxes.

"What do you think? Should we arrange them alphabetically or by genre?"

"Genre, then alphabetical," I said. "I'd hate for someone to accidentally pick up a teen vampire romance when they were really looking for a teen werewolf romance."

Nate laughed. "Those both sound *awful*."

"I've read my fair share," I admitted. I handed him a stack of literature textbooks that I'd had to get for school. "They all start to blend together after a while."

Nate slid the textbooks onto the shelf, then pulled one free. "Poe," he murmured.

"Yeah, I had to read that for school…" I trailed off as shadows slid across his face. I bent over to see the page he'd opened to.

"Annabel Lee." My heart jerked and shuddered. "'In a kingdom by the sea,'" I whispered. "That's where she got the name."

Nate looked up. I didn't want to notice that his eyes glistened. In the silence before he spoke, I heard the Catch, rippling through the sadness in my heart. "She said..." He stopped to clear his throat. "She said her mom used to read it to her when she was little." His hand stroked the page like it was something sweet and precious. "She said she used the name because she had to believe there were still beautiful places in the world."

My breath left my body in one *whoosh*. I closed my eyes with the force of its leaving. Behind my eyelids I saw Annabel's kingdom by the sea, the make-believe fairyland she imagined from the poem. *Turrets rise high over ocean cliffs, colorful banners waving from each tower. Elaborate stained glass windows shine multicolored in the sun, splaying reds and blues and golds on the floor of my castle. I run through tapestried halls, my laughter echoing off the stone walls. And I'm so there, so in that place, that I laugh for real, and the man on top of me takes it for fun, that I'm actually enjoying myself with him... I squeeze my eyes tighter and go back to my castle. Because he might own my body—at least for the next hour—but he can't capture my mind.*

The memory slid away and I was sickened in its wake. God, I could actually feel the weight of that man... I shuddered. She'd lied to Nate. She used the name because this place, this imaginary kingdom by the sea, was the place she escaped to when she was with men. It was the only beautiful place left for her.

A warm weight on my knee made me open my eyes. Nate's hand rested there, and he was looking up into my face. "Are you okay?"

"I—" I tasted salt in my mouth and caught the tears on my tongue. "No. No, I'm not okay."

Nate moved from the floor to sit beside me on the couch. "This stuff has really gotten to you, hasn't it?"

I shifted so that I sat cross-legged on the cushions, facing him. He had no idea how deep I was in, how far down "this stuff" had gotten to me. I waved my hand over the boxes. "I brought all this crap, and what good is it? It didn't help Annabel. I was so stupid to think that a new sweater or a book could make a difference."

"It *does* make a difference." Nate took my hands. "Do you know how many people don't care enough to even do that? At best, they write a check to ease their guilt—and hey, there's nothing wrong with money—but what you're doing is so much more valuable. You're here, educating yourself. You're writing that article, and maybe that will make other kids at your school get involved—"

I squirmed. But I couldn't very well tell him I was here because of Annabel's heart. Like he would believe me anyway. I looked at my hands, enclosed in his. "Why do you come here?" I asked, my voice low and quiet. "What makes you come here every day?"

Very slowly, deliberately, Nate pulled his hands away from mine. "I…went through kind of a dark period a couple of years ago. During that time, I found this place, and it…saved me."

"Oh." I hadn't expected him to tell me the real reason, but somehow it hurt that he was lying to me. Well, not lying exactly, but not telling me the whole truth. I slid my hands under my legs. A crazy thought popped into my head. "Hey, what are you doing on Valentine's Day?"

"Uh…" He lifted one shoulder. "I'm, not sure. Do you, um—"

"My parents have a party every year," I said and his shoulders relaxed. "It's huge and yes, there are adults there, but it's really fun. You should come. You know, if you're not doing anything."

"I'm not," he said quickly. "And I'd love to."

"Great." Now I'd have to find something cute to wear to the party. I glanced at the trash bags full of clothes. *Maybe I'd been too hasty…*

The door to the basement opened, sending a blast of cold air through the room. "Hey," I said, "isn't that Char?"

Nate swung his legs off the couch. "She *never* comes here." I followed him toward her.

As soon as she saw us, she marched over and we met in the middle of the room. "I got a message for you," she said, loud enough that a couple of people glanced toward us. "From Jules."

I took in a sharp breath, but Nate just reached out and touched Char's arm. She winced. "Why don't we get you some hot chocolate while you tell me?" he said. Char looked around the large room and wrapped her arms around her middle as though she was protecting herself from some invasive attack. "It'll just take a minute." Nate tugged her arm gently. "We have marshmallows."

Char narrowed her eyes at him. "The big fluffy ones or the crappy mini kind?"

Nate laughed. "The good ones. Come on."

As I walked behind them toward the kitchen, I saw why FAIR Girls wanted him around. He was good. *Really* good. Totally easy and casual and nonthreatening. He made *cocoa*, for crap's sake.

"Have a seat," Nate told her, indicating one of the chairs at the kitchen table. She sat, still hugging herself. I went to help Nate at the counter but he gave a barely-there shake of his head. "Talk to her," he muttered, only loud enough for me to hear.

I walked back to the table where Char sat and tucked myself into the chair across from her. What the hell should I say to her? Somehow "What's up?" seemed ridiculously out of place. Especially now that I had experienced—*vividly*—what went through a prostitute's mind when she was on the job. My stomach turned.

"What's with all the trash?" Char asked.

I blinked and looked over to where she was pointing. "Oh! It's clothes that I brought in. You should go through them, see if there's anything you want."

"I don't need your cast-offs," Char snapped.

"That's not what I meant." I picked at a gouge on the seat of the plastic chair beneath my legs. "You know, I shop at the Salvation Army all the time," I said. "You can find some really good stuff there, and for super cheap. I go there almost every Saturday with my friends."

Char raised an eyebrow. "Which one do you go to?"

"Usually the one in the South End."

"I've never been to that one." She chewed at her lip and glanced at the bags. "You got any sweaters in there?"

"Uh-huh. Some cashmere."

Char's gaze lingered on the bags before she shrugged. "Maybe I'll take a look."

"Here we go." Nate set down three mugs of hot chocolate, all with several big marshmallows floating at the top, and slid into the chair next to me.

Char picked up her mug and cradled it in her hands. I noticed how her eyes never stayed focused on one thing for more than a few seconds. She was always looking everywhere, and she sat on the edge of the chair like she was prepared to bolt at any instant.

"So what's the mess—" I started to ask but Nate knocked his knee against mine.

"Where are you staying these days, Char?"

"I got a place." She took a sip of her cocoa and slurped in one of the marshmallows.

"You getting enough to eat?" Despite Char's unfocused gaze, Nate never took his own eyes off her face. She shrugged in response to his question. "We have packets of ramen noodles if you want to take some."

She shrugged again. I tapped my foot against my chair; I wanted to hear Jules's message. Nate glanced at me. My foot froze, and I got it. As soon as Char delivered the message, she would leave. As long as we kept her plied with hot chocolate and talking about everything else, she would stay. And if she stayed long enough, she would come back again.

"I brought books too," I said. "If you want to borrow one."

Char snorted. Then her eyes brightened. "I read this one book about a girl who turns into a bird or something, and it ended on a total cliffhanger. You have the next book?"

"Yeah, I do!" I jumped up. Char trailed behind me as I knelt beside the boxes and rummaged through them. "It was actually a trilogy." I handed her all three books.

She stroked her finger along the worn spines. "Thanks."

"No problem." When we went back to the table, Char stuck the books in her bag. As I slid into my chair, I caught Nate smiling at me. I buried my face in my cup and pretended the heat in my face was from the steam.

Char drained the last of her cocoa. "Do you want some more?" Nate asked. She nodded. As Nate stood, the door to the basement opened. Char jumped, knocking her chair over. Even when she saw it was just another kid, she stayed on her feet, trembling.

"I gotta go," she said.

"Char, wait," I said, reaching for her arm.

She jerked away. Now her eyes were focused, their espresso depths drilling into me as she pushed up the sleeve of her coat. I had to tear my own gaze away from hers to look at her arm.

At first I thought I was seeing a tattoo because the marks were perfectly circular. But as I looked closer I saw they were red and angry. Like cigarette burns. Recent cigarette burns.

Still looking at me, Char rolled one sleeve up as high as her bicep and then the other. My stomach turned over. Nate sucked a breath in between his teeth.

The burns ran the length of both her arms, wine-colored against her dark skin. The little circles were evenly spaced, like someone had carefully measured out exactly where to place them. It was not the work of someone who was angry or rushed. It was the work of someone deliberate, someone who had held her arm in place and taken his time.

I swallowed hard. "Jules did this to you?"

Char nodded.

I tore my gaze away from the burns and looked at Nate. "Shouldn't we go to the police or something? Can't they do something? Arrest Jules?"

Char snorted and shoved her sleeves down. "Yeah, you do that. You go to the cops and see how far that gets you."

Nate sighed. I looked back and forth between him and Char. "Half the time when you try to report a pimp, the cops wind up arresting the girls," Nate explained. "And even if they do get the pimp, they usually don't have enough to keep him locked up for very long." His jaw tightened. "It's complicated."

"No, it's not," Char said, her voice hard. "It's pretty simple, actually. Don't come near me again. That's the message." She turned to go.

I rounded the table and blocked her path. "Wait. Annabel—what did he do to her?"

"Annabel? What does she have anything to do with this?"

"I don't know. Maybe nothing." *Maybe everything*, but I didn't say that out loud. "But she's dead now, isn't she? Doesn't that make you wonder?"

Char stared at me. She drew a long, shaky breath. "No," she said. "I don't wonder. I don't think. That's how I stay alive. Maybe Annabel thought too much, and that's what killed her." She took a step away and turned back over her shoulder. "Thanks for the books."

She stalked back across the room, her chunky-heeled boots thunking against the floor. I watched her leave, my rib cage squeezed tight. When the door had slammed shut behind her, I whirled around to Nate. “We have to do something. There must be someone we can report this to.”

He took my elbow and guided me back to the couch by the bookshelf. “I can talk to some of the FAIR Girls counselors. But we have to be very, very careful.”

I saw the burns in my mind’s eye, and even though I wanted to go charging after her, I knew he was right. “I know she said that she was only here to warn us,” I said, “but I could feel that she wanted help.” I met his gaze. “I’m not wrong, am I?”

He shook his head and half smiled. “You’ve got good instincts, Georgie.”

I looked away. Once again, everything jumbled up inside me. These weren’t my instincts. This was Annabel’s territory. I was just a visitor in her land.

CHAPTER ELEVEN

I was putting on lip gloss when Ella burst into my room. "I *love* the decorations this year! So much better than last year."

"Thanks. My grandma did it all." I smacked my lips together and turned away from the mirror. "Do I look okay?"

Ella shifted the neckline of my top so that it bared a shoulder. "Now you do."

I piled my hair on top of my head. "Up or down?"

"Definitely down." She narrowed her eyes at me. "You got a date coming or something?"

I laughed but didn't answer, just grabbed my brush and ran it through my hair a few times. I hadn't told anyone about Nate, but I knew once he showed up, Ella and Toni—not to mention my parents—would be all over me about him. My stomach gave a little flutter.

"Seriously, do you?" Ella pressed, her eyes narrowed at me in the mirror.

I gave her a little smile and winked. "Who knows?" And really, who did? He might not even show up. I gave myself one last appraisal in the mirror. "Okay, let's go."

"Who is he? Come on, tell me!" Ella pestered me until we got downstairs and the flurry of noise and activity drowned her out. Patsy Cline warbled from the surround-sound system about walking after midnight. The doorbell rang over and over as people arrived. I stood in the hall with movement all around me and veered into the kitchen.

"Georgie, where are you going?" Ella called after me.

"I'll meet you out there in a minute," I told her. The kitchen door swung shut behind me, cutting off the noise from the living room. I closed my eyes and breathed in the scent of chocolate and vanilla extract.

"Need any help?" I asked Grandma, who was bent over the oven. She straightened, a sheet of just-baked cookies in her oven-mitted hand.

"Would you mind frosting those?" She nodded at the cooled cupcakes on the table, half of them naked without frosting.

"Sure." I picked up the pastry bag and went to town. The repetition of the movement was soothing, and from my seat at the table I had a good view of the front hallway through the window in the kitchen door. No Nate yet.

"Aren't your friends here yet?" Grandma picked up a spatula and carefully transferred each cookie from the tray to the waiting plate.

"Yeah, they're out there somewhere." I finished one plate of cupcakes and moved on to the next one. These were red velvet. I iced one and bit into it, savoring the dark chocolatey taste of it. I licked the crumbs off my fingers one by one before frosting the rest. Red velvet was my favorite—mine and mine alone. It was good to delineate what belonged to me and what belonged to Annabel. I raised my eyes to the door again. Where Nate fell, I still wasn't sure.

"Why don't you go join them? I can finish that."

"It's okay." I pushed the plate of red velvet cupcakes away and pulled the last plate—pink vanilla—toward me. "It's a little crowded out there."

Grandma turned and leaned against the counter. "And since when did you become so claustrophobic?"

I shrugged without looking up. "I'm not claustrophobic."

"Then why are you avoiding your friends?"

At that, I did look up. "I'm not—" I bit my lip. I *was* avoiding my friends, and I wasn't sure why. At past Valentine's Day parties, I'd held court with them in the center of the room, dominating the scene. But that was when I used to tell them everything and they knew everything there was to know about me. Now, I felt like I couldn't talk to them at all.

Grandma grasped my elbow with fierce gentleness and propelled me toward the door. "Go. You should be with your friends, not hiding out with your old grandma." She gave me a kiss on the cheek and a swat on the rear and pushed me out into the hall.

The front door opened with a harsh gust of wind that swirled around me. At its center, I heard the Catch, whispering something inside me that I couldn't quite hear. I craned my neck around the two figures who had just come in, sure that Nate was behind them. But they were alone.

"Hi, Mr. Lowell," I said as the two people shed their coats and hats. "Hi, Michelle."

"Georgie!" Mr. Lowell boomed out. "It's great to see you up and about!"

"Thanks." I took his coat. I hadn't seen him since before my surgery, but Detective Lowell was the neighborhood cop who was friends with everyone on the block (and knew everyone's business). His daughter, Michelle, had gone to my school. "How's B.U., Michelle?"

"Good. Hard." She unwrapped a long tasseled scarf from her neck, her dark brown hair falling around her shoulders. I'd always envied her hair. I'd sworn it was the reason Josh Harris had dumped me and started dating her three years ago. We hadn't spoken much since that happened, and then she'd graduated. I gritted my teeth as I took her coat. I'd thought I was over that—it *was* three years ago—but my insides were all clenched up now as I looked at her. Guess part of me was still holding on to that anger after all.

"Come here and let me give you a hug," Detective Lowell said, pulling me into a big bear embrace. "Did you get the flowers we sent?" he asked when he released me, still holding on to my hands.

"Yes! They were beautiful. I'm sorry I haven't sent a thank-you note."

"Oh, please. You've had a lot going on." He squeezed my hands tight. Something bit into my skin and I winced. "Sorry!" Detective Lowell dropped my hands and held his up. A silver claddagh ring with a deep emerald set in the center flashed in the fairy lights strung along the staircase. "A Christmas present from Michelle."

"It's a really nice ring," I said to Michelle.

"Yeah well, my dad is always bragging about being Irish," she said, punching him lightly in the arm. "Figured he should have something to show for it."

"My little girl's so modest." He threw his arm around her shoulders and kissed the top of her head. Michelle rolled her eyes at me. "She had a 3.9 GPA last semester, did she tell you?"

"Daa-aad. You're embarrassing me."

"Curt!" My father charged into the hall, a wineglass in one hand, the other extended to Detective Lowell. "Great to see you!"

"You too." Detective Lowell gave Michelle a little push toward my dad. "You're up, kiddo."

"What is it, Michelle?" Dad tried to look serious, but given that he was mildly tipsy, it didn't work so well.

Michelle tossed her hair and straightened her shoulders. "Well, um, I'm applying for an internship and was wondering if you would write me a recommendation." She gave him a lopsided smile. "I mean, a recommendation from a Harvard dean would be really, really helpful."

"Of course! I would love to." He tapped her arm. "Call my office on Monday so that my assistant puts it on my to-do list. Now let me get your dad a drink."

They disappeared into the throng of people in the living room, leaving me and Michelle alone. We stared at each other while I shifted from one foot to the other. "So, B.U. is good?" I asked, at a loss for anything else to talk about.

She shrugged and gave a slight nod. "You still planning to go to Juilliard?"

"That's the plan. I still have to audition."

"I'm sure you'll get in. You always get everything you want," she added, leveling her eyes at me.

I opened my mouth to ask her what the hell that meant, but the front door flew open and a small crowd of people tumbled in. My mother barged through me and Michelle to greet them. I turned on my heel and headed into the living room where my friends were, feeling Michelle at my back as she followed. What the hell was her problem? Didn't the fact that I'd *almost died* prove that I actually didn't get everything I wanted? Michelle had been popular at Hillcoate but always had a little chip on her shoulder about being there on scholarship. Looked like that chip had gotten bigger over the last couple of years.

I made a beeline for the oversized armchair that Ella was treating as her throne. Toni and Sydney shared the ottoman like a pair of lapdogs, and a couple of boys from our school perched on the wide arms of the chair. "Hey guys, look who's here." I plastered a smile on my face as I gestured to Michelle. A few years ago, my parents had had to institute a no-drama rule at their parties, and I was determined to abide by it.

"Michelle!" Sydney jumped up and gave her a hug. "So nice of you to join us precollege slugs."

Ella and Toni both smiled at Michelle but didn't get up. They hadn't forgotten the Josh Harris incident either, and I couldn't wait to tell them about her snide remark. "How's college?" Ella asked, her voice tight.

"Hard."

I glanced sidelong at Michelle. That was the second time she'd said how hard college was. In the sparkly pink fairy lights that ringed the chair, I could just make out the dark circles under her eyes. Jeez. I got that college could be stressful, but the girl could lighten up a little.

"I hear B.U. parties are off the hook," Sydney said.

"I don't really go to parties," Michelle said.

"Oh, come *on*." Sydney nudged her. "You can't study *all the time*."

"You try taking chemical engineering," Michelle said. "And my dad's not paying thirty thousand dollars a year for me to goof off."

Wow. Ella and I exchanged a look. I ducked around Michelle and snuggled in next to Ella in the armchair. When we were little, we used to fit perfectly side by side in this chair. Now our backsides were crammed up against the armrests. "Looks like all work and no play makes Michelle no fun at all," Ella muttered in my ear.

"Wait 'til you hear about the attitude she pulled with me in the hall."

"Ugh, whatever. She's in college now. We shouldn't have to put up with her crap anymore."

"Right?" I glanced at Michelle. She chewed on her nail and stared out the window. "Why did she come anyway?"

"Her dad probably dragged her. You know how he likes to show her off."

I elbowed Ella. "That's mean."

"Oh please. You know it's true."

"I know, but..." I shimmied my shoulders a little. "Whatever. Let's not let her ruin our night. Besides, you know the rule—"

"No drama!" we said in unison and dissolved into giggles, earning a trio of dirty looks from Toni, Sydney, and Michelle who weren't in on the joke. Ella poked me in the side but my laughter died away. The Catch rang in my ears, louder than the music. I pulled away from Ella, the pulse in my throat quickening. *Nate*. Nate was here.

"Georgie!" Mom's voice rose over the noise but I didn't need her to tell me. My heart fluttered like moth wings. I scrambled out of the chair and pushed my way through the crowd. It was thick now, wall-to-wall people with half-drunk wineglasses in their hands.

When I reached the hallway, Mom's head was bent low to Nate's, and he was talking into her ear. "—friend of Georgie's from All Saints."

Mom caught sight of me. "What's All Saints?"

"It's where I'm doing all the research for that article I told you about." I tucked my arm into hers and smiled up into her face. "Nate's been helping me out a lot, so I thought it would be nice to return the favor and invite him to the party."

"My little social butterfly," Mom said with a little eye roll to Nate. Her cheeks were tinged red; she'd had a couple of glasses of wine already. "Well, enjoy yourself."

"Thank you, Mrs. Kendrick."

"Oh please, call me Liv." She waved her hand like it was a wand and twirled off into the living room.

Nate and I looked at each other. For the first time all night, there was no one else in the hallway. We glanced away and then back again at each other. "Can I, um, take your coat?"

"Sure." He shrugged it off. I laid it carefully on top of the towering pile of coats on the bench. He leaned forward and peered into the kitchen, then leaned back to look up the stairs. "Nice house."

"Thanks. It's, like, a hundred and thirty years old or something. By the way," I said in a low voice, "I told my parents that All Saints is in Jamaica Plain."

Nate laughed. "They're not so keen on Murderpan, huh? Fair enough. By the way," he said, his voice like velvet and silk, "you look great."

I flushed beneath his blue eyes, but I didn't look away. "So, um, do you."

"Listen." He stepped in close to me. "I may have found something out. I'm not sure what it is or if it even means anything. Another girl came to All Saints today—I've seen her before on the street, and I know she's one of Jules's girls."

My gaze hadn't left his eyes and I barely registered what he was saying. The fairy lights and the romantic music and the sound of laughter filled me. At that moment, Annabel didn't matter. She wasn't here. *I* was.

I grabbed his arm and pulled him toward the kitchen. "You want a cupcake?"

"Sure." He let me drag him along. "So she told me about this place—"

I plucked a cupcake from the tiered platter and held it up to him. "You like red velvet?"

"Yeah, I do." He took the cupcake but didn't bite into it. "So this place she told me about—"

"Nate."

He stopped and squinted at me. "Yeah?"

"It's a party. Let's have fun."

"Oh." He looked around him and took in the twinkling lights, the loud music and merriment. "Right."

I took his arm and led him back toward the living room. "You do know how to have fun, don't you?"

He halted in the middle of the hall. "You know…it's been a long time since I've had some fun. I'm always working or at All Saints."

My heart squeezed. I fought the urge to hug him hard and just touched his hand instead. "Well, tonight it's your job to forget all that." I pointed at the cupcake in his hand. "Sugar always helps."

Without taking his eyes off me, Nate took a big bite, leaving a dollop of frosting at the corner of his lip. Before I could stop myself, I wiped it off and licked my finger. His eyes darkened to such a deep blue that I couldn't breathe. "Georgie…"

"Hear ye, hear ye!" Dad's voice made us both stumble away from each other. We gravitated toward the threshold of the living room and watched Dad climb onto a chair. The room quieted and Colt turned down the music. "Liv and I have this party every year, but this year it has particular meaning for us." Dad leveled his gaze at me. "Someone once told me, just before Georgie was born, to get ready to wear my heart outside of my body. And it is true. Our children are our hearts manifested."

In the twinkling light, his eyes were shiny. "And there is nothing scarier than almost losing your heart, as we almost lost Georgie." His voice quavered a little. I shifted from one foot to the other, uncomfortably aware of Nate's eyes on me. "But we didn't, and so tonight we celebrate the heart and the power of love. To Georgie!"

"To Georgie," the room echoed. Colt turned the music back up and the chatter began again.

I grabbed a cookie off a nearby plate and bit into it, avoiding Nate's stare. He reached around me and took a cookie for himself. "What was that all about?"

I took a long time chewing and swallowing the rest of my cookie. "Remember I told you I was sick?"

Nate searched my face. "I didn't realize it was that serious."

"It was pretty bad," I admitted. "But I'm fine—"

"Georgie!" Ella came up from behind me and draped her arms around my neck. "We almost lost you!"

Nate backed away as Ella and Toni tackled me, mimicking my dad's sappy speech. "Yeah, yeah," I said, "you can't get rid of me that easily." I disentangled myself from them. At the same moment, they spotted Nate.

"Hi," Ella said, extending her hand. "I'm Ella."

"Nate."

Ella grinned as she pumped his hand, flicking her gaze between him and me. "Nate, huh? Funny...Georgie hasn't mentioned you."

"Does she tell you everything?" Nate asked.

"Pretty much."

"Okay, okay," I said, stepping in between them, which forced Ella to drop Nate's hand. "I don't tell you *everything*."

"Clearly." The wicked grin was still on her face, but I could tell there was an undercurrent of hurt beneath it because I *hadn't* told her about Nate. "Guess she wanted to keep *you* a secret."

I slid an impatient look at Nate and pulled Ella into the corner, out of earshot. "I met him at that church I've been going to. You know, to research that article."

Ella squeezed my arm. "Why didn't you tell me you met a guy? That's major!"

"I know, I just..." I couldn't come up with an excuse fast enough. "I'm sorry."

"You can make it up to me by giving me all the details." She pinched me. "And I do mean all."

I swallowed. That would be a challenge...

"Tomorrow," Ella added and spun me around to give me a little push toward Nate. He was chatting with Toni, who kept glancing over her shoulder at us. We joined them and I introduced Nate around to my other friends. The guys sized him up and the other girls looked him over, asking him all sorts of inappropriate questions.

Only Michelle seemed uninterested. She was nursing a long-necked beer in the shadows, even though I was pretty sure she wasn't twenty-one yet. Seriously? With her cop father in the same room? She met my eyes over her beer, her gaze hard and challenging. I shrugged. Whatever. Like I told Ella, I wasn't going to let her ruin my night.

As I turned away, blood pumped through me with the same beat as the music. The sounds in the room faded and the Catch rose up in their place. Its whisper grew louder and louder until it hurt my eardrums. Beneath its reverberations, I felt something else, something sharp and sickening. It slithered through my ribs and wrapped itself around my heart. I turned in a small, fast circle, the room a blur. The thing was dreadful, spreading itself to every corner of my being.

It was fear.

Not anxiety. Not I-haven't-studied-for-this-test kind of fear. Not even standing-on-top-of-a-black-diamond-trail-when-you're-only-a-green-trail-kind-of-skier fear. It was the bone-crunching fear of facing down death and knowing you're going to lose. I'd felt this fear before. I'd felt it when they wheeled me into surgery.

But why was I feeling it now?

The music slowed and dropped into a slow, sexy rhythm. With knife-edge clarity, I realized the fear was not my own. It belonged to Annabel. But why? I turned again and found Nate. He was right next to me; he had never left my side. Without thinking, I took his hand.

Instantly, he dropped the conversation he was having with Sydney and bent toward me. His thumb stroked my palm. I tilted my head up to meet his eyes. "Do you want to dance?"

He didn't answer, just encircled his arm around my waist and pulled me in. Patsy Cline sang about being crazy, and Nate rocked me back and forth. With each sway, I softened in his arms and the bands of fear loosened. I rested my head on his shoulder and closed my eyes. He moved me across the floor, and the fear disappeared. Whatever Annabel had been afraid of, Nate was the cure.

Then why hadn't she gone to him before she'd jumped off that balcony?

I sucked in a breath and let it out slowly. It was part of the mystery I had to unravel. Once I did, I'd be able to see Nate with my own eyes and sort out which feelings were mine and which were Annabel's. I pulled back a little, but Nate tightened his arms around me and held me close. He dipped his head. "You're really all better now? Not sick anymore?"

Oh yeah, I was great. I was losing my memories, my body could reject my new heart at any moment, and I had a scar the size of a Cadillac on my chest. "I'm fine," I murmured into his shoulder.

"Good." His mouth was so close to my ear that his breath tickled my skin. "Because it would suck if you died after I've only known you for a couple of weeks."

"Yeah, that would suck. More for me than you, though."

He laughed, and the sound reverberated into my chest, into my heart… I stiffened a little. Always that reminder that I was no longer just Georgie. There was someone else inside me that I had to compete with. I lifted my head from his shoulder. Nate's eyes were soft on my face. "Do you like me?" I asked.

Nate blinked. He looked even more surprised than I felt at the boldness of the question. But he didn't hesitate when he answered. "Yes."

"Why? What is it about me you like?"

His brow furrowed, but when he spoke, it was without confusion. "You have guts. I like how willing you are to get involved with FAIR Girls." He smiled. "You have a good heart, Georgie."

I felt his words in my gut, heard them echo inside me along with the Catch. I laid my head back down and swallowed hard to fight the tears. A good heart. He liked my good heart. But it wasn't mine.

CHAPTER TWELVE

When I woke up the next morning, I lay for a long time staring at the ceiling. Early sunlight streaked the walls. I watched it stretch along the wall like a living thing. With each passing minute, the light brightened, but the shadows also darkened.

I touched the scar on my chest, lightly running my finger along its length. Dr. Harrison said it would never go away completely. There would always be a mark on my skin. But what about beneath the skin? Would Annabel always be marked on my heart too? When would my life be my own again?

The previous night replayed in my head in snapshots. The dollop of frosting on Nate's lips. His hands around my waist as we danced. Him telling me that he liked me…and that I had a good heart.

A stolen heart, more like. Maybe all the good he could see in me belonged to Annabel. Maybe everything else was worthless. What good had I done with my life? How could straight A's at Hillcoate compare to the work Nate did with FAIR Girls?

I lowered my head into my hands and massaged my temples. She was making me doubt myself to my core, shaking me off my anchor like a storm-swept sea. I had known what I wanted to do with my life since I was ten, and she wasn't going to take that away from me.

I tossed my covers off and grabbed my oboe off my desk chair. While the rest of the household awoke in post-party slow motion, I sank into the intricacies of the Poulenc concerto, reworking the same five measures over and over until they were second nature. The smell of pancakes wafted up to the second floor, but I stayed in my room, lost to the music. Keeping myself tethered in this storm. Drowning out the Catch. Staking my claim in my own heart, the place where my music lived.

When I finally felt secure enough to let go, I put my oboe away and went downstairs. At the door to the kitchen, I paused. The remnants of breakfast were strewn across the kitchen table. Dad read the newspaper; Mom scribbled notes in her journal; Colt played on his iPhone; and Grandma flipped through a *Real Simple* magazine. I peered through the round window in the door. Everyone was in their own little world, and their worlds seemed so much more peaceful than mine. It almost felt like an act of war to push the door open and intrude.

I was just about to back away when Mom spotted me. "Good morning, sweetie."

"Morning." I edged into the kitchen but didn't sit.

"You sounded good," Dad said. "Is that the piece you're playing for Juilliard?"

"That's the plan. I could go with something easier…"

"Don't you dare," Dad said. "If you can nail the hard piece, you'll have a better chance of getting in."

"I guess." I chewed on my cuticle and imagined for an instant what my parents would do if I told them I wanted to drop out of school and get my GED like Nate. The house would probably explode.

"There are leftover pancakes," Grandma said.

"Thanks." I was being dumb. Going to Juilliard was my idea, not my parents. They just wanted me to do well. I headed to the counter, where a plate with a short stack of pancakes sat. Out of the corner of my eye, I saw Mom nudge Dad and nod to me.

"So, Georgie," Dad said, "did you have fun last night?"

"Yeah. Great party." I drizzled maple syrup over my plate and carried it to the table. I sat next to Grandma, who patted my knee without taking her eyes off her magazine.

"Did your friends have fun?"

"Everyone had a blast." Except Michelle. She'd spent most of the night being antisocial, until she finally tore her dad away from telling his umpteenth cop story and got him out the door.

"They want to know who the boy is," Colt said loudly. One headphone dangled from his ear and his fingers flew over the iPhone screen. "That's all they've been talking about."

"Okay, Colt, that's enough." Mom snapped her journal shut and twisted in her chair toward me. "But you can't blame us for being curious."

"He's just a friend," I said, picking at my breakfast.

Dad laid his newspaper down with a loud rustle. "He looked mighty friendly with you."

"Oh, *Dad*." I rolled my eyes at him. "We were just *dancing*. Trust me, we are just friends."

"Honey, we've known all of your friends since you were six," Mom said. "So when a new one shows up out of the blue, I think we have a right to know who he is."

"Okay," I said, "his name is Nate. He volunteers with the organization that helps trafficked girls, and he's been helping me with my research. Anything else you want to know?"

"Where does he go to school?" Dad asked, his eyes laser-focused on me.

Here it comes. I shoved a forkful of pancakes in my mouth and took a long time chewing. "He doesn't. He works at Starbucks and he volunteers at the church."

"Did he graduate?"

"He got his GED."

Dad folded his arms across his chest. "And he's working at Starbucks to save for college?"

"I don't know. We haven't really discussed it."

"Does he plan to go to college at all?"

"You know, Dad," I said, my voice climbing a little high, "college is not the end-all, be-all."

"That may be true, but it's still very important—"

"The work that Nate does at All Saints is a million times more important than college," I said. My temper had slipped away from me and was out of control now. "He literally saves lives every day. How many lives do you save every day in your ivory tower at Harvard?"

"Georgie!" Dad slapped his palm against the table, making Colt jump. "That is a very rude thing to say."

I jabbed my finger at him. "Well, I don't appreciate you insinuating that Nate is a bad person because he doesn't go to college."

Mom sighed. "That's not what we're saying at all. We just want to know who he is, because you two looked awfully close last night."

My jaw tightened. "Well, we're just friends. We are nothing more than friends. If anything more happens, I'll be sure to tell you all about it *right away*." I stormed out of the kitchen. I shouldn't have gone in there in the first place. I should've stayed on the other side of the door, instead of trying to be a part of a world where I didn't belong anymore.

Once upstairs in my room, I grabbed my phone off my nightstand. Are you at All Saints?

No. Working till 3, came the almost instantaneous reply.

Can I come by? I promise to order something.

Sure. I make a mean latte.

I started to get dressed, then grabbed my phone again. This time I texted Ella. Remember how you said you didn't mind covering for me? I was fully dressed by the time the reply buzzed through.

Only because he's so freaking cute.

The Starbucks that Nate worked at had a much different clientele than the one in Brookline. Instead of the cluster of moms with their eight-hundred-dollar strollers and college students working on their brand-new MacBooks, there were a homeless woman and a nerdy boy who looked way too young to be drinking coffee.

Nate spotted me as soon as I walked in and gave me a big smile. "Hey there."

"Hey." I leaned on the counter and studied the menu on the wall, even though I knew everything that Starbucks offered.

"Thanks for inviting me last night. I had a good time."

I could feel his eyes on me so I lowered my gaze. When I looked at him, I couldn't help smiling. "I did too."

We were standing there, looking sort of goofy at each other, when a voice broke us apart. "You gonna help her or flirt with her all day?"

Nate flushed as a woman emerged from behind the Employees Only door. She looked like she was in her late twenties, with flyaway blond hair and oversized glasses. The little name tag on her green apron read Jan. She snatched a croissant from the microwave just as it dinged and ducked under the counter to deliver it to the homeless woman.

Nate cleared his throat. "So, uh, do you want anything?"

"Sure." I leaned into the counter, looking up at the menu again. "But I can't have caffeine."

"Oh. How come?"

"Doctor's orders."

He raised an eyebrow but didn't comment further. "I can make you a tea latte from one of our herbal teas."

"That sounds good."

I stood at the coffee bar and watched as he brewed the tea and steamed the milk. His hands were sure and practiced, and he took the same care with making a latte that he did when he was recounting facts and figures about trafficked girls. I tilted my head, my spine warm and tingling. No matter what Nate did, he did it one hundred percent and he did it with pride. I admired that. It was so different from the guys at Hillcoate who expected to half-ass their way to success.

When he was done, he handed me the cup with a flourish. "Okay if I take my break, Jan?" he asked. She waved at him and went back to stocking the bakery case. Nate directed me to one of the comfier-looking couches and sat down beside me.

"Careful, that's hot," he warned me as I lifted the cup to take a sip.

"Thanks." I took a cautious sip. "Oh, that's delicious."

He smiled and settled back on the cushions. "So what's up?"

"Nothing much." I rolled my eyes. "My parents were all over me this morning about you."

"Sorry," he said. "But at least they care."

"They are so annoying!" My hands were shaking. I carefully set the cup down on the low table in front of me to keep from spilling it. "They have such a narrow view of the world. I never noticed it before, but now it's so obvious. They seem so threatened by someone who doesn't follow their prescribed life plan." I glanced at Nate. "My dad was giving me the third degree about why you're not in college."

"Oh." Nate leaned forward and rested his elbows on his knees. "Well, money mostly. But also I just didn't get my act together fast enough to apply."

"You mean after you got your GED."

"Yeah." He pushed his hand through his hair. I watched it travel behind his ear and down his neck and drop back to his knee. I wanted to follow it with my own hand and touch his hair, his ear, his throat. I took another sip of my tea to hide my flush.

"I just wasn't ready to plunge myself into the college world," Nate went on. "I needed to take some time off and figure out what I want to do."

"Have you?" I asked. "Figured out what you want to do?"

"I think so." Nate took a deep breath, like he was about to say something he didn't say out loud often. "I want to go into child psychology. I want to help kids, especially at-risk teens."

"You would be amazing at that," I said.

He grinned with obvious relief. "Thanks." He hunched his shoulders a little. "I still need to save a little more money but I'm hoping to apply for next year."

"Your parents won't help out?"

"My parents…" Nate exhaled a long breath. "They'd help if they were able to. They're just not, right now." He tapped his knee against mine. "What about you? What do you wanna be when you grow up?"

"Oh." I chewed at my lip. "Have I told you that I play the oboe?"

"The *oboe?*" Nate raised his eyebrows. "That's not an instrument you hear every day."

I half smiled. "Yeah, exactly. That's how I got into it. My music teacher convinced me to switch from flute to oboe because nobody else was playing it and he needed one to fill out his orchestra."

"And it stuck."

"Yeah, it stuck." I scrunched my face up little. "I'm actually… really good."

"And that's what you want to do with your life?"

In the late-morning sunlight, Nate's eyes looked even bluer than usual. The color reminded me of the way the Atlantic Ocean looked on a really sunny day. My breathing slowed as I looked into their depths, and for the first time since I'd felt Annabel in my heart, I said the thing that I was most scared to admit.

"For as long as I can remember, I've wanted to go to Juilliard and play in an orchestra like the BSO or the New York Phil. It's always been the only thing that mattered. But now, ever since I got sick…I don't know. I feel like it's too trivial. I should be doing something more important with my life."

"Bringing music and art to the world is important," Nate pointed out. His eyes leveled with mine and the world slowed down. There could have been a hurricane around us and I don't think Nate would have looked away. That's how intense his gaze on me was. "But there's nothing like nearly dying to make us rethink everything."

"Yes," I breathed. Without breaking eye contact with him, I reached up and unfastened the top few buttons on my cardigan.

Nate started and glanced around to see if anyone was watching. "Uh, Georgie—" Then his eyes fell on the scar that peeked out from the top of the sweater. He stared at it for a moment and lifted his eyes to my face.

"My heart failed," I whispered. "When I had the pneumonia. It happened very suddenly. I was going to die. I had a heart transplant," I finished, my voice just a wisp of breath, of air, of almost nothing. I swallowed hard, watching Nate's face as he digested the information.

He raised his hand and, haltingly, reached out to touch the scar. His finger was like a butterfly's wing, soft and fluttering and oh so warm. "Does it hurt?"

"Sometimes." I licked my lips; they'd grown dry and cracked in just the last minute. "When I overexert myself. Like…the first night we met. When I almost collapsed in the street. That's why."

"But you're okay now, right?" He looked in my eyes again, the ocean-blue enveloping me like soft rain. "You're not going to die on me anytime soon, are you?"

"I hope not," I said and we both laughed nervously. "I have to take medication for the rest of my life so my body doesn't reject the heart."

"'Reject the heart,'" Nate murmured. "There's a metaphor in there somewhere."

He had no idea.

With some reluctance, I buttoned my cardigan back up, closing off Nate's touch. "So, that's why everything's changed.

Everyone…my parents and friends…all just expect me to be the same old Georgie. But I woke up from the surgery—"

"—a different person," Nate finished for me.

Heat tightened my throat. Tears prickled behind my eyelids. *He got it.* "Wow." I sniffled. "Not even my own parents can see that."

"It's because they've known you for so long. They're too close." He used his thumb to swipe away one of the tears that had fallen on my cheeks. I leaned into his hand, pressing my skin into the contour of his knuckles. "I've only known the post-op Georgie so it's easier for me to see."

"I kinda like that you've only known the post-op me," I said. The tears had stopped but his hand still cradled my face. "Is that weird?"

"No." His palm was so warm against my cheek. "Because it feels like we've known each other for a long time." I couldn't see anything past the dark ocean of his eyes. "Doesn't it?"

I nodded. My heart thudded in my rib cage, like Annabel was trapped inside and pounding with her fists to get out. *It's her*, I thought. *It's her he knows, not me.* "Nate…"

"You ever coming back to work, Romeo?" Jan's gravelly voice interrupted my thoughts. Nate glanced at the clock above the coffee bar and sighed.

"I'm sorry," he said. "Duty calls."

"That's okay." His hand dropped away from my face. A chill swept through me.

"I'm off at three," he offered.

"I think my parents would ground me for life," I said.

He laughed. "All Saints tomorrow afternoon, then?"

"Definitely."

We stood up and looked at each other awkwardly for a moment. "Screw it," Nate muttered and pulled me against him. His hand wound itself deep into my hair and he tilted my head back, bent over me, and lowered his lips to mine.

My whole body woke up singing, every nerve blazing with golden light. I felt him everywhere—inside my veins, filling my head, surrounding my heart...my heart—*No, this is mine, mine*—I wrapped my arms around his neck and crept my fingers into his hair. He was kissing *me*, not Annabel...this was *mine.*

After a long moment that felt too short, he released me. I stumbled back a step, slowly becoming aware that Jan and the homeless woman were clapping and the nerdy boy was whistling. I flushed and bit my lip, still tasting Nate there. I was pleased to see that he was breathing hard and had a little red in his cheeks too.

"So, um, tomorrow then," he said. I walked backward to the door so that I could watch him duck under the counter.

"Tomorrow," I promised and backed out onto the street. Blinking in the bright sunlight, I touched my mouth. He had kissed me. *Me.* But what I still wasn't sure about was who had kissed him back—me or Annabel.

CHAPTER THIRTEEN

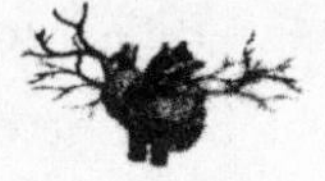

After I left Nate at Starbucks, I wandered for a while. My brain was on fire with a million thoughts. I had never fallen so hard for a boy, and I didn't know if it was my own leap or Annabel pushing me off the cliff. But I couldn't deny that kissing Nate had felt amazing.

I stopped at a street corner, tapping my foot against the curb as I waited for the light to change. Now all the doubts started to creep in, the what-ifs and worries. If we started something, I *had* to tell him about Annabel. I couldn't base our entire relationship on a lie. And he could help me find out who Annabel was. Unless…he thought I was a crazy, nuthouse girl. Which was the more likely scenario.

The light changed and I crossed the street, head bent against a gust of hard wind that blew up. "Okay," I said out loud, earning an odd stare from a guy walking his dog past me. I'd table the issue of telling Nate the truth for another day. I'd work on finding out Annabel's real identity on my own. The sooner I did that, the sooner I could get her out of my head—and heart—and know for sure if the thing with Nate was real.

But I was pretty sure I'd need help, even if it wasn't from Nate.

I stopped in the middle of the sidewalk and spun around, my

strides purposeful now. Nate couldn't be the only one at All Saints who had known Annabel. She used to go there a lot, he said. She'd even been to the holiday party. Someone else had to have known something about her, and maybe that someone would be there now, while Nate wasn't.

But when I pushed open the door to the basement, a scene very different from any other time I'd been there greeted me. The place was overrun with toddlers running and screaming and climbing everywhere. A handful of adults tried to wrangle them, but they were no match for the deafening energy of the little kids. I stood openmouthed in the doorway until I realized that it was Sunday. Church day. The congregation must run a daycare while the kids' parents were upstairs in services.

I was about to leave when I spotted Tommy in the farthest corner, her skinny black jeans and Madonna: Blond Ambition World Tour T-shirt in complete contrast to the miniature suits and fancy dresses. I skirted the edge of the room, nearly tripping on several three-year-olds, until I reached her.

"Tommy, right?" She looked up from her magazine and smiled at me. "You're Nate's friend, aren't you? Nice to meet you officially," I said and shook her hand.

"You too. Are you looking for Nate? He's not here."

"I know—I just saw him at Starbucks." I waved my hand at the room. "Um, I wasn't expecting this, though."

Tommy laughed. "I like to come here on Sundays and completely freak the parents out." She scooted over on the love seat. "Take a load off."

"Thanks." I watched two little girls playing tea party with their baby dolls. "I thought this was, like, an all-inclusive church."

"Everyone is all-inclusive until the transfolk walk into the room." Her laugh was so throaty that a couple of the adults looked over at us, their eyes narrowed.

"That must really suck, having to deal with that kind of prejudice." I stared back at the kid wranglers until their attention got pulled away by a boy throwing a Tonka truck at the wall.

"It's not fun," Tommy agreed. "Sometimes I think people are just afraid to ask the awkward questions they have to ask in order to, you know, educate themselves. But I wish they would."

I bit my lip. "Actually, I have an awkward question."

"Shoot."

"Why do you still call yourself Tommy?" I shrugged one shoulder as she leveled her gaze on me. "Why not change it to something—I don't know—more feminine?"

The corner of Tommy's mouth turned up. "Because I don't deserve it yet."

"Oh, come on—"

"No, seriously." Tommy tossed her long hair and it shimmied over her shoulders. "I've been doing so much work *on me*—kicking my addiction, dealing with how I react to people's prejudice—that I feel like until I work through that shit, I haven't earned my new name." She kicked one leg out in front of her and flexed her foot. "When I get my surgery—when I emerge from that cocoon a beautiful butterfly—then I'll christen myself with a new name."

"Wow." I breathed in deep. "I think I just got chills." I touched her arm. "Just please…don't name yourself Chrysalis."

Tommy laughed again. "How do you laugh so easily?" I asked before I could stop myself. "After all you've been through?"

"Because if I don't laugh, I'll cry and then I'll ruin my mascara." She winked at me. "No one likes a raccoon."

We both laughed. It was infectious, and it felt good after the roller coaster I'd put myself on for the last day. Tommy tossed her magazine aside. "So if you didn't come here to see Nate, what are you doing here?"

"Oh." I cocked my head. "Did you know that girl Annabel who used to come here?"

The slight smile that lingered on Tommy's lips died away. "Yeah. Yeah, I knew her." She blinked several times, fast. "Now I really will cry," she said. "Thinking about Annabel always makes me cry."

I touched her arm. "I'm sorry. I shouldn't have brought it up."

"No, it's okay." Tommy fanned her face with her hand. "You're writing an article about her, right? Nate said something to me about it."

"Yeah," I said, looking away. Tommy was so upfront about who she was. It was hard to lie to her face. "I'm trying to figure out what drove her to the streets in the first place."

"Jeez." Tommy sank back into the cushions. "It could've been anything. I know this one girl who was sold by her friend's father during a sleepover."

I gasped and pressed my fist to my mouth. "That's *sick*."

"It's just a lethal combination, the system plus low self-worth. Then some hot guy comes in and tells you how beautiful you are, how he's going to take care of you..." Tommy's jaw hardened as she looked beyond me at a past she'd escaped. "And he really does take care of you at first. And you would do anything to repay that." She snapped her gaze back to my face. "Even allow him to sell you."

I shivered. I remembered what Nate had told me, that Annabel didn't think she deserved anything better. Jules must've spotted that a mile away. "Do you think..." I trailed off as Tommy's words sank in. "What do you mean, 'the system'?"

Tommy blinked. "You know. The foster system."

"Foster?" I sat up straight, my breath caught in my throat. "Annabel was a foster kid?"

"Well, sure. A lot of the girls here are," Tommy said, and I remembered that Nate had said something similar the other day. The wheels in my brain churned, clicking the bits and pieces I'd collected so far into place.

"Annabel was eighteen, right?" My words tripped over one and another.

Tommy peered into my face. "Are you okay?"

"Right? She was eighteen?"

"Yeah, I think so... I mean, none of the girls here are really forthcoming about their age."

"Of course!" I jumped up, startling a small girl who had wandered close to our corner. She ran to the nearest adult, who gave us a dirty look and directed the girl to a pile of blocks. "Foster kids age out of the system when they turn eighteen, right?"

"Well, yeah." Tommy watched me pace back and forth in front of the couch, a nervous look on her face.

"That's why she was a Jane Doe! That's why she didn't have any parents to claim her!" I slid to a halt and whirled to face Tommy. "Her parents! What happened to them, do you know?"

"I…I have no idea." She reached out and touched my wrist. "Um, seriously, are you okay?"

"There's got to be a record of it," I murmured. "If she was in the system, there must be."

"Hey." Tommy's fingers tightened on my wrist and she shook my arm. "What's going on?"

I dropped back down to the couch and hugged her. "I just had a breakthrough, thanks to you."

She hugged me back. "I guess you're welcome."

Annabel was eighteen when she died. Presumably the foster kid system held on to records for at least a year after a kid aged out. Which meant that somewhere in the jungle of government offices in the city of Boston, there was a file with Annabel's real name on it, along with her last known address.

Dinner that night was accompanied by a symphony of forced chitchat and a long review of the book Dad had just finished. I tapped my foot against the table for the length of the meal, and as soon as I'd cleared my plate, I escaped upstairs.

I sat on my bed and opened my journal. On one page, I wrote

down all the memories Annabel had given me: strawberries, her bedroom, the cemetery, her kingdom by the sea, Nate. I started to write down the memories of my own that I'd lost, but I tore the page out and crumpled it up. This wasn't about me right now. I needed to decipher Annabel's side of things first, and when I'd done that, I could figure myself out.

Besides, who knew how many memories I'd lost if I couldn't remember them?

On the opposite page, I wrote all the things I'd learned about Annabel through my research: 826 Emiline Way, Jules, Annabel Lee, Nate's work at All Saints, foster kid.

Then I drew lines. When I was done, I had a crazy *Beautiful Mind*-like map. But everything was connected. And it was starting to make some sense.

I stared at the words "foster kid" and circled them over and over with my pen, my brain trying to make sense of them. Under what circumstances did a kid get turned over to the foster system? When no one else could take care of them, like if both parents died… My throat tightened as I imagined my parents no longer around. My whole body hurt at the thought of it. But in that situation, Grandma would take me in, or my Aunt Bobbi who lived in Chicago, or even the myriad of friends that my parents had. Someone would step forward and take me and Colt in. Annabel had no one.

I took a deep breath and grabbed my laptop from my desk. I was on the verge of finding something out. I could feel it. A quick Google search brought me to the Massachusetts Department of

Children and Families page. I drummed my fingers on the side of the computer. I might be on the verge, but where the hell did I go from here? An internal search of the website wouldn't exactly yield personal information about a former ward of the state. Still…I let my fingers hover over the keys. It looked so easy in the movies when people hacked into mainframes to get the information they needed.

My phone buzzed, making me jump. I looked at the screen with its lit-up picture of Ella on her last birthday. I reached for it but my hand froze before hitting the answer button. If I talked to her, I'd wind up telling her about Nate. And I wasn't sure I wanted to yet.

The phone stopped buzzing, and an instant later, a text popped up from Ella. You around?

Doing homework, I responded. My lessons with the tutor start tomorrow.

I hear ya. I have a ton. After a moment, another message zinged in. Wanna meet up tomorrow afternoon?

Can't. Going to All Saints to do research.

Research??? Is that what the cool kids are calling it these days?

Ha-ha.

Seriously, tho, when am I gonna see you? Feel like you're avoiding me.

My insides twisted as I read that. I'm not! I wanted to respond right away, but I couldn't. I *was* avoiding her. I was avoiding everyone from my pre-op world. No, I lied. I just have a lot on my mind.

No you don't. You have a cute boy on the brain.

I half smiled. Even through texts, she could read me like a book. And you never told me what exactly I was covering for today, she added.

I'll call you tomorrow. <3 I shut off my phone. I stared at the black screen for a moment. A month ago if I'd kissed a boy, I would've texted Ella the minute we came up for air. But Nate… he was different. He was on the outside of my leaf-lined world, and I wanted to keep him separate.

He belonged to Annabel, and she belonged to me.

My throat tightened. No, I had that wrong. She owned me, heart and soul. I was chained to her, and until I broke that chain, Nate would never be mine and I would never be free.

CHAPTER FOURTEEN

My insides were in knots when I went to All Saints the next day. All through my first lesson with my tutor, Mr. Blount—or Mr. Blowhard, as I secretly nicknamed him within the first ten minutes of meeting him—I'd obsessed about seeing Nate. I had no idea what to say to him, or what he would say to me. When I got out of the cab, I spotted him standing on the little patch of lawn next to the side entrance to the basement. My hands shook as I fumbled with the cab door. Was he going to tell me it had been a mistake?

As I walked toward him, I shoved my hands in my pockets and hunched my shoulders against the cold. Fine, whatever. I'd just get as much information out of him about Annabel as I could and never see him again. I was ten feet away from him when he jogged forward, his breath white mist in front of his face. He didn't stop when he reached me. We collided into one another and I felt myself lifted off the ground, held tight in his arms.

"I couldn't wait to see you," he said, his voice muffled against my hair.

I laughed out loud and hugged him around the neck. He lowered his head so that our noses touched. When his lips finally touched mine, the kiss was sweet and possessive at the same time.

I swallowed my doubts and pressed myself into him. He held me fast, his hands splayed across my back, and I could feel the heat of him even through all our layers.

When at last he let me go, my skin was on fire. I certainly had experience kissing, but most of the boys I'd kissed were clumsy and awkward. This was on a whole other level. "Can we just stay out here and do this for a while?"

Nate smiled against my mouth. I breathed him in, tasting coffee and spices and winter. "I wish," he whispered. "But there's someone inside you should meet. I wanted to tell you about her the other night at the party, but we, uh—"

"Got distracted."

"Yeah." Nate took my hand and led me toward the door. "She's another one of Jules's girls. I'm pretty sure she knew Annabel. I saw them on the street together a couple of times. But she never set foot in All Saints before the other night."

"Why do you think she's come here now?"

"I don't know. Fear?" Nate hunched a shoulder. "The other night when she came in, she seemed pretty freaked out about something, but I couldn't get her to talk." He squeezed my hand. "Maybe you can."

"Me?"

He dipped his head to look into my eyes. "You're good at it. You got Char to talk."

"I got Char to threaten. There's a difference." His head was still so close to mine that I couldn't resist. I reached up and pulled him all the way to my mouth.

"Stop doing that," he said when we separated, "or we'll be out here all night."

"That's my evil plan." I grinned, but when we reached the door to the basement, I swallowed it down. Nate's work here meant a lot and I didn't want to distract him. Too much. Just before he opened the door, I put my hand on his. "Hey, Annabel was a foster kid, right?"

Nate raised his eyebrow. "Yeah, why?"

"I just wondered if you knew anything about her case. I mean, I know she aged out of the system but there's got to be a file on her somewhere, right?"

He nodded slowly. "I guess so. But it would be at Social Services, wouldn't it? Why does it matter?"

I chewed my lip. "That file has her real name on it. Her last known address. What happened to her family. That file has answers in it."

"Yeah, but you'll never get it. I mean, it's not like you can just waltz in there and ask for it." He pulled open the door.

Somehow, the fact that Nate said it couldn't be done made me want that file more than anything. I followed him into the basement, let the warmth blast out the cold, and unbuttoned my coat. Tommy was at the kitchen table, chatting with a couple of other girls. I waved to her as Nate led me over to the couch by the bookshelf, where a slight redheaded girl sat with a book open in her lap. As we got closer, I saw just how thin she was. I could count the ribs that appeared above the low neckline of her shirt, and her collarbones stood out sharp and prominent. Her skin was almost translucent; she was like a whisper of a person, or an echo.

The book she had in her lap was one I'd donated, a vampire romance that Ella had swooned over and made me read. "That's a good one," I told her, even though it wasn't.

She looked up. Her eyes were bottomless, pale blue like faintly colored glass. "The vampire is an idiot," she said. "Why doesn't he just bite someone already?"

I laughed and took that as an invitation to sit next to her. "What other books do you like?"

Her mouth pressed so thin it almost disappeared. "I don't read much," she said, tucking a long strand of her stringy red hair behind her ear. I examined her profile. She couldn't have been more than fifteen at the most. What was I doing when I was fifteen? Spending my summer at Interlochen and worrying about my math grade.

"So what brings you here?" I asked. Nate squeezed onto the couch beside me. I tried to ignore the heat of his thigh pressed against mine.

"Annabel told me if I needed a warm place to go, the basement was usually open." She shrugged. "I got kicked out of my usual place so I came here."

"Where was that?" Nate asked.

She glanced at him. "The halfway house over on Lexington. But they got these stupid rules."

Nate nudged me and I followed his gaze to her wrists. They were so thin that the wide sleeves of her shirt kept falling back, and when they did, I caught a glimpse of the bruises on her skin. I jerked back and looked at Nate. "Track marks," he muttered in my ear. "The halfway house kicked her out for using."

I stared at her wrists, unable to contain the horror I felt inside. Nate had told me that most of the girls he dealt with were drug addicts too, but seeing it firsthand—those bruises were not movie makeup—hit me right in the gut. She was so young, her whole life ahead of her. And she'd spend it trying to get clean.

I dragged my gaze away from her arms. "So, what else did Annabel tell you?"

She shrugged. "Not much." She narrowed her eyes toward the kitchen. "She said you got food here too."

Nate jumped up. "I'll get you something."

I watched him head to the coffee machine, then turned back to the girl. "So—"

"He's cute," she said, flipping another few pages. "He your boyfriend?"

"I..." I looked back at Nate, who was taking a mug down from the cabinet. "I don't know. It's kind of up in the air."

"I don't think so," she said, still not looking up. "I saw the way he was looking at you when you guys walked in together."

"Really?" I bit my lip. I wasn't here to dish with this girl about Nate. Then again... "We just met. It's hard to say what's going to happen."

She slammed the book shut and peered into my face, her eyes like orbs. "You trust him?"

I watched Nate put three mugs, a plate of cookies, a banana, and an apple on a tray and try to balance it. "Yeah. Yeah, I trust him."

"You just make sure he deserves your trust." She traced her forefinger over the outline of the vampire on the book's cover. "I trusted a guy once. Biggest mistake I ever made."

"What happened?"

She hunched her shoulders. "He...promised me the moon, or whatever the saying is. And when I ran away with him, he didn't exactly deliver."

I put a hand on her knee. "Is that what happened to Annabel? Did she meet some guy who did the same thing to her?"

"There's always some guy." It was unnerving, how she didn't seem to blink. "Every girl's story is the same."

"But it doesn't have to be," I said, leaning in. "You don't have to end up like Annabel."

The girl hugged herself, her thin arms wrapped like wire around her middle. "I liked Annabel," she whispered. "She was nice to me."

Nate returned with the food. He dragged a side table in front of the couch and set the tray down. The girl grabbed one of the mugs, dumped five sugar packets into it, and took a long sip. She glanced around the room. "Can I sleep here too?"

"Sorry, no." Nate handed me a mug. "This one's herbal tea."

I smiled up at him. "Thanks."

He settled himself on the floor next to the table, the third mug in his hands. "We can help you find a place to stay," he said to the girl, who was dumping more sugar into her coffee. "But you'll find they have the same rules as the halfway house."

The girl shoved a couple of cookies into her mouth and didn't say anything.

"We can help with that too," Nate said. His tone was so easy and gentle, like he was coaxing a kitten out of a closet. "You have a lot of options."

She choked, sputtering crumbs. "Are you fucking serious? I got no options. I got nothing." She started to get up. "This was a mistake."

"No, wait." I put a hand on her shoulder. She looked back and forth between me and Nate. "Hear him out." She sat on the very edge of the couch, ready to bolt at any second.

"Where are you from?" Nate asked.

It took a long moment but she finally answered. "Baltimore."

I started at that. She'd followed this guy so far away from home, and then he'd made her a prostitute. A sick taste rose up in the back of my mouth.

"Are your parents there?"

Her jaw clenched, but she nodded.

"We can get you back there."

She breathed heavy, in and out. "Jules says if I try to go home, he'll kill my family."

I swallowed hard. Even if that wasn't true, all Jules had to do was make this girl believe it, and she would stay put. Nate set his mug down on the floor and laid his hands on the girl's knees. "Then we can bring them to you. And you can go someplace safe together."

She looked from him to me and back again. "I–I don't know. I gotta think about it."

I squeezed her shoulder. Her bones were sharp beneath my fingers. "Something brought you here. Not just a warm bed. You can tell us."

Her eyes were wild, looking everywhere except at our faces. She half rose from the couch. "No. He'll kill me."

"He doesn't have to know," I said. "Who's going to tell him? Not us. Not you."

She wavered halfway between standing and sitting. "I should go." But she didn't move.

"I can get a place for you to stay," Nate said.

After a long moment, she sat. Nate and I moved closer to her so that she wouldn't have to speak much above a whisper. "I overheard him. Jules. On the phone."

"Was he talking about Annabel?" I asked.

She shot me a look like I was an idiot. "No."

I clenched my fingers into a fist and released them again. Not everything was about Annabel—at least not to this girl or to Nate. Annabel was the road to someplace bigger for them. For me, she was the place that all other roads led to.

"What was he talking about?" Nate prompted.

"I don't know exactly. But he called it 'the Warehouse.' And when he got off the phone and caught me listening, he just said I'd know what it was soon enough." The girl narrowed her pale eyes at Nate. "Do you know what it is? Because I don't think I want to go there."

The Warehouse. I let the words roll silently on my tongue, and fear rose like bile in the back of my throat. A pit of pure dread settled in my stomach. *The Warehouse*. I closed my eyes and pulled up all of Annabel's memories that I'd gotten. The Warehouse was not among them but I could feel it there, just out of reach. Annabel knew this place. But how, exactly, I wasn't sure. "I don't think you want to go there either," I murmured, opening my eyes.

"Look," Nate said, sliding a card out of his back pocket. "Go to this address tonight. She'll have a bed for you, and she can keep you safe." The girl reached for the card but Nate held it back from her. "But you can't stay there if you're not clean."

The girl's face pinched tight. She pulled her backpack into her lap. After digging into an inside pocket, she took out a little box and slammed it into Nate's palm. He didn't drop his hand. She sighed hard and dug into another pocket, extracting a little bag, and practically threw it at him. He caught it neatly.

The girl shrugged herself into her coat, took the banana and the apple off the tray, and shoved them into her pockets. She stood to leave. "Did she—Annabel—ever tell you anything about herself?" I asked. "Anything at all?"

She shook her head. "She used to let me stay with her sometimes. But we never talked much."

"Where? Where did you stay with her?"

"She squatted at a building not far from here," she said. "On Emiline."

Again, 826 Emiline. That explained why she'd jumped from there. "Thanks."

The girl took a step away from the couch, then twisted back.

"Strawberries," she said. Her voice was quiet and hushed. "She used to bring me strawberries. Even in winter."

I closed my eyes and the memory rose up. *The holes in my gloves let the cold in to touch my skin, freezing my fingers as I pick through the strawberries. The cobblestones beneath my feet are littered with rotting fruit and broken crates. By the time my little basket is full, my fingers are numb. I pay the wholesaler out of my precious stash of cash. I'd have to make up the difference tonight, but as I bite into one of the strawberries and let the juice dribble down my chin, it's worth every cent.*

My vision blurred with tears. "They were her favorite," I whispered.

"Yeah," the girl said. "That's what she told me." She hugged herself. "Thanks for the cookies."

As she walked away, Nate pushed himself up onto the couch. "How did you know that?"

I brushed the tears off my cheeks. "I…just figured if she was buying strawberries in the middle of winter, she must've really loved them."

Nate took my hands in his and rubbed them. "Are you okay?"

No. No, I was not okay. What memory had I just lost? "I'm just glad she'll have a place to sleep tonight," I said, nodding toward the door where the girl had just left. "And that we got more information." But I couldn't swallow the hot lump in my throat, and not just because of the memory. All these girls, following some phantom dream, only to be smashed. To find themselves standing on a lonely street, waiting for a stranger to pick them up in a silver sports car. Like this girl, like Char.

Like Annabel.

CHAPTER FIFTEEN

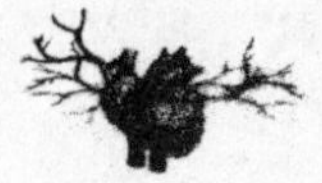

That night, I lay wide awake, staring at the ceiling. What the hell was the Warehouse? And why didn't I get the memory of it when the redheaded girl mentioned it? Instead I got a memory of buying strawberries in winter. Where the hell was that going to get me?

"If you're going to screw with my brain," I said aloud to the shadows on the wall, "at least give me something I can work with."

The only answer I got was the clacking of bare branches on the tree outside my window.

I sighed and rolled over toward my nightstand. I flipped on the light and slid my journal onto the bed. It fell right open to the page with all my scribbling on it. The memories-lost and memories-gained map was as inscrutable as ever. I stared at it until the lines blurred, hoping that something useful would pop out the longer I contemplated it. Finally I grabbed my pen. I added the Warehouse at the bottom of the page.

Whatever went on at the Warehouse, it couldn't be good. Maybe Annabel had found out about it, and it was so bad that she'd rather commit suicide than face it. That was the biggest thing I'd gleaned from our conversation with the skinny redheaded girl.

I laid the pen in the crease of the journal and ran my finger down the list of memories I'd gained. What did it all mean? Why were these memories imprinted on Annabel's heart? What were they leading me to?

As I touched the indentations of my writing, the tip of my finger tingled. They *did* make sense.

They were in order.

They were in chronological order. I was remembering her memories in the order that they happened. I was living her life over again, gaining each memory when the heart wanted to reveal it to me.

Or when it was provoked. The memory of Nate had come to me as soon as I'd met him. Annabel's kingdom by the sea had been stirred up by Nate reading the poem. All of the memories so far had occurred *before* she'd learned about the Warehouse or been there.

I rolled onto my back and gazed at the small circle of light my nightstand lamp made on the ceiling. If this was true—if the heart only gave me each memory in the order they happened—then I wouldn't know why Annabel had committed suicide until the heart revealed all the memories that preceded it. I laid my hand on my chest, heartbeats reverberating against my palm. I was powerless against this organ, completely at the mercy of its will. I just had to believe that when I reached the end of her memories, when I figured out who she was and why she jumped from that balcony, it would all end and I could go back to normal.

Whatever normal looked like now.

I shoved my journal in my nightstand drawer and brought

my laptop back into bed. The covers pooled around my waist as I pulled up the Department of Children and Families website again. Maybe just staring at it would magically make Annabel's file appear. I clicked on every link I could but it was like the big hedge maze at Tanglewood. Everything kept leading me to a dead end.

"Dammit," I muttered and clicked on the "Fostering Kids, Fostering Futures" headline again. It took me back to a page spouting some bullshit about how invested they were in every child's future potential. Yeah, they sure hadn't been in Annabel's. I ran the mouse down all the links below the banner and stopped at something called the Teen Crisis Line that I hadn't clicked on before. The link opened to a new page.

Volunteers needed

Volunteers are needed to help answer the Teen Crisis Line. Looking especially for teen volunteers so that callers can talk to their peers. Apply in person at the Department of Children and Families, 600 Washington Street, Boston, during the hours of 10 a.m. to 2 p.m., Monday through Thursday.

Well. I sat back and stared at the little square box advertising for volunteers. My insides jittered like I'd had too much coffee. It wasn't Annabel's file, but it was a way in the door.

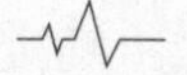

The Department of Children and Families offices in Downtown Crossing were in a tall building made of glass and steel that badly needed cleaning. The windows were grimed up and the silver door handles had long since lost their shine. I stopped at the reception desk. The receptionist's hair flew in all different directions and half-covered the headset she wore over one ear. She held up a finger without looking at me, pressed about a dozen buttons on the huge dashboard-like phone that took up half her desk, and answered one of the blinking buttons. "Please hold."

She tilted her chin up to me. "Can I help you?"

"Department of Children and Families—"

"Which department?"

"Children and Families—"

"Which department in the Department of Children and Families?" Her words practically tripped over one another in her rush. "Who are you here to see?"

"Oh, um, I don't have a name—"

"I can't help you without a name." She pressed the blinking button again and transferred the caller, who apparently did have a name.

"I'm here to apply to volunteer for the Teen Crisis Line," I said in one breath before she pressed another button.

"You want the Adolescent Office," she said, slapping a Visitor tag on the desk. "Fourth floor."

"Thanks," I offered, but her head was already down, focused on the blinking dashboard in front of her.

I expected to encounter another receptionist when I got off the elevator on the fourth floor, but instead I found an open office space filled with endless cubicles. File boxes were stacked up in every available corner. The sound of ringing phones filled the air. I peeked into the first cubicle I came to. It was empty except for a half-drunk cup of coffee. At the next one, I found a woman hunched over her phone, and even though I stood in front of her for a good three minutes, she never looked up.

I moved on to the third, fourth, and fifth cubicles, where I finally found a squat little man typing at his computer with only his two forefingers. "Excuse me?"

"Yeah?"

"Um, I'm here to apply for the Teen Crisis Line? To volunteer?"

"Good for you." He pointed down the length of cubicles. "Sally Klein. Second cubicle from the end."

"Thank you," I said very pointedly. He didn't get it.

I found Sally Klein's cubicle. It was empty, but there was a half-eaten bagel by the keyboard that indicated she had just stepped away. A box hung on the side wall with a sign that read, "If you are here to apply for volunteering, please fill this out." An arrow pointed down into the box.

I drew out one of the applications, grabbed a clipboard and pen from Sally's desk, and looked for a place to sit down. The only other available chair besides the desk chair was piled high with files. Carefully, I moved them to the floor and sat in the chair. On impulse, I bent over the stack of files, looking at the tabs.

"Can I help you?"

I straightened so fast my neck cricked. "Hi—I'm here to apply."

It was idiotic to think Annabel's file would just be sitting there, waiting for me to find it.

"For the Teen Crisis Line? That's great." She slid into her chair. "We need more teen volunteers. Studies show that kids are more likely to talk to other kids about their problems rather than adults."

"I'd—love to help out," I said weakly. I'd memorized a whole spiel about how I wanted to give back to the community, but the script disappeared from my brain. On this gray floor filled with gray cubicles, Sally was the only one with some color. For some reason, I didn't want to disappoint her.

"Just fill that out and then we'll chat." She picked up her bagel and took a bite.

The application was pretty straightforward. I handed it to her when I was done. Sally looked it over and raised an eyebrow. "The Hillcoate Academy? That's very impressive."

"Thanks. I have a copy of my last report card if you want to see it." I drew it out of my bag and handed it to her.

Sally looked it over for a minute and then back at my application. "You're a senior?"

"That's right."

"And you..."—her eyes scanned the paper—"play the oboe?"

"Yes."

She peered at me over the clipboard. "What are your plans for college?"

"I'm auditioning for Juilliard."

"Oh." Her eyes widened with surprise. "That must be very competitive."

"It is. Only two or three get in every year. If that." I tightened my fingers in my lap. "Last year, they didn't let any in."

"Wow. Any backups?"

"Eastman, New England Conservatory, Manhattan School of Music. And well, Curtis, but that one is so hard to get into that you don't even pay tuition." I half smiled at her. "But my dream has always been Juilliard."

"Well, you're not afraid of a challenge. That's obvious." Sally set my application and report card down on her desk. "And you'll have no shortage of challenges working the Teen Line."

"What sort of calls do you get?"

"Oh, everything from 'My boyfriend dumped me and I'm sad' to 'I'm standing here with a razor and want to slit my wrists.' It can get intense."

I wondered what would've happened if Annabel had called the Teen Line before she jumped off the balcony. Would she still be alive? And if she was still alive, would I be dead? I shivered.

"So, Georgiana—"

"Oh, please call me Georgie." I wrinkled my nose. "Georgiana sounds way too British."

Sally laughed. "Okay, Georgie. Tell me, why does a senior like you want to do this? You've obviously got your future figured out, and your grades are excellent. You've already sent in your applications so you don't need this for a good extracurricular activity. You're probably spending all your free time practicing for your auditions. Why do this?"

"Because—" I stopped. I swung my gaze around the depressing

gray walls. Had Annabel come here to meet with her case worker? Was this another place I was walking in her footsteps? "Because—" The lies I'd prepared died on my lips. "Because I knew a girl."

Sally crossed her arms over her chest and leaned back. Her chair creaked.

"I knew a girl who committed suicide. And I just think that maybe if she'd called a crisis line like this, if she'd talked to me, I could've stopped her."

"Jeez." Sally sighed, shaking her head. "I'm really sorry. I like to think that we could've prevented that from happening too."

"There are so many kids out there who need help," I said, thinking of Char, of the skinny redheaded girl with track marks on her arms. I wasn't lying anymore, giving Sally a bullshit line to get what I wanted. These girls really did need help, and I could do it. "And they believe they have no one to turn to, no one who can help them. If they could know that there are people out there who can help, who *care*…"

Sally nodded, her bobbed salt-and-pepper hair shaking in front of her face. "Yes, exactly. That's why I created the Teen Crisis Line to begin with."

"You created it? Wow." I glanced around her chaotic cubicle. She was clearly overworked and understaffed—I mean, she had to get volunteers for a crisis line that should be staffed by certified counselors—but she still cared enough to get a project off the ground to help more kids.

All of a sudden, I really, really wanted to do this. Yes, I wanted

Annabel's file, but I also wanted to stop the next Annabel from jumping off her balcony. "Hey, can I ask you something?"

"Sure."

"The girl I knew—who killed herself—she was a foster kid. Well, she had been. She was eighteen, so she'd aged out of the system. Right? When kids turn eighteen, they're no longer your—I mean, the Department's responsibility?"

"Yeah." Sally's face screwed up and she let out a long sigh. "It's such bullcrap—pardon my French." I shook my head to let her know she wasn't offending me in the least, and she went on. "I mean, these kids clearly need our help past their eighteenth birthday, but the State just cuts them off. We have a couple of programs in place to track them, but only if they're receiving a grant or tuition aid or something like that." She clenched her jaw. "It's *ridiculous*."

"Right? It is!" I threw my hands in the air. "I'm practically eighteen and I'm not nearly ready to be on my own. My mother still does my laundry, and I couldn't even tell you what button turns the washer on. How can the State expect these kids to just fend for themselves?"

"You have no idea how much this issue means to me," Sally said. She sat up straighter and set her shoulders. "I actually tried to petition the State to get the law changed to keep kids in the foster system until they're twenty, but it went nowhere." She pointed her finger at me. "It is very astute of you to recognize this problem. We need people like you around here."

"Does that mean—I have the job?"

"Yes. I know you must be busy with your auditions, so whatever time you can give us would be great."

"Thank you!" I smiled and danced a little in my chair. "I just have to talk to my parents about my schedule. It might have to wait until after my Juilliard audition, but that's only next month."

My stomach squirmed. Less than a month before the audition. Somehow, I hadn't been as obsessed with it the past few days.

"That's great. Just give me a call and let me know when you can start." Sally handed me her card and stood. "I'll walk you to the elevator."

It was only when we arrived at the elevator bank that I remembered I'd come here for an entirely different purpose. While Sally pressed the down button, I scanned the directory on the wall. "RECORDS, 10TH FLOOR," it said.

Crap. That was up. The elevator dinged. *Please don't get on with me*, I thought feverishly at Sally.

"It was really nice to meet you, Georgie," she said, sticking her hand out. "Call me when you have a better idea of your schedule."

"I will," I promised, shaking her hand. "Bye."

I hit the second-floor button. I'd get off there and go back up to ten. But just before the elevator doors closed, Sally thrust her hand in. "I need coffee something awful," she said. "The sludge they have here is undrinkable."

The doors closed. I slumped against the wall a little. Sally hit one. "Oh—did you hit the second floor by mistake?" she asked, pointing at the lit-up second-floor button.

"I must have. Oops."

We rode the elevator down in silence. My cheeks flamed as I tried to think of how to get back up to the tenth floor. When the doors opened on the first floor, I had no choice but to follow Sally out. "Can I buy you a latte?" she asked as we walked to the front entrance.

"Oh—no, thanks. I have to get home."

"Okay. Great to meet you, Georgie," she said as she held the door open for me. I ducked through it and walked toward the T stop. Thankfully, Sally was going to a coffee place in the opposite direction.

I stood for a moment, watching her disappear into the crowds of Downtown Crossing. Before I could hesitate or think it through, I dashed back in through the grimy glass door.

"Can I help you?" the receptionist asked as I breezed past her.

"Oh. I was just upstairs," I said, waving my Visitor badge. "I was meeting with Sally Klein? And I forgot something."

She narrowed her eyes at me but then her phone rang. "Go ahead," she said in the same breath as she answered her phone.

A bunch of people piled into the elevator behind me. I shrank into the corner, hoping I was invisible. I crumpled my Visitor tag in my hand and shoved it into my coat pocket. If someone stopped me, I didn't want them to think I didn't belong.

If the fourth floor was a wasteland where office drones go to die, the tenth floor was the Mount Doom that lorded above them all. I got off behind a couple of women and followed them through a door that could only be accessed with an ID card. That door led to a long hallway with a dozen rooms, each with the same electronic swipe pad protecting the contents within.

Dammit.

I kept following the two women, all the way down the hall. As we passed the locked doors, I noticed a sign on each of them. Closed Files, 1990–2000. Closed Files, 2000–2010. And so on. At last we came to a desk at the end of the hall with a lonely computer sitting on it.

One of the women bent over the computer and typed something on the keyboard. I turned and swept my gaze down the long hall. Which room had Annabel's file? Was she even here? She'd aged out of the system not that long ago; maybe she hadn't even been filed yet. And what the hell was I supposed to do with that computer? Why hadn't I paid more attention to all those stupid spy shows Colt made me watch?

A printer next to the computer spit out a sheet of paper and the woman straightened. "It's in Room C," she told the other lady. They brushed past me.

Okay, one thing I *had* picked up from those shows was that sometimes it was best to hide in plain sight. I took a deep breath and arranged my features into my best damsel-in-distress expression. "Excuse me?"

The ladies turned. "Yes?"

I bit my lip. "Um, I just started an internship this week and my boss sent me up here for a file and I have no idea how to find it. Can you—" I gestured to the computer.

The woman with the paper handed it to her coworker. "You go ahead. I'll help her."

"Oh, thank you so much!" I gushed as she stepped over to the computer. She gave me a tight smile and leaned over the keyboard. "By the way, I love your sweater. Did you knit it yourself?"

The woman straightened again, this time her smile stretching wide. "I did! Thank you so much."

"It must've taken forever, with all those little baby bunnies," I said, widening my eyes with what I hoped was an expression of admiration. "I wish I could knit."

"Oh, it's easier than people think. You should take a class. That's what I did."

"What a great idea!" I sidled next to her and put my hand on the computer. "So, you use this to find a file?"

"Yes." She tapped a couple of things and a search screen popped up. "You just type in the name you're looking for, and it will give you the file's location."

"Cool." I gave her a worried face. "But the thing is, these doors are all locked and I don't have my ID yet. So how do I—"

"Oh, you poor dear. Your boss really threw you to the wolves, didn't he?" She gave me a sympathetic pat on the arm. "I'll wait while you type in the name and we can find the file together."

My insides clenched. Crap. I had no idea what Annabel's real name was; I couldn't just type it in. "Um…okay." I leaned way over the keyboard, trying to position my shoulders so they blocked the screen from my helper's view. I typed in "Lee" on the off chance that was her real last name.

It took ten seconds for the search results to come back with about five thousand Lees. I pressed my lips together, trying to control the shaking of my fingers. I was so freaking close…

The door to Room C opened and the other woman emerged. "Got it. Let's go."

"Just a minute. I'm helping this young lady," said my hideously sweatered friend.

"We're going to be late for the meeting."

She turned to me. "Did you find it yet?"

"Oh—no, but…" I glanced at the locked room closest to us. Closed Files, 2010–2020. "It would be in that room, though. If you could—"

"Sure, dear." The woman swiped her card in front of the keypad and the door clicked open.

"What'll you do in 2020, when you're out of space?" I asked.

"Purge the files from the 1990–2000 room," she told me. "We only keep them for twenty years. Good luck on your first week."

"Thanks so much for your help."

When she got to the door to the elevator bank, she turned back to me. "Oh, don't forget to leave a printout of which file you took in the box on the back of the door. That way we have a record of which files are checked out and who took them."

"Oh—right. Thanks." I waited until the two women were on the elevator. Once I was safely alone again, I ducked into the room she'd opened for me and shut the door.

File cabinets lined all the walls and filled the center of the room. How would I find Annabel? I walked around the room until I found the cabinet that contained the *Ls*. It was the only place to start. I pulled open the drawer and thumbed through to Lee. There was an entire row of them. I walked my fingers over the tabs, moving quickly past the boy names. But the girl names... it could be any of those. I tapped my foot on the ground as I went through the entire drawer. I pulled out a few possibilities—Lee, Michelle and Lee, Olivia and Lee, Samantha—but the dates didn't match up.

I rested my forehead on the cold metal edge of the drawer. She wasn't in here. I could feel it. Or rather, I *couldn't* feel it, couldn't hear the Catch telling me I was on the right track. I put the files back, slammed that drawer shut, and opened the next one.

This one had several Lees at the front and then started to branch into Leed, Leefer, Leek, and Leeland.

Leeland. My body went hot and cold. The Catch stirred to life. My fingers stopped at the first Leeland file.

Leeland, Anna Isabel.

My hand shook. I touched the name on the file and felt those letters burn into my fingers. It had to be her. There was no way that it wasn't her. I pulled the file out of the drawer and held it against my heart. The Catch was so loud in my ears that I could swear it was playing through a surround-sound system hidden in the corners of the room.

"Anna Isabel Leeland," I whispered. I touched the edges of the folder, almost afraid to open it. What would I find?

The door to the file room slammed open. "Was that you searching 'Lee' on the computer?" asked a short guy with glasses as he stomped into the room. There were multiple stains on his brown tie. "Because you need to clear the search history when you're done. For confidentiality reasons."

"I'm sorry," I said. I clutched Annabel's file to my chest and closed the drawer I'd gotten it from. "I'm new."

"That's not an excuse," he said, sliding a file drawer out with such violence I thought it was going to come off its tracks. "Your boss should train you better."

"Okay, I'll tell him that," I said and ducked out of the room.

"Hey, you forgot to leave a printout in the box!" he called after me. I ran to the elevator, pressing the down button over and over. The elevator dinged and I stepped on just as the guy came striding down the hall. I jabbed the button to close the doors and they slid shut just in time.

I breathed out and sagged against the wall. Before the elevator could stop on another floor between here and the ground, I shoved the file up under my sweater and buttoned my coat over it. The elevator carried me directly down to one.

But when I stepped off it, the first thing I spotted was Sally Klein chatting up the receptionist, who looked especially annoyed at being interrupted from her constantly ringing phone. I stepped back into the elevator and hit the button to keep the door open. I couldn't ride the elevator up and down until she left. I peeked out again. She was still there, now showing the receptionist something on her phone. *Crap*.

Another elevator on the opposite side of the bank opened and half a dozen people spilled out. I bolted into their crowd and hid myself between two gray-haired ladies and a middle-aged guy. Thankfully, Sally didn't look up as we moved out the door and onto the street.

I didn't stop until I was safely down the stairs into the T station. Only when I was on the train did I let myself relax. My fingers itched to pull the file out from under my sweater, but I couldn't begin to think how wrong that would look to everyone else on the crowded train. So I just counted the stops back to Brookline, repeating her name over and over. *Anna Isabel Leeland. Anna Isabel Leeland.* She had a name, a real name. She wasn't just a figment of my imagination. She existed, as sure as the manila folder digging into my skin.

"Anna Isabel Leeland," I whispered, and the name wrapped itself around my heart.

CHAPTER SIXTEEN

When I got home, I ran straight up to my room. Grandma's voice floated up behind me. "Georgie, Mr. Blount will be here in a few minutes!"

"Be right there," I called down and closed myself behind my bedroom door. I flung my coat on the floor and, at long last, slid the file out from under my clothes. I sat on the floor with my back against the door and flipped it open.

The first thing my eyes fell on was a picture stapled to the inside of the folder. It showed a girl of about seven with long blond hair, her brown eyes wide and staring at the camera. No smile adorned her mouth. In fact, her lips were pressed together in an expression far too wise for a seven-year-old. I traced my finger over her features, around those wide eyes, down her slanted cheekbone, and over her hair, as if I could comfort the teenager she would become.

I shuffled through the rest of the file, looking for a more recent picture, but there wasn't one. I went back to the first page and began to read. *Leeland, Anna Isabel. Born July 20, 1995. Mother: Eliza Marie Leeland, incarcerated for life without the possibility of parole. Father: Karl Michael Leeland, deceased.*

Downstairs, the front door opened and I heard Grandma's

voice greeting Mr. Blount. With great reluctance, I closed the file and carefully slid it between my mattress and box spring. Sitting through my lessons would be torture.

I wasn't wrong. "Georgie, that's the third one you missed," Blowhard said, tapping his pen on my paper. "Where's your head today?"

Upstairs with the file of the girl whose heart I got. I gave him a weak smile. "Sorry." I tried to concentrate, but after I missed two more calculus problems, Blowhard gave up and switched to English lit.

Colt came home from school, and Blowhard was still grilling me about *Crime and Punishment*. I excused myself to the bathroom and texted Nate. Help! My tutor is holding me hostage!

He texted me back a sad face. Tomorrow?

Hope so. Will text you later.

Blowhard finally left at four, but not before Mom emerged from her office and sat down with us to powwow about my progress.

"She needs to focus more," Blowhard said. I folded my arms and glared at him. I was sitting *right there*. He could at least address me.

Mom nodded, either unaware or choosing to ignore my mounting annoyance. "Well, she has been spending a lot of time on that article for the school paper."

Blowhard raised an eyebrow. "What article?"

Oh, crap. I sat up, my boots scuffing the floor. Mom glanced at me, then back at Blowhard. "The article on human trafficking."

"Georgie never told me she was writing an article."

They both looked at me. I squeezed my arms even tighter across myself. "Sorry," I said, rolling my eyes, "I didn't realize I had to clear it with Blow—Mr. Blount."

He blinked. "Well, honestly, it does seem to be getting in the way of our lessons."

"But it's for school. Both my social studies and English teachers are giving me credit," I lied.

Mom and Blowhard stared at me for a moment longer. "Well," Blowhard finally said, "if she's getting credit for it at school, then I suppose it's all right. But she still needs to focus more on her studies with me."

"Absolutely," Mom said. "I'll make sure she does."

"And I will too," I said. "After all, Georgie can't be trusted to study on her own. She can't take responsibility for herself. She needs to be treated like a child even though she's almost eighteen."

"Georgie!" Mom shot an embarrassed look at Blowhard. "I'm sorry."

"It's okay." He stood up and put a hand on my shoulder. "It must be hard to be away from your friends at school and your regular routine. Just remember..."—he squeezed my shoulder—"being treated like an adult is something you have to earn. And you won't earn it by acting like a child."

I fought the urge to shove his hand off my shoulder and gave him a sugary-sweet smile. He picked up his briefcase and headed to the front door. I started to get up, but Mom put her hands on my knees and held me down. "That was incredibly rude, Georgie."

"Yeah, well, it's incredibly rude to talk about me as if I'm not sitting right next to you." I met her eyes blaze for blaze. Her shoulders slumped a little.

"What's gotten into you lately?" she asked.

"Gee, I don't know. Maybe a *new heart*," I snapped.

"Oh, baby." She squeezed my knees. "You're still the same person. I know what happened to you was traumatic, but you can't use it as an excuse to behave badly."

I clenched my jaw for a long moment before I realized she was right. No matter how confused or angry I was about what was happening to me, it wasn't her fault. "I'm sorry," I said. "I just… don't feel like the same person. I feel different."

"Different how?" She leaned closer to me. "Should we go see Dr. Harrison?"

"No, no, it's not that—"

"Then what?" Her eyes softened. "Do you want to talk to someone? Like a therapist?"

"Oh my God. *No*." The thought of sitting on a shrink's couch, trying to explain that I was getting some dead girl's memories while losing my own, seemed worse than torture. "I just need space. Space to figure out who I am with this new heart."

"Georgie, you're still the same." I narrowed my eyes at her. She was saying it for the second time, almost as if she needed to convince herself of it more than me. "You still have the same dreams and hopes, don't you? You're still dying to go to Juilliard, aren't you?"

"Yes, but—"

"Then you're still the same."

Again that word, "same." *I'm not the same*, I wanted scream, but I knew I couldn't tell her the real reason why. I patted her hands that were still on my knees. "I know. It's just been a hard adjustment. And I need everyone to lay off. Okay?"

She sighed, her shoulders drooping. "Okay. Fine." The doorbell rang. "Oh, that's Joel. Can I trust you to treat him with a little more respect than you showed Mr. Blount?"

"Yes," I hissed and went upstairs to grab my oboe. Normally, I would be bouncing with excitement for my lesson, but all I wanted at that moment was to be locked away in my bedroom with Annabel's file. We ran through the Poulenc a dozen times but he still wasn't satisfied at the end of the lesson. "I want that one trouble spot perfect by Friday," Joel said as we packed our oboes away. "You won't get into Juilliard with it sounding like that."

"I know." I wished everyone would ease up on the Juilliard talk. As I walked Joel out, I wondered if my parents would be as excited to learn that I got a job helping prevent teen suicide as they would be if I got into Juilliard. Probably not. I'd been talking about Juilliard for so many years that there were so many hopes, so much expectation.

As soon as Joel was out the door, I booked it up the stairs to get my hands on Annabel's file. I'd barely gotten to the top when Mom called me back down for dinner. All I could think about while we ate was that folder burning a hole in my mattress. As soon as the dishes were in the dishwasher, I made a beeline out of the kitchen, but Colt blocked my escape.

"Game of Hearts?" he asked, juggling a deck of cards.

"I have to practice."

"You just had a lesson," Colt said. He slung his arm around my shoulders. "Just for an hour. You can practice after."

I cast a longing look up to my room, but when I caught Mom's gaze on me again, I let Colt propel me into a chair. If I spent this hour with the family, she'd probably stay off my back for the rest of the night.

"You all better watch out," I said, snatching the cards away from Colt. "I'm feeling pretty feisty tonight." I shuffled the deck and began to deal.

"Hey, remember that Christmas we all spent in New Mexico?" Colt asked. "When it snowed?"

"Oh, that was the worst blizzard I've ever seen," Grandma said. "We were snowed in for days."

"And we had that Hearts tournament where Georgie crushed us," Colt said.

"Not to mention that epic game of Risk that lasted for three days," Dad said. "*I* won that."

"I just remember eating so much chili because all we had were canned beans," Mom said.

"And we sent Grandpa to the grocery store and he got stalled at the end of the driveway." Grandma's eyes misted at the memory. "By the time he got back to the house, he looked like the abominable snowman."

"That was one of the best Christmases ever," Colt said.

"That was the last Christmas before your grandfather passed," Grandma said, her voice soft.

I dealt out the last card, letting their voices, their memories, wash over me. They didn't seem to notice that I was silent through their reminiscing, offering nothing of my own memories. Because I had none to offer. Any memory I had from that Christmas was gone.

I fought the rising panic inside me. When would it stop? What had I gotten for the memory of my last Christmas with my grandfather? Buying strawberries in winter. It wasn't fair. I tossed the cards out to everyone. "Should we start?"

Without even trying, I shot the moon during the first round, which sent Colt into sore-loser mode. "Fine," I said, pushing back from the table. "I don't need to play."

"Aw, come on," Colt whined. "Sit down."

"No, I really do have a lot of homework."

Dad sighed, but before he could say anything, I ducked out of the kitchen and climbed upstairs. Inside my room, I leaned against the door and breathed in and out, in and out. I had to believe Annabel was leading me somewhere—and that even if I didn't know where that was, it would be worth it. That once we got there, she would go away. That once she went away, I would be Georgie again.

I pulled the file from its hiding place and sat on my bed. Finally, I would get some answers. I spread my schoolbooks around me, in case I was interrupted. Under the cover of my calculus textbook, I opened the file.

Mother, incarcerated. Father, deceased. I turned the page to find a sheet titled "Case History," and a long paragraph typed beneath it. I bent over the page and read.

On March 4, 2002, DCF was called to... The address was blacked out. *Case was a seven-year-old female. Mother was taken into custody for the double homicide of her husband—Case's father—and his girlfriend. Mother confessed to crime at the scene, having called the police herself. Case witnessed the crime but was unable to provide any kind of comprehensive report. Case taken into DCF custody for immediate placement with a foster family.*

I wanted to cry but everything inside was frozen. I flipped back to the picture of seven-year-old Anna with her wide, staring eyes. She wasn't staring at the camera. She was staring into a future without a mother and a father, a future where she would have to take care of herself. I went back to the page with the case history and read it again. This time I did cry, large teardrops splattering on the yellowed paper. What kind of a mother abandoned her daughter like that? She hadn't killed two people that night. She'd killed three. She'd killed her daughter too.

With shaking fingers, I turned the page. The next few pages contained the names and addresses of the foster families Anna had been placed with. The first family had moved out of state and couldn't take Anna with them. The second family had wound up having twins of their own and couldn't handle the extra burden. The third family had sent her back within only six months. I peered at the dates; Anna had been a teenager by then and was probably too unruly for them. She'd been with the last family for two years before she was emancipated. There was an address. It was in Mattapan.

I splayed my hand across the address, covering it and uncovering it. I wasn't sure I wanted to go there. But I knew that if I went, I couldn't face it alone. I reached for my phone. I found out more stuff about Annabel, I texted Nate. Tell you tomorrow when I see you.

OK, he sent back. Have a good night.

I smiled and held the phone to my chest. I lay back on my pillows, wishing that Nate was here next to me, his knee touching mine as we went through the file together. I wished I could tell him everything.

A knock thudded on my door. I shoved Annabel's file under my pillow in the instant before Mom opened the door. "Sweetie? Ella's here."

"What? Why?" I scrambled off my bed and nearly collided with Ella as she sidled into the room.

"*That's* the greeting I get?" she said, tossing her hat onto my desk.

"I'm just surprised to see you, that's all." I gave her a hug that she half returned.

"Not too late, girls. Okay?" Mom shut the door as she left.

Ella surveyed my room as if she didn't already know every inch of it. "So you really do have a ton of homework, huh?" she said, nodding to the pile of textbooks on my bed.

"You think I was lying to you?"

"Well, I don't know, Georgie!" Ella threw her arms into the air. "I mean, you're never around anymore. You never call—"

"I texted you the other night," I protested, shifting my weight between my feet. Anytime Ella and I fought, she always gave herself the upper hand.

"Yeah, after I texted you and called you. And you said you'd call me the next day and never did." She folded her arms and blew a hard breath out. "What is going on with you, Georgie?"

"Ella, I'm sorry." I sank onto my bed. "But please try to understand. I have someone else's heart inside my body. Do you not *get* that?"

"I get it, okay?" She ran her hand through her hair. "But I mean, did I do something? Did Toni do something? Why don't you want to hang out with us anymore?"

I picked at a loose thread in my bedspread. "No, you didn't do anything. It's not you."

"What is it, then? Is it this guy?" She half smiled. "No guy is worth changing yourself for. How many *Seventeen* articles have told us that?"

"I'm not changing myself for him." I looked at her for a long moment. "But I'm not the same old Georgie. I'm just not. I woke up from that surgery different—"

"So, what? The new you doesn't want to hang out with your friends?" Ella planted her hands on her hips.

"No, that's not it—"

"You'd rather hang out with druggies and hookers?"

"Ella!" I jumped to my feet. "That's a really mean thing to say."

"You're right. I'm sorry." She brought her fingers to her temples. "I would've thought that after a near-death experience, you'd want to be with the people you love even more. Not less."

"I do want to hang out with you guys." My voice climbed higher and higher. "But I've got other things going on in my life—"

"What other things? Clue me in!" Ella glared at me. "That's what friends do, Georgie. They share what's going on in their lives. They ask for help."

"You can't help me with this. Trust me, if you could, I would've asked for it a long time ago." I folded my arms and leaned back on my pillows.

Ella stared at me for a searing, stretched-out minute. "So that's it, then?" she said finally. "You're really not going to tell me what's going on?"

"Ella..."

"Fine." She started buttoning her coat, shaking her head. "I can't believe you, Georgie. I thought we could tell each other anything. I guess I was wrong."

"Ella, please." I launched myself off my bed. My chest tightened and I had to steady myself on my feet. "Please just trust me on this."

She snorted. "Yeah. *Trust you*. Okay, Georgie. Whatever." She jammed her hat on her head. "I'm sorry you had to have a heart transplant. I'm sorry you don't feel like the same person anymore." Ella bit her lip. For a second, I thought she was going to cry. "But I'm really sorry that the new Georgie doesn't feel like she can trust her friends. Because I would've trusted the old Georgie with my life." She flung open the door. "The new one? I'm not so sure."

CHAPTER SEVENTEEN

Right after Ella left, Mom knocked on the door but I didn't answer. I stood in the middle of the room, my whole body shaking, my scar prickling. It wasn't the new *Georgie* who couldn't trust her friends. It was Annabel, insinuating herself into me. Annabel couldn't trust anyone, and she'd imprinted that instinct on her heart.

I shivered and wrapped my arms around myself, trying to get warm even though the cold came from inside me. There was no place that was off-limits to her, no place where she didn't knock me out of the way and take over. Playing Hearts with my family, dancing at the annual Valentine's Day party, hanging out with my friends…either the Catch or the discovery of a lost memory interrupted. Nowhere was safe.

I blinked. There *was* one place she couldn't enter. I marched to that corner and dragged my music stand to the center of the room. When I fit my oboe together, the keys were warm beneath my fingers, the heft of the instrument so right in my hands. I ripped through a set of scales and went right into the Mozart concerto, gliding up and down the notes as if I'd been playing them since I was in the womb.

Warmth spread up my spine. The old Georgie was still here.

As my fingers danced over the keys, any shred of Annabel left me. She had no place in this world, the world of reeds and symphonies and intricate fingerings. This was my world, the one I'd always felt at home in.

I played for so long that Dad had to knock on the door and tell me to stop because everyone was going to bed. After he left, I sat on the floor and pulled the oboe apart to clean it. I took a long time, polishing in between the keys until the rosewood gleamed. Then I nestled the pieces back in their velvet-lined case and sat with the case open on my lap.

I really did want to volunteer for the Teen Crisis Line. I really did admire the work Nate did with FAIR Girls, and I wanted to help him. But as much as I knew that, the oboe was still who I was. I was still destined to go to Juilliard and play with the New York Phil. Music was still my core, and not even Annabel could change that.

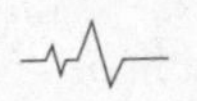

The next morning, I texted Ella to apologize. I didn't expect to hear back right away; she was at school and Hillcoate had a strict no-cell-phone policy. That didn't stop me from tapping my foot against my chair and glancing at my phone every other minute during Blowhard's lesson.

She still hadn't texted back by her lunchtime, when I knew that she always sneaked a peek at her phone. *Fine*, I thought and went upstairs to grab Annabel's file after Blowhard left. I texted Nate that I'd meet him at Starbucks instead of All Saints and headed out. I just wanted one of those delicious tea lattes, I told myself. It had nothing to do with what Ella had said last night.

When I passed from the bitter cold sidewalk to the warm coffee shop, Nate emerged from the back. He'd taken off his green apron and was buttoning up a non-uniform shirt. "Hey."

"Hey." I nodded to the couch. "Can we sit for a minute?"

"Sure. You want something?"

"Can I get the same thing you made me last time?"

"Sure."

I waited on the couch while he made the latte. A couple of teenage girls were hanging out at the table in the corner, but otherwise the place was empty. When Nate returned with my drink, I pulled my bag onto my lap and slid Anna's file out. Without a word, I handed it to him. He flipped it open and his eyes went wide. "That's Annabel," he breathed. He scanned down the page and looked up at me. "How—where did you get this?"

I shrugged. "I have my ways."

"Seriously, Georgie, this is a big deal." There was shock in his tone but the expression on his face was impressed. A little squiggle of pleasure squirmed through me.

"I wanted to know who she was," I said. "For real. Not just her street name."

He sifted through the papers in the file for a few minutes, then lowered the folder to his lap. "You're amazing," he said, reaching for my hand.

"No, I'm not," I said, but I let him take my hand and stroke my palm. "I just need to know who she really was. For the article," I added, but Nate raised his eyebrows.

"It's not just for the article, is it?"

"What do you mean?" My heartbeat skittered.

"You're like me," Nate said. "You have to get to the bottom of things. You can't just leave it alone."

"No," I murmured, and my heart returned to normal. "No, I can't."

We sat for a long moment, our eyes devouring each other, distinctly aware of the two teenage girls and Jan, who stood at the counter reading a book. If we kissed, we'd have an audience, and I was definitely ready to make this a more private show. With a pang of reluctance, I picked up the file. "But the real reason I wanted to show you this was because it has the address of her last foster home."

"Yeah?"

"I want to go there. But I don't want to go alone." I squeezed his hand. "Will you go with me?"

Nate sucked in a breath. "Are you sure this is a good idea? What is talking to these people going to accomplish?"

I looked at our entwined hands. I couldn't tell him the real reason I needed to go there, but lying to him so much made my insides twist. "I don't know. I feel like...maybe they can give us a clue as to why she killed herself. Why she got on the streets in the first place." I swallowed hard and met his eyes. "Maybe it won't help much, but it might help us understand why a little bit more."

Nate lifted my hand to his mouth. "Okay," he said, his lips moving against my knuckles. "Let's go."

He led me up the street to the bus stop and wrapped his arms around me to keep the wind away. I leaned my cheek against his chest, listening to the steady *thump-thump-thump* of his heart. The old Georgie would've stopped to think this through, to question how wise charging off to an address would be without knowing what she might find there. Sense probably would've gotten the better of that Georgie, and she would've stayed home.

But now I had this new heart, propelling me forward without stopping to overthink. Was that how Annabel lived her life? Was she teaching me to do the same? I couldn't be sure whether that was a good thing or a bad thing. Nate's heart beat strong and solid beneath my cheek. At least I wasn't charging ahead alone.

The bus barreled up the street and screeched to a stop in front of us. We took two seats in the back, and I watched the streets blur by, boarded-up storefronts and liquor stores with bars on the windows. The houses were old and shabby here, like they'd once been great but had long since passed their prime. I thought of my old Victorian, like a grand old lady—but only because my parents could afford to replace the plumbing with copper pipes and install central air.

At last, Nate reached up and pushed the stop button. We came out of the bus onto a deserted sidewalk with a vacant gas station and a doughnut shop that had gone out of business who knew how long ago.

"It's a couple of blocks from here," Nate said. "Come on." He held my hand tight and kept me close to his side. Across the street, a couple of guys in hooded jackets watched our progress. Nate nodded to them, and they turned away.

We headed up a hilly street lined with crumbling brownstones, the yards out front patchy and covered with piles of trash. I hugged in closer to Nate. My neighborhood, with its pristine facades and English-garden lawns, was just a handful of miles from here. How could one city contain so much contradiction?

Nate halted in front of a brown and white house, its paint peeling so that raw wood showed through. One of the windows on the second floor was broken and boarded up. Yet a BMW sat in the driveway. I stared at it until Nate nudged me. "This is it."

My belly coiled itself. I touched the chain-link fence that ringed the lot, expecting a flood of memories to rush in. But my mind was blank. Annabel was curled inside me, hiding from this place. She didn't want to remember.

We walked up the path to the front porch. Inside, a television blared. My hand shaking, I raised my hand and knocked.

A moment later, the door opened a crack and the sliver of a man's face appeared. "Yeah?"

"Mr. Sutton?"

"Who's asking?"

I found Nate's hand. He clenched my fingers. "My name's Georgie and this is Nate. We're friends of Anna's."

"Anna?" The single eye that was visible through the crack squinted. "Anna who?"

I jerked back, my insides cold. "Anna Leeland. Your foster *daughter*."

"She don't live here anymore." He started to close the door, but

Nate put his hand flat against it and pushed. Sutton stumbled back to avoid getting knocked over by the door. "Hey!"

"Can we come in?" Nate stepped over the threshold without waiting for an answer. I followed him, listening closely to my heart. But the Catch was silent. I touched the wall just inside the door. Still nothing.

"I didn't say you could come in." Sutton planted himself in the middle of the living room.

"We need to talk to you about Anna," Nate said, squaring off to him. He glanced at me.

I didn't say anything, just turned in a small circle to take in the room. A large HDTV hung on the wall across from a leather couch and a fancy armchair, one of the ones that had a cooler built into the bottom. A plush rug covered half the floor. I leaned forward and peeked into the kitchen off to the side of the room. The cabinets seemed new but the appliances were old and a stack of pizza boxes sat on the small seventies-era table. I rubbed my arms. Something was off here, and I didn't need the Catch to point it out to me.

I looked back at Sutton. "Where are the kids?"

"They're around. Not that it's any of your business." He crossed his arms. "What about Anna? I ain't seen her in—"

"Since her birthday, right?" I said. "Since you kicked her out on her eighteenth birthday."

Sutton narrowed his mud-brown eyes at me. "Now wait a minute. I didn't kick her out. The State don't give me money to keep them here after they turn eighteen. That ain't my fault."

"And that's all you care about," I said. "The money."

Sutton's jaw tightened. "Get out."

"She's dead." Nate's voice was strangled. I tore my gaze away from the strange luxury of the living room to look at his face. His skin was mottled, his brow knitted together with anger. "Did you know that? She died over a month ago. All alone."

"How was I supposed to know?" Sutton ran his hand through his thinning hair. "I hadn't seen her in months. What was I supposed to do?"

"Care about her!" Nate roared before I could even open my mouth. "Did you have any idea what she was doing? That she was a prostitute, even when she lived here? Did you?"

"Don't fucking yell at me in my own house!" Sutton bellowed back.

Beneath their furious voices, I heard the Catch. Annabel unfurled inside me. I tiptoed away from the two men. They were so preoccupied with yelling at each other that they didn't notice me creep upstairs.

A print of Monet's *Water Lilies* hung at the top of the stairs. There was only one bedroom up here, and it was just as comfortable as the living room, with a rich mahogany sleigh-bed and a huge vanity that I'd seen in Pottery Barn. The master bathroom had a Jacuzzi tub and a marble sink. I stared at my reflection in the mirror above the gold faucets. What the hell?

I closed my eyes and listened to the Catch. *The basement.* My eyes flew open. Of course. How could I be such an idiot? One of my first memories from Annabel was of her dank, windowless bedroom…in the basement.

I galloped down the stairs, past Nate and Sutton.

"If you had cared one tiny iota, maybe she wouldn't have turned to the streets—"

"That girl was whack from the minute she got here! She wouldn't listen to nobody!"

"Because nobody ever talked to her—"

I raced through the kitchen and pulled open the basement door. The stench of dank sorrow washed over me. My insides cracked open and Annabel flooded in, her pain and loneliness saturating every nook and cranny of my being. My knees buckled and I caught the rail before I could fall. It shook beneath my grip as I made my way down into the dimness.

An old couch stood in the middle of the room, its cushions stained and sagging. There was no rug on the floor down here, just the cold concrete. *My toes are always cold...* I squeezed my eyes shut but I couldn't keep the memories from tumbling over one another. *Having to pretend we're allowed upstairs in the living room whenever a social worker comes over...getting screamed at for daring to touch the BMW...sneaking in to take a bath in the Jacuzzi when the Suttons are out...*

I opened my eyes. My ribs ached with the effort to breathe. Five doors ringed the basement, one room for each of the kids they always had in rotation, bringing in six figures a year from the state that they spent on themselves while the kids had holes in their shoes.

All I needed was love, and there was never any to spare here.

The darkness closed in on me. I fled up the stairs, my scar

searing like a physical manifestation of everything Annabel had endured in this house. I collided with Nate and clung to him, my body racked with sobs.

"Georgie! What's wrong?"

"Get me out of here," I moaned and Nate half carried me to the door. Just before we escaped, I turned back to Sutton. "Someday you'll pay," I whispered. "Someday you'll pay for what you did to her."

We made it to the sidewalk before I sank to the ground, fighting for breath, fighting to find myself inside Annabel's abyss. I couldn't contain her; she had come out of hiding and was everywhere. The darkness was going to swallow me whole, eat me alive…

"Georgie. Georgie." Warm hands cradled my face and I opened my eyes. Nate pulled me close and kissed the tears that had frozen on my cheeks, my eyelids, my forehead, my temples. "It's okay. It's okay."

"No," I gasped. "It was never okay. It was never okay for her here."

"But you're not her," Nate murmured into my hair. "You're okay."

I hung on to him, trying to bring myself back to the surface. Nate kissed my lips, soft and gentle, and light began to edge out the darkness. Bit by bit, breath returned to my body. I was Georgie. I had a home with two loving parents. I forced everything else out as Nate held me, his hands moving slowly up and down my back. *I am Georgie. I am Georgie. I am Georgie.*

Somehow, Nate found a cab and got me inside. I curled into

him, not paying attention as the cab wound through streets I didn't know. I was going to make sure Sutton paid. I'd tell Sally Klein about him the next time I saw her. I'd get him investigated...

The cab ground to a stop and I looked up. "Where are we?"

Nate helped me out onto the sidewalk in front of a purple-and-red Victorian house. Neat boxes filled with holly adorned each of the windows, and the front lawn had a burbling koi pond. It looked like an Alice-in-Wonderland version of a gingerbread house. "This is my place."

I started and pulled back from him. "What, the whole house?"

Nate laughed. "No, just the parlor level. My landlords live on the upper floors."

I peered down the street. "What neighborhood is this?"

"Hyde Park. Come on."

I followed him through the intricate wrought-iron gate and up the front steps. "I guess I just assumed you still lived with your parents."

"No, I moved out after I got my GED." He unlocked the front door. The main hallway was brightly lit by a dangling crystal chandelier. A Persian-style runner ran along the floor, and a massive walnut sideboard stood against the wall. "This way." He unlocked the first door in the hallway. Before I followed him inside, I peeked up the stairs. Another chandelier hung on the second floor.

"Nice apartment building," I said.

"It's not really an apartment building," Nate said. "It's more of an illegal duplex that my landlords converted so they could get a little income to pay their mortgage." He flicked a light switch, and the room lit up with a warm, golden glow. Another crystal chandelier hung in the center of the room. Nate caught me looking at it and flushed. "That's more my landlords' style, not mine."

"I like it." I plucked my gloves off. The room was sparsely furnished—exactly what you'd expect from an eighteen-year-old guy—but it was comfortable and lived in. Nate took my coat and hung it on a peg by the door. I sat on the couch—which was actually a futon—and curled my knees up to my chest. I could still feel Annabel swirling inside me, her pain an ache in my chest that would not ease. All she had wanted was love, to feel safe and cherished like she had before her mother had shot it all to hell. My throat tightened again and I laid my cheek on the top of my knees.

Nate handed me a glass of water and sat down next to me. His eyes never left me as I took a long sip and set the glass down on the floor next to the futon. "Are you okay?"

I nodded even though I was far from okay. "It was just...upsetting."

"I know." Nate ran his hand through his hair but I still felt his eyes on me. "But that was still a, uh, pretty extreme reaction."

I swallowed and didn't say anything. I couldn't lie to him anymore—but I couldn't tell him the truth either. I took another sip of water. I felt stretched in all directions, like my skin couldn't quite cover my bones.

"Georgie," Nate said, and I looked up to meet his eyes. "What *was* that back there?"

"What was what?" I asked, even though I knew exactly what he meant. My insides squirmed but I didn't look away.

"Look, maybe this is just too overwhelming." His brow furrowed. "I love that you've gotten so into the program at All Saints. But you've got to have enough info to write your article by now. Maybe you should...take a break from coming to the church."

"No!" Nate started; I hadn't meant to speak so loud and sharp. "I don't want to stop coming to All Saints."

"Why?" He shifted closer to me, his eyes searching deep into my own. "Why does it mean so much to you?"

Time slowed, and the only thing I could hear was his breath. I had stopped breathing, and I couldn't even hear my own heartbeat. Now was the time to tell him. Now. *Tell him...*

"Because I love you," I said instead. Nate blinked. I still couldn't breathe. It wasn't a lie. There was love inside me for him, but whether it was my own or Annabel's, I still didn't know. I reached out and took his hand. "I–I'm sorry... I shouldn't—"

He grasped my hand and pulled me onto his lap. "Don't apologize," he whispered and kissed me. His lips were gentle at first, but it was almost like we became aware at the same time that we had nothing and no one to interrupt us. With one breath, we closed in on each other. I wrapped myself around him and let him devour the darkness out of me. In his arms, there was no Annabel. There wasn't even Georgie. I could just disappear into his light.

Warmth spread to the outer reaches of my body. He tilted me backward until we lay pressed together on the futon. His mouth descended to the hollow of my throat and I twined my legs through his. I arched up into him and a moan escaped me as his hands crept up under my sweater. His fingers were like butterfly wings on my skin—soft, warm, and impossibly gentle. I kissed the side of his neck.

"Don't stop," I murmured into his ear, my voice little more than a breath that raised goose bumps on his skin. I slid my hands up his back and under his shirt, feeling every curve and contour of his muscles and bones.

He didn't stop; there was no one to tell us no, and all my barriers were down. I'd just told him I loved him. Those three little words had broken down any walls I might have still had up. *You still haven't told him the real truth*, niggled a little voice in my brain, but I told it very firmly to shut up and pulled my sweater off.

He kissed the length of my scar and covered my bare skin with his mouth. I tugged his shirt over his head and held him against me. I wanted to melt into the heat of him. I wanted to dissolve into his flesh. I wanted…I wanted… I had never *wanted* so badly. I shifted so the full weight of him was on me and wrapped my legs around his hips. For a moment that was sheer bliss, he moved against me, our bodies molding into one. *Yes…yes…* I reached between us and began to undo his belt.

He stopped.

My whole body shuddered with disappointment. Nate sat back on his knees and I scrambled up. "What's wrong?"

He ran his hand over his face. "We can't do this," he said, his breath ragged.

"Why not?" I reached my arms around his waist and tried to draw him down to me again, but he was immovable.

"Because you're upset," Nate said. His voice was becoming stronger, his breathing normal. "You're not in the right frame of mind to make a decision like this. It would be wrong."

All the warmth he'd generated inside me went cold. That wrongness he felt… It was Annabel. He could sense *her* even as he held *me* in his arms. I shrank away from him.

"Hey," Nate said, reaching for me. "Hey, hey, hey. It's not that I don't want to. Trust me, *I want to.*" He tried to pull me in to him, but I pushed him away. "Georgie…"

"*Don't.*"

I wanted to tell him that it wasn't him, it was me…that I was a monster with someone else's heart. That the part of me he wanted didn't belong to me at all. But my mouth wouldn't form the words. We stared at each other, a sudden gulf between us where just a moment before we had been melded together. My brain was all jumbled, my body firing messages that my mind couldn't compute.

Nate rubbed his face with his hands. "Look—"

A loud buzzing cut him off. We both looked around wildly for a moment before I realized it was my phone. I dug into my bag and pulled it out; it was a number I didn't recognize. More to avoid Nate than out of curiosity, I answered it. "Hello?"

"I'm looking for…George?" said a gravelly male voice from the other end.

"Do you mean Georgie?"

"Oh. Yeah. Yeah, that's right."

"That's me."

"You left me a note. About the apartment."

I scrunched my face up. "Apartment?"

"At 826 Emiline Way."

I bolted to my feet, the confusion in my brain blasted away. "Yes. Yes, I did leave you a note."

"Are you still interested?"

"Yes—definitely," I said. Nate got to his feet and nudged me, but I ignored him. "Can I come see it now?"

"Now? Uh, yeah. I'll be there in fifteen."

"Great. See you soon." I tossed my phone back into my bag and pulled my sweater over my head.

"What was that about?" Nate asked.

I didn't answer as I put my coat on. I could feel Annabel creeping back in, grappling for my heart again, and I let her. It was easier to deal with than whatever I was feeling for Nate.

"I have to go," I said and turned to the door. It was only after I was in the hallway that I heard the door close and his footsteps behind me, and I let him follow me out into the cold, darkening night.

CHAPTER EIGHTEEN

I called Manny to pick us up in his cab. His friendly chatter covered the tense silence between me and Nate. I also called Mom to tell her I wouldn't be home for dinner, and I actually told the truth. "I'm out with Nate," I said when she asked who I was with.

"Well, I guess that's okay," she said. "You took your meds this morning, right?"

"Yeah. I feel fine."

"Alright. Be home by ten."

Nate watched me as I hung up the phone and stashed it back in my bag. "Where are we going?"

"Someplace near All Saints," I said, peering out the window. Long streams of headlights flashed by. In the reflection of the glass, I saw his eyes on me, his pupils dark and unreadable.

Manny pulled up in front of 826 Emiline Way. I paid him the fare and climbed out. Nate grabbed my arm halfway up the litter-strewn path.

"This is where it happened, isn't it?" His voice quivered; with anger or sorrow, I couldn't tell. I met his eyes and didn't say anything, but I didn't have to. "This is where she died," he whispered.

I pulled my arm out of his grasp and continued up the stoop.

A shadowy figure moved inside the door and pulled it open. "You Georgie?"

"Yes." It was dim inside the vestibule, lit only by a single bulb that swung naked with the rush of wind from outside.

"I'm Harvey," the landlord said. He pulled a ring of keys out of his kelly-green Celtics jacket and clicked through them with his pudgy fingers. "The apartment's upstairs."

A handwritten sign on the elevator read "Out of order." Harvey led us to the stairwell. "It's five flights," he said, "but you two are young. You can handle it. Me, on the other hand..." He patted his sizeable gut. "It's probably good for me. Wife keeps telling me to exercise."

At the third-floor landing, I put a hand on the wall, my breath short and shallow. My scar burned. "Wait," Nate said, and Harvey turned. "She needs to rest."

Harvey squinted at me. "You okay?"

"She had surgery recently," Nate said. I flashed him a pinched look, but he ignored me. His shoulders were hard set, his jaw tight. I could feel the anger just beneath his surface. Whatever happened on the fifth floor, whatever we found, I'd have to tell him something. Something real.

"Let's go," I said.

As we rounded the landing on the fourth floor, Harvey glanced at me over his shoulder. "How'd you know there was a vacant apartment in the building?"

"Uh, I didn't." I gulped in air. "I was just, uh, passing by, and the building looked nice so I left a note."

He stopped and faced me, his hands on his hips. "This place is a shithole."

"Yeah, she's lying," Nate said. I stared at him, my mouth open. "We're friends of the girl who died here. We need to see it."

Harvey shifted so that he blocked the last set of stairs we needed to climb. "Hey, I ain't running a sideshow here."

"For fifty bucks, you are," Nate said and fished a few bills out of his wallet. Harvey stowed them in his pocket and moved aside.

A creeping blackness stole into me with every step upward I took. When we reached the fifth floor, tremors overtook my body. Nate grasped my arm. "Are you okay?" he muttered.

I shook my head, my teeth chattering. A terrible ache spread across my heart, reaching its fingers out until every inch of my body was in pain. It wasn't a physical pain; it was deeper than my skin and muscles, deeper even than the marrow of my bones. I followed Harvey to the door of the apartment, each step an effort.

He unlocked the door and stood aside for us to enter. "I gotta fix the place up," he said. "Apparently she was squatting for a while before she... Well, you know."

"And you didn't know she was staying here?" Nate asked. He stood just inside the door, taking in the room.

"I ain't here much," Harvey said. The two of them moved deeper into the apartment, leaving me on the threshold.

Deep down, I knew if I walked through that door, everything would change. There was something in there that I wasn't sure I wanted to know. But I had to know it. I lifted my foot and stepped into the room.

The memory washed over me like the sea. I closed my eyes to take it in. *I place the picture on the little mantel against the wall, where a fireplace would be if this apartment were nicer. I touch the picture, tracing my five-year-old face as I lean forward to blow out the candles on my huge strawberry shortcake. My gut twists as I move my finger to touch Mama and Daddy's faces. I drop my hand and turn to look at my new domain. A sleeping bag and a duffel with my clothes...that's all that's mine in this borrowed home. But it's more mine than any other home I've ever been dumped in...*

I open my eyes. And there were windows. Not like the dank basement at the Suttons'. Windows that she looked out of every night, searching the stars for a future that would never come.

A bittersweet taste filled my mouth. It wasn't that Annabel was happy here—she had never been happy, not since her mother killed her father—but this was the first place she'd ever lived where she didn't have to answer to anyone else. The small joy of that independence echoed inside the Catch as I walked in her footsteps. I stood in the place where she put her high heels on every night, where she sat next to her little space heater and ate ramen noodles.

From across the room, I felt Nate's eyes on me as he let Harvey lead him around. I looked toward the one place I had avoided—the balcony. My heart beat quickly. If I stepped out there, would it all be over? Would I remember the night she died? Would she let me go? I moved until I was right at the glass door to the balcony, until my fingers could just reach the knob. I stretched my hand out.

"Oh, you can't go out there." Harvey's voice was right behind me. I became aware that he and Nate had followed me to the door. The Catch crescendoed inside me as I turned the knob. "It's still loose. It's too dangerous."

His voice was muffled, drowned out by the Catch. I could hear nothing else but Annabel's whisper. *Open it. Open it.*

She wanted me to know. She wanted to let me go.

Two pieces of crime-scene tape crossed the doorway. I tore the tape aside and stepped out.

"Georgie," Nate said, his voice sharp.

He sounded far away. The cold air slapped me, whipping my hair across my eyes. The moon was clouded, the stars veiled. I tasted moisture on my tongue. It would snow soon.

The wrought iron creaked beneath me as I took another step. Nate said my name again. I barely heard him. I was listening, listening, listening inward…trying to pull forth the memory that I wanted, the one that would release me from her hold…

But no memory of Annabel's came. It was just out of reach, like the Warehouse. I had come to this place too early, before she gave me the other memories that she needed me to know.

I pressed my hands to the side of my head, trying to squeeze the memory out. The Catch ripped through me, its insistence almost violent. Another memory rose to the surface, but it wasn't Annabel's.

It was mine.

A great big push, two invisible hands shoving me back into consciousness.

I gasped, sending a shot of icy air to my lungs. The very first thing I'd felt when I woke up after my surgery. A great big push. Like someone pushing me back into life.

I reached out and touched the rail lightly. "Georgie!" Nate's voice was right behind me. "Stay back!"

"No," I breathed. The frozen iron burned beneath my fingertips. My heart swelled with the force of the Catch. And then, like the nickname I'd given it, I caught on.

I hadn't been pushed into life.

Annabel had been pushed out of hers.

The heart was made to be broken.

—Oscar Wilde

CHAPTER NINETEEN

My fingers curled around the rail. I looked up into Nate's face. His nose and cheeks were bright red in the cold. "I get it," I whispered. "I get it now."

"Get what?" He gripped my elbow. "Come back inside."

"Don't you see?" I resisted him, forcing him to look down at the rail. "She didn't jump, Nate. She was pushed."

Nate stared at me. I marched past Harvey and out of the apartment. Warmth and light spread through me, taking over all the bittersweet darkness that had seeped in. When I got down to the street, I turned my face up to the sky. Snow was coming.

I should've been angry that Annabel had given me a mystery that I now had to solve. But all I could feel was a sweet sense of triumph that I had figured it out. Now I knew why she couldn't let go. She hadn't chosen to die. She'd been forced into it.

This was her purpose all along, the reason so much of her still echoed inside me. If I solved her murder, if I brought her killer to justice, she'd release her hold on me. The memories would stop… and maybe my own would even come back.

Nate joined me on the sidewalk, his face a wordless question that I couldn't quite answer. A few flakes of snow drifted down between us. I dug out my phone, activated the location search feature, and found a diner a few blocks away where we could at least be warm and fed while I figured out what to say to him.

"Come on," I said to Nate and walked in the direction my phone told me to.

Nate fell into step with me. "Georgie," he said, "you can't seriously think that Annabel was murdered."

I glanced over at him. "Yes, I can. I know it."

His breath puffed out in white mists. "How? How can you possibly know that?"

I didn't answer. A block ahead, I saw the neon sign of the diner and sped up. But I was certain, with every ounce of everything that I had ever known was right, that Annabel had been pushed. The feeling in my heart, the resonance of certainty, told me I was right.

Bells jangled overhead as I pulled open the diner door. Red leather booths lined the interior. A bored-looking waitress barely looked up from her post at the counter as we entered. "Anywhere you like," she said.

I led Nate to a booth in the corner, far away from anyone that might overhear us. The exhilaration over getting this huge piece of Annabel's puzzle was dissipating, replaced with anxiety. I was going to have to tell Nate the truth. There was no way out of it now. I dug my fingernails into my palms as I took my coat off. What if he didn't believe me? What if he walked out of this diner and out of my life forever?

We avoided each other for several minutes by examining our menus. I kept peeking over the top of mine to look at Nate, to drink him in if this was the last time I was ever going to see him.

My heart hammered against my ribs. Maybe I could talk my way out of it.

The waitress sauntered over. "I'll have the meatloaf," I told her. "With mashed potatoes." Dr. Harrison would not approve, but if there was ever a time to forego the diet for comfort food, this was it. Nate ordered a grilled cheese with fries and the waitress shuffled off, tucking her pen behind her ear.

"Listen," I said before he could open his mouth. "It makes sense. You even said yourself that despite her situation, she never seemed suicidal."

"I did say that, but why was she murdered?" Nate said. "Who would do that to her?"

"Jules. Someone in his network. Maybe even one of the other girls." I pressed my palms flat on the table. "There are any number of suspects. Maybe she found out something about the Warehouse that she shouldn't have." I reached for his hands. They were freezing. "We have to at least look into it."

"Don't you think the cops would've found something when they went over the crime scene?"

"Not if they assumed it was a suicide." I squeezed his fingers. "On the surface, it was so obviously a suicide." Without thinking, I touched my scar, as though I could speak to her through all the muscle and bone and consciousness that separated us. "You knew Annabel and the world she lived in. You have to help me figure out who killed her."

Nate opened his mouth, but the waitress came over with our food. The meatloaf smelled like a childhood memory restored, but my appetite slipped away as I waited for Nate to speak. The waitress left. Nate didn't touch his food either.

"I will help you," he said, "but first you have to tell me why you care so much. Why you are so invested. And I don't buy that it's for a school newspaper article. And—and—" He swallowed. "You may love me, but that's not the reason either. Not the real one. I need the real reason before I can go any further."

I threaded my fingers together, kneading my palms. I couldn't talk my way out of this. I had to tell him the truth. The words were stuck in my throat. I looked away from him, out the window where snow had started to fall. I moved my hand to my chest, to the place where he knew the scar was hidden beneath my sweater, and swung my gaze back to him.

"My heart," I whispered, my eyes on his. "My heart. It's hers. It's Annabel's."

Time froze, like the diner was inside a large snow globe and we were just two little figurines, stuck in this booth forever. Nate's jaw worked. I could see all the words and sentences and questions churning on his face, but all he managed to get out was, "What?"

"It's anonymous," I said. "Organ donation. Except, you know, like when your brother gives you his kidney or whatever. But most of the time, it's anonymous. I didn't know who she was. But I had to. She'd saved my life by dying. I had to know who she was."

Nate's chest moved up and down with short, jerky breaths. I went on. "I found out she was a Jane Doe. No one knew who she was. I started to do some research. That's what led me to 826 Emiline."

His eyes were still on me, but they were seeing something past me. "You—Annabel's—heart is—in you?"

I nodded. He blinked fast. I laid my hand on top of his. He jerked his hand away so fast that I gasped. "Nate, please—"

"How could you not *tell* me this?" Nate ran his shaking fingers through his hair. "All this time you've been lying to me? About some goddamned article that never existed?"

"Because I didn't think you'd believe me—"

"Why? Why wouldn't I believe that you wanted to know who your heart donor was?" He slammed his hands down on the table. The waitress looked over. "I get that, Georgie. Who *wouldn't* want to know? Now I get it, why you care so much. But why couldn't you trust me with that? After everything that's happened—between us—"

"Because…" I swallowed hard, my throat like sandpaper. "There's more."

"More than—"

"I remember things."

His eyes narrowed. "What things?"

"I remember things…about her life." Nate's mouth opened but I rushed on. "That's how I knew who you were. And that's how I know, without a doubt, that she was murdered." I balled my hands into fists so tight my knuckles turned white. "Nate, there's one more thing. Every time I remember something from her life, I lose a memory from my own."

He flattened his palms on the table and took a deep breath. "Georgie, I'm sure having a heart transplant is a traumatic thing to go through—"

"And what? You think I'm going through some sort of post-traumatic stress disorder?"

"Maybe." His voice was gentle, like he was talking to a scared child. "And maybe you do have Annabel's heart, and you think you're remembering things—"

"*Think?*" I leaned across the table toward him. "I *am* getting her memories. How else can you explain how I knew your name before you told me, or where the cemetery was, or that Annabel loved strawberries—"

"Those are all things you could've found out."

The softness of his voice made me want to punch him. "How?" I demanded. "How could I know all those things?"

"Georgie—"

"And I know about your sister."

The blood drained from his face.

"You told Annabel about her. Isn't that right?" I went on. He sat still and silent, staring at me. "To get her to trust you. Didn't you?"

He was still frozen, but at last he spoke. "You could've found it out some other way." His voice was like a wolf's, more animal than human.

"How? You've never told anyone, and I've never met your parents. Annabel was the only one who knew."

"She must've told someone."

"Who? When she wouldn't even tell anyone her real name?"

Nate slid to the edge of the booth and pushed himself to standing. "I–I can't—*process* this. I don't know how you know about my sister, but it is *not* because you have Annabel's heart. If you even do." He grabbed his coat and hustled toward the door.

I snatched my coat off the booth seat and dashed after him. "You kids still need to pay!" the waitress yelled. I ignored her and followed Nate into the cold, snowing night. Flurries blustered all around us, muffling the world except for the tense snow globe that he and I seemed to exist in.

"Nate, I'm telling the truth. You have to believe me—"

"Why should I? When you've been lying this whole time?" The tip of his nose shone bright red, but whether it was from cold or anger, I didn't know. "Who the hell *are* you? How do I know you're not after something else?"

"What? How could you think—"

"Do you know how many crackpots came after my family after my sister went missing?" He stalked toward me. I could feel his rage just below the surface, ready to explode. "I give you points for creativity, using Annabel's heart to get close to me—"

"I'm not lying!" My voice shattered the peaceful snow falling around us. I struck my fist against my chest. Pain shuddered down my scar but I didn't care. "I have Annabel's heart. I know things about her no one else does. She was *murdered*, Nate. That's why she's hanging on. Why she's giving me her memories. She wants us to figure out who killed her."

Nate held up his hand. "This is insane—"

"I am not crazy!" That word...*that word*...I wanted to strike it from the dictionary of my life. "I have to find out what happened to her. And I need your help." I reached out toward him, but he backed away, his eyes wide and wild on me. "Please, Nate. You're the only one I can talk to about this. Remember when you said you only know the post-op Georgie? You get me. You're the only one. Please." My voice was thin and scared, coming from that place inside me that was desperately trying to hold on to all my memories before Annabel took them. "Please. I need you."

Nate covered his face with his hands. His knuckles were red and raw from the cold. I touched him lightly on his wrist. He jerked away with such violence I almost fell over.

"Don't, Georgie." The danger in his tone sent a shiver down my spine that had nothing to do with the cold. He dropped his hands and his gaze froze the world around me. "I liked you. I think I could've fallen in love with you. But I don't know who you are now, and I don't think I want to know."

He turned and walked away so fast that within seconds, the snow had swallowed him from view. I think I called after him once, twice, or three or a hundred times, but the wind tore my voice into shreds. He never turned back, and soon I was all alone on the sidewalk, drowning in a storm of snow and tears.

CHAPTER TWENTY

I stumbled back into the diner to pay the bill and made my way home. Nate's words kept twisting and turning around in my head. Every time I heard them, I closed my eyes in red-hot shame. I should've been honest from the beginning. I should've told him I had Annabel's heart. I should've told him the truth about her memories.

He wouldn't have believed you then either, my brain reasoned.

But it wouldn't have hurt so much, I answered. Not back then before I knew who he was, before he'd kissed me, when the only feelings I had for him were Annabel's. Now my own were tangled up inside with hers, and my own heart was broken.

—\/\/—

When the dawn finally broke the next day, a foot of snow blanketed the world, making my street look like a row of sugar-covered gingerbread houses. I sat on my windowsill, looking down at the still, silent world. I'd sat there most of the night, watching the sky change from dark to light.

My heart hurt, a fierce ache that I knew was my own and not Annabel's. But whatever the pain or the cost, I'd decided on something in that long, long night: I had to go on.

I'd lost Nate, but I'd gained the real reason why Annabel was still imprinted on my heart. I knew my direction now, and I couldn't stop just because Nate had left my side. I wasn't angry at Annabel anymore. It wasn't her fault she had died, and she'd gotten my attention the only way left to her. She'd hijacked my memories to get me to piece together her own. Once I did, once I solved the puzzle, she'd give me my memories back. I had to believe that.

Next to me on the pink cushion, my phone buzzed. I picked it up to read a text from Toni. Hillcoate had a snow day, and she and Ella were going to our favorite brunch place. Did I want to join them?

My fingers hovered over the keyboard, about to type *no effing way*—I mean, what kind of passive-aggressive game was Ella playing, putting Toni in the peacemaker middle?—but I froze. I couldn't go back to All Saints. I'd confided in Nate and he'd rejected me. A fresh wave of heartache twisted through me. Ella and Toni were all that I had left. Maybe I *could* trust them with this.

What time? I responded.

My bedroom door burst open. "No school! Best birthday *ever!*" Colt crowed and did a silly little jig all around my room. "Mom says I can do whatever I want today. Within reason, of course. I'm thinking that within reason means skiing up at Gunstock. It's only a two-hour drive." He vaulted onto my bed, sending the pillows several inches into the air. "What do you think?"

"I can't go skiing, silly," I said. "No strenuous activity, remember?"

"Aw, crap." Colt's face fell. "I guess I could just stay home and play *Skyrim*."

"Don't be a dummy," I said, punching his arm. "You should go. Enjoy your snow day. It's the first one this year, isn't it?"

"First snow day and my birthday all in one. I am a lucky boy." Colt bounced off my bed and started poking through the stuff on my desk and dresser. "Wonder what the big sis got me this year." He shot me a wicked little grin. "Is it in the closet?"

"Is what in the closet?" My heartbeat jolted my rib cage.

"Duh. My present."

I looked wildly around the room, my eyes settling on a primly wrapped package with a bright blue bow on my dresser. "That's it," I whispered.

Colt snatched up the box and shook it. "Ooooh. Is it a an Xbox 360 with 4GB Kinect?"

I forced a laugh. "Yeah." And for all I knew, it could've been.

"The anticipation is killing me," Colt said, clutching the package under his arm. He bolted out the door, calling back, "Mom's making pancakes!"

I pressed my hands against my chest, fighting for breath. I had no idea what was in the box. I must've bought it days ago and set it out yesterday to give to him today...but in that span of time, I'd gotten the memory of Annabel's days at the Sutton house, of her apartment at 826 Emiline...and now Colt's birthday was gone. Not just the date. I scrambled backward to the day my parents had brought Colt home from the hospital as a baby. It must've been there at some point...but now it was gone. Another fragment of my life removed. Another reason why I had to solve Annabel's murder.

Heat crept up the side of my neck, anger and fear and sorrow stealing through me. *Couldn't you at least have told me something useful in exchange for taking my brother's birthday away from me?* I thought at whatever was left of Annabel inside me. *Like, who pushed you off the balcony?*

There was no answer, of course. There never was. There were only more questions.

Colt went skiing with Dad and Grandma. At breakfast, my parents had reminisced about the night he was born, that it had snowed that night too, and my dad had been stuck at the airport waiting for my grandmother's delayed flight for hours and hours. I had been very young, but I should've remembered. And I didn't.

Colt loved the present I'd gotten for him, but that seemed like a very meager reward for the fact that I didn't remember the day he was born anymore. I sat at the window in the living room and watched them pack the car up, pile in, and drive off to Gunstock. I wished I could go with them. I wished I could forget everything for a day and fly down the side of a mountain, the wind at my back.

"What are you going to do today?" Mom asked, squishing in next to me at the window. "I'd love to spend the day together but my damn deadline is in a week."

"It's okay. Ella and Toni want to meet at Zaftig's, if that's okay."

"Sure." She put her arm around my shoulders and squeezed. "Don't worry—you'll be skiing again next year."

Yeah. If I hadn't lost the memory of how to ski by then. I leaned into her for a moment, also wishing that I could tell her what had happened with Nate, that I could spill everything over our favorite comfort food. But it was going to take more than homemade mac-and-cheese and a pint of chocolate chocolate chip to make this go away.

"I'd better go lock myself in the office," Mom said, peeling herself away from the window. "Are you going to practice for a while before you meet the girls?"

I shrugged, ignoring the underlying suggestion of *you should be practicing* in her tone. "Maybe." I felt her eyes on me for a minute longer before she headed upstairs to her office.

Once I was sure she was safely ensconced in her cocoon of writing, I went to my room and stood in the middle of it. I was all twisted up inside and it made me twitchy. I had a couple of hours before I had to meet Ella and Toni, and I *should've* been practicing, but when I reached for my oboe, I just couldn't make myself put it together and play. There was something else I needed to do instead, another decision I'd come to in the night, and Nate was no longer around to discourage me from it.

I got dressed fast, told Mom I was heading out to run errands before brunch with the girls, and left the house. The snow had stopped and it was now just cold. That otherworldly quiet that comes after a snowstorm still hovered over the streets, and I breathed it in as I made my way to the heart of Brookline.

The stately brick building on Washington Street was practically empty when I walked inside. A couple of cops milled around and barely looked up as I opened the door. Somewhere inside one of the offices, a phone rang over and over. The chair at the reception desk was empty so I wandered past it, checking names on the offices along the corridor. File cabinets lined the wall opposite the offices, and halfway down the hall, I almost tripped over an open drawer.

"Oh, sorry about that!" A woman kneeling on the floor in front of the drawer got to her feet. Her black hair was neatly braided and pulled tight at the top of her head, emphasizing the strong cheekbones that cut across her cocoa skin. Though she was dressed in plainclothes, a badge flashed from the inside pocket of her blazer when she moved. "Can I help you?"

"I'm looking for Detective Lowell."

"He's two offices down." She pointed and bent over to pull open another drawer.

Lowell's door was closed, so I knocked lightly and waited. From inside, I heard papers rustling and the rumble of Lowell's voice, although I couldn't make out what he was saying. I glanced up the hall. All the other detectives' doors were open; Lowell's was the only one that was closed. I knocked again, louder this time in case he hadn't heard the first one.

"Just a minute!" His voice sounded harried.

The female detective straightened, her rich brown eyes narrowed at his door. When the door opened, she bent back over her filing. But the person at the door wasn't Detective Lowell. It was Michelle.

"Georgie?" Her eyes narrowed as she looked me up and down. That same heavy feeling that I'd felt around her at the party settled in the pit of my stomach. Inside my chest, the Catch slithered awake. "What are you doing here?"

"I came to see your dad. I didn't realize you'd be here." I tried to look casual and unconcerned. "Were your classes canceled today too?"

"Yeah. I brought my dad breakfast." She jerked her head and I saw the desk inside the office littered with coffee cups and an empty bag from Kupel's. "Why do you need to see him?"

"Let her in, Michelle." Detective Lowell appeared in the doorway behind Michelle. He opened the door wider and stepped back to let me into the office. I had to sidle beneath Michelle's gaze to get into the room, and I felt her eyes hot on the top of my head.

I turned and gave her a smile that didn't reach my eyes. "Actually, I have something for you too." I dug into my bag and pulled out my dad's letter of recommendation that I'd had the presence of mind to grab before I left the house. "What's it for, by the way?"

"An internship," she said, taking the envelope from me. "Some big corporation that's building a hydroelectric power plant in Maine. They came recruiting to my engineering class last semester."

"Cool." I rocked on my heels. "I hope you get in. Maine's really pretty in the summer."

"Never been." She slid the letter into her back pocket. "Tell your dad thanks." She darted a glance to her father. "So did you just come here to deliver that? Your dad could've mailed it."

I pressed my lips together for a moment and sucked in a breath through my nostrils. I hadn't forgotten what she'd said to me at the party about things coming so easily for me, and my tolerance level for her attitude was in short supply.

"I came to talk to your dad, actually. About an article I'm writing. For the *Banner*." I waved my hand toward the breakfast remnants. "But maybe I should've called first. I'm sorry I interrupted daddy-daughter time."

"No problem!" Lowell cleared his throat and started to clear some of the trash off his desk. "You know you're welcome here any time. Unless you're in trouble," he added, wagging his finger at me.

"Oh, Georgie's not in trouble." Michelle leaned against the door frame, her arms crossed. One side of her mouth curved in a half-smile that I couldn't quite read. "In all the years I've known her, Georgie's never been in trouble."

I met her half-smile with one of my own. "Maybe I'll use that as my yearbook quote. 'Never been in trouble.'" I cocked my head. "What was your yearbook quote, Michelle? Something about bringing joy and light to the world?"

She straightened, dropping her arms at her side. Lowell cleared his throat and sat in the big chair behind his desk. "So, Georgie, you said you're writing an article. What's the topic?"

I turned my back on Michelle and sat opposite him. I could feel Michelle's presence as she hovered in the doorway, like a black cloud on the horizon threatening rain. I wasn't too keen on talking about Annabel with her around, but I couldn't very well kick her out of her own dad's office. "Sex trafficking."

Lowell's eyes widened and a little tick started at the bottom corner of his left eye. "That's a pretty heavy issue."

"I guess." I reached into my bag and laid the printout of the article on Annabel's suicide from the BPD website onto the desk. "See, I started writing about teen suicide. I was going to use this case as the focus, but then I found out this girl was trafficked so I decided to write about that instead."

Lowell took the paper from me and read through it, his lips pressed into a thin line. "How do you know she was trafficked?"

"Well, I went to the address mentioned there and found this church nearby where this organization, FAIR Girls, has a chapter. And they knew her—she, you know, worked near there."

"So she was a prostitute." Lowell put the paper down and gave it a slight shove back to me across the desk.

"No," I said and pressed my palm flat over the article to keep it from drifting onto the floor. "She was trafficked."

"Well, it's pretty much the same thing—"

"No, it's not," said a voice from the doorway. I turned. It was the woman I'd practically tripped over in the hallway. She edged into the room. Michelle shrank into the corner, her face tight as she listened to the conversation.

"Are you eavesdropping again, Lucy?" Lowell kept his voice light but I could hear the undercurrent of annoyance.

Lucy laughed, either not noticing Lowell's attitude or choosing to ignore it. "Yeah, well, you know me. I never met a trafficking case I didn't want to crack." She crossed the room, holding her hand out to me. "Detective Lucy Russell."

"Georgie Kendrick." I shook her hand. Her palm was warm and calloused.

"Detective Russell works on our sex crimes unit," Lowell said.

"I'm trying to establish a protocol here that treats the girls like the victims they are, instead of criminals," Lucy said. "But it's hard to get the old guard to change their ways," she added with a wink to Lowell.

"The prostitutes are still breaking the law," he said. The undercurrent of annoyance in his voice came to the surface.

"But many of them are underage," I said. Lucy raised her eyebrows. "And none of them are choosing to be there. What little girl do you know that wants to grow up to sell herself on the street?"

"Exactly," Lucy said.

Lowell gripped the edge of his desk. "So what does this have to do with the article you're writing, Georgie?"

"Oh. Well, um, I did a little digging and I think..." I took a deep breath and looked back and forth between him and Lucy. Somehow having her in the room made this easier to say. "I don't think she committed suicide. I think she was murdered."

Lucy whistled low under her breath and leaned over to pick the paper up off the desk. Lowell scrunched his face up and said, "Why do you think that?"

I hunched my shoulders. I couldn't answer the question honestly without sounding insane. "Just from talking to the people who knew her at FAIR Girls, she didn't seem suicidal."

"She was a prostitute." We all started and turned to the corner where Michelle stood, her back as straight as a wooden totem. "That alone would make someone suicidal."

"I have to agree with Michelle," Lowell said. I wanted to roll my eyes. Of course he'd agree with his perfect little 3.9-GPA daughter. "This case wasn't in our jurisdiction, but I remember it. Everything at the crime scene indicated a suicide."

"Well, if she'd been pushed, that would be hard to tell, right?" I looked to Lucy for confirmation.

She chewed her lip thoughtfully. "Possibly. I mean, in this case, it would be hard to tell. Especially now that there's no longer a body to examine."

Without thinking, I touched my scar. If it wasn't for me, there might still be a body to examine. Instead she'd been carved up, her organs recovered for those whose lives they could still save. Lowell leaned forward. "Are you okay, Georgie?" he asked.

"What? Oh, I'm fine." I dropped my hand into my lap. "It's just become a habit."

"Well, you should probably go home and rest. I'd hate for your parents to think I was slowing your recovery." He glanced at Lucy. "Georgie had a heart transplant several weeks ago."

"Really? You look great," Lucy said.

"I'm doing fine," I said. My cheeks prickled with heat at being reminded, once again, how *not normal* I was. I pointed at the article that Lucy still held in her hands. "So, you'll look into it?"

"Sure. By the way, when is your Juilliard audition?" Lowell stood and came around the desk. "It's coming up, isn't it?"

"It's in a couple of weeks—"

"Shouldn't you be focusing on that instead of writing this article?" Michelle said.

I really wished she'd keep her mouth shut and her nose out of my business. "Well, I'm not in school right now so I have time to do both."

I buttoned up my coat and swallowed hard as I looked at both of them. Other than delivering Michelle's recommendation letter, this had been a waste. *Nate was right*, I thought with an ache in my chest. And Char. *You see how far that gets you*, she'd told me. Yeah, it hadn't gotten me very far at all.

"Um, it was nice to see you both," I lied. "Good luck with the internship," I told Michelle and bolted out of the office.

I was halfway down the hall when a voice stopped me. "Georgie, wait." I turned to see Lucy half jogging to catch up with me. Behind her, Lowell's office door was shut tight once more. She slid to a stop in front of me and held up the article. "Lowell could care less about this. Like I said, he's old guard. But this is an issue that I'm very passionate about. I've been working with the CATW to institute an in-house program to help get the girls off the street instead of arresting them."

"CATW?" I asked. "What's that?"

"Coalition Against Trafficking in Women," Lucy said. She waved the article in front of my nose. "Do you by any chance know who this girl's pimp was?"

"Some guy named Jules," I said. "Some of the girls have talked about this place he runs called the Warehouse. Have you heard of it?"

Lucy looked off in the distance and nodded slowly. "Actually, yes. Another girl came in here several weeks ago and reported something similar. But when we went to investigate the address she told us, there was nothing there."

Another girl. "Detective Russell," I said, my words trying keep up with my brain, "I think that was her." I pointed to the paper. "I think she knew too much, and her pimp killed her for it."

She folded the paper into quarters and tucked into her jacket pocket. "I will look into this. And I'll do a more thorough job than my 'old guard' colleagues." She plucked a card out of the same pocket she'd put the article into and handed it to me. "If you find out anything else, call me." Lucy took my elbow and walked me to the front door. "But Georgie, please don't go looking for more information. It's not safe."

"I won't." I thanked her and stepped back out onto the street. The sun had come out by now, thin streams of light dappling the snowbanks. I wrapped my scarf tightly around my throat and headed to Zaftig's to meet Ella and Toni. Maybe the trip to the cops hadn't been a waste after all.

But at the end of the day, the cops didn't know what I knew about Annabel. They could only go so far. I was the only one who could finish whatever it was she had started.

CHAPTER TWENTY-ONE

Toni and Ella were already sitting at our favorite table by the window when I got to Zaftig's. Toni half stood and waved but Ella stayed put, her eyes glued to her phone. I clenched my jaw. Really? They invited *me*, not the other way around. Fine, whatever. I squared my shoulders. If I had to play the part of the bigger person, so be it.

"Hi, guys," I said when I got to the table. "Happy snow day."

"Happy snow day!" Toni said, a little too loudly.

With a ridiculous flourish, Ella set down her phone and looked up. "Hey."

With a sigh, I realized that I just didn't have it in me to play this game. "Ella, if you didn't want me to come, you shouldn't have invited me."

Ella folded her arms over her chest. "I didn't. Toni did."

"Fine. I'll leave." I started to get up but Toni put her hand on my arm.

"No, Georgie, stay." She looked back and forth between me and Ella. "Come on, you guys. This is so middle school." Ella looked out the window. I picked at a chip in the table. Toni sighed. "Look, both of you are right, okay? Ella, you need to be a little more sensitive to the fact that Georgie had a near-death experience."

"I didn't—" I started to say, but Toni kept right on going.

"I've read about heart transplants, and people are always changed afterward. So are we going to support her through this, or are we going to abandon her? Support her, right? And Georgie"—she turned to me—"you need to not shut us out, okay? We're here for you. Use us."

I took a deep breath. "Okay."

Ella sighed melodramatically and faced me. "Okay. I'm sorry."

"Me too." There was an awkward silence while Toni grinned at both of us. I rolled my eyes at her. "Can we order already?"

I ordered oatmeal and herbal tea while the girls ordered jumbo omelets and lattes. "So how are you feeling about the audition?" Ella asked.

"Okay, I guess." I took a sip of tea and dumped another packet of sugar into it. "Joel's still nitpicky about my piece. What about you?"

"Ugh, I'm in panic mode." Ella spooned a dollop of foam from her latte into her mouth. "I was practicing all last night and this morning. I've got a lesson later today too. I've been having them every other day."

"You'll be fine," I assured her even as my own stomach fluttered. What had I been doing last night and this morning? Chasing Annabel's ghost. With a jolt, I realized that old Georgie would've been panicking just like Ella. But new Georgie... "I mean, is it really the end of the world if we don't get in?" I said before I could stop myself.

Toni's jaw dropped. Ella's spoon froze halfway to her mouth. "Um...*yes*," she said.

"Georgie, the first thing you ever said to me on the first day of sixth grade was 'Hi, I'm Georgie Kendrick and I'm going to Juilliard,'" Toni said. "You've had this all planned out since you were ten. And we *all* know how you are about your plans."

"We've been dreaming about Juilliard since fifth-grade wind ensemble," Ella said. I could hear the hurt below her words, the frustration that once again "new Georgie" was interfering. "I know it's stressful, but you *are* going to get in."

The waitress came with our food, and I shoved a few huge spoonfuls of oatmeal into my mouth so I didn't have to talk. It wasn't stress that was making me talk like that. It was Annabel.

"I just meant," I said after a minute of tense silence as we all chewed our food, "that if I didn't get in, I would survive. I'd figure something else out." Like maybe not go into music at all. Like maybe do something to help girls like Annabel.

"Well, of course," Ella said. "I mean, even if you don't get into Juilliard, you'll definitely get into Eastman or NEC."

I ducked my head. Easier to let her believe that was what I meant than to reveal the truth.

"I'm so glad I already got my early acceptance into Brown," Toni said. "I don't think I could handle this pressure."

I sucked in a sharp breath. My insides had started twisting the moment Juilliard had come up and now they were all knotted up tight. I tried to call up the feeling I had when I held my oboe, of my lifeline tethering me to my old self, but all that came up were the ache in my chest over Nate and the Catch. I was spending too much time in Annabel's world. I was losing myself.

"What's going on at school?" I asked quickly, trying to ground myself. "Did Sydney get into Yale?"

"She hasn't heard yet. Not a lot of people have, except for the early admissions," Toni said. "Oh, but now she thinks she wants to go to Princeton. Because of *Kyle*."

"It's so lame," Ella said, "following a boy to college. As if they're not going to break up during orientation anyway."

"That's if Kyle even gets in," Toni said. "His SATs were not the best."

"Yeah, but he's a legacy," Ella replied. She forked the last bit of omelet into her mouth. "All his dad needs to do is make a call and he's in."

Toni wrinkled her nose. "Ugh. He's so spoiled."

"Um, hello? Your mom went to Brown. Who's spoiled now?" Ella laughed, snorting coffee out her nose. It splattered the table with little brown droplets.

"Ewww!" Toni yelled, throwing a handful of napkins at Ella, who was almost falling off her chair with laughter.

I watched them like I was watching a play, like they were onstage and I was the audience and a thick fourth wall separated us. It all seemed so trivial, this world of SATs and Ivy Leagues and legacies. Not when there was a world full of girls fighting for their lives and losing. I stared out the window while Toni and Ella bickered playfully back and forth. No matter how much I wanted to be normal again, I never would be. Our threesome would never be the same. I was like a warped puzzle piece now, unable to fit with the others anymore.

"—Colt's birthday?"

Ella's voice yanked me back. "Huh?"

"Isn't it Colt's birthday today?"

"Oh." I cleared my throat. "Yeah. He and my dad and my grandma are all up skiing at Gunstock. I couldn't go, of course." I waved my hand in front of my chest.

"I can't believe he's fourteen," Ella said. "You know, I actually remember when he was born."

My stomach bottomed out as I stared at her. "You do?"

"Yeah." She tilted her head. "It's actually one of my earliest memories. But it's very vivid. There was a snowstorm and your dad had to go to the airport to pick up your grandmother. He dropped you off at my house so my mom could watch you. And then later when he picked you up, your mom came into the house carrying this tiny baby, and I thought it was a doll." Ella laughed. "I kept saying, 'I want to play with the doll! I want to play with the doll!' Isn't that so weird that I remember that?"

My eye sockets ached with all the tears I was holding back. "Yeah…weird," I whispered. I blinked fast and hard. *Ella* remembered my brother's birthday.

Toni peered into my face. "Georgie? Are you okay?"

"Huh? Yeah." I ran my hand through my hair, praying they didn't notice how much I was shaking. "I'm getting kinda tired, though. I should probably go home and rest. And practice," I said with a forced smile.

"God, me too." Ella checked her phone. "Crap, I didn't realize how late it was."

We paid the bill and ventured back out into the cold. I walked Ella home, numb while she chattered on about her audition and the dress she was planning to wear and whether she should wear heels or flats. I hugged her good-bye outside her house and watched her disappear through her front door. Fourteen years ago, I'd been in this very house, waiting for my parents to bring my baby brother home. It wasn't fair that Ella got to keep that memory and not me.

I turned toward home but I couldn't make myself go there. There were too many things in my own house that I didn't remember, from the dream catcher to the pictures of last summer in Nantucket to my own brother's birthday. And there was no one—*no one*—I could talk to about it.

The Catch whispered inside me, as loud as the wind through the bare trees. There was one person I could talk to. It didn't matter that he didn't want to talk to me. I just needed to see him.

Before I could think it through, I was on the T to Hyde Park. I walked several blocks in the wrong direction before I found the purple and red Victorian. The downstairs apartment was dark. I checked my phone; it was only two-thirty, and Nate wouldn't be off from Starbucks for another hour.

I sat down on the wooden bench on the porch and shrunk into my coat to wait. I knew this was stupid, that he'd probably just tell me to leave, but I didn't know where else to go. I hugged myself to keep warm but the chill dug deep inside. How many memories made up a person? I tucked my knees up against my chest and rested my head on them. How many were you allowed to lose before you were no longer yourself anymore?

"Georgie?"

I looked up. Nate climbed the steps to me. My eyelids were heavy with icy tears. "I don't remember my brother's birthday."

"What?" He was at the top of the steps. "What are you doing here?"

I shook my head. "I don't remember the day he was born. Fourteen years ago today. I should remember that. But I don't. Not anymore." I wasn't sure I could move. My body felt frozen into this position.

"How long have you been sitting out here?"

"I mean, what makes you *you?*" I asked. I was so cold it hurt to breathe. "Is it our memories? Is it our past or our future? Because my past is slowly becoming Annabel's." I tightened my arms around my knees. "Pretty soon my future will belong to her too."

"Georgie, I thought I made it clear last night—"

"I know you said you didn't want to see me. I don't blame you. I'm a mess. This whole thing is a mess. But I was out with my friends, and they were going on and on about things that I just don't care about anymore. And then Ella said she remembers the day Colt was born and I don't, not anymore. It got taken from me last night when I remembered the basement at the Sutton house and the apartment at 826 Emiline, and it just doesn't seem fair, you know? You don't know what it's like to not remember something so important."

I glanced up. Nate was standing right over me. "It's like you're a cabin built out of Lincoln Logs and someone keeps taking one log out at a time. And pretty soon, so many logs will be gone that the whole structure will just collapse in on itself." I couldn't breathe. "I should be the one to remember Colt's birthday, not Ella. Me." I pounded my fist against my chest with each word. "Me. Me. Georgie."

"Okay, okay, stop." Nate caught my arm before I could hit myself again. "Jesus, you're freezing." He pulled me up and helped me through the front door. The heat shocked me with such a jolt that I felt dizzy. Pain prickled my fingers and toes as blood stole back in. Nate unlocked his apartment and ushered me inside. When he closed the door, we stood staring at each other for a long moment.

"I–I shouldn't have come." My teeth chattered. "You d–don't need to be involved in t–this."

Nate rubbed his hand over his face and took off the navy woolen hat that brought out the blue in his eyes. "I'm already involved." He threw the hat on the little table by the door. "I got involved the day Annabel walked through the door at All Saints."

I remembered that day. It was there, clear as a sunlit morning, bright in my mind where the memories of Nantucket and New Mexico, a strawberry allergy, a snowstorm in February fourteen years ago, and the last Christmas with my grandfather should've been. "You teased her for putting honey in her coffee."

Nate stumbled back until he hit the side of the refrigerator in the kitchen. "How the hell do you know that?"

I blinked. "I told you. I have her heart. And her memories are imprinted on it." I pulled my scarf higher up on my neck, trying to get my ears warm. "Everything about you that she knew, I remember."

Nate's chest heaved up and down, up and down. "Then tell me about my sister," he said, his voice hoarse. "What's her name? Tell me the last time I saw her. Because no one knows that, not even my parents."

I reached inside for the memory that Annabel had given me on the night I'd first met Nate, the memory I'd tucked away until I needed to pull it out. Until now. "The last time you saw Sarah was two years ago in Philadelphia. You tracked her down and met her under the arrivals board at the train station. You tried to get her on a train home with you but she'd been followed there, and the two of you got separated on the way to the platform."

Nate closed his eyes.

"That's why you dropped out of school, isn't it?" I said. "To devote all your time to trying to find her. That's why your parents don't have money for college. They've spent it all trying to find her. That's what brought you to All Saints. That's why you want to help those girls." My voice broke. "Because they could all be Sarah."

Nate slid down the refrigerator until he hit the floor. He lowered his head to the tops of his knees. I came to kneel in front of him and reached out, but I didn't dare touch him. "I'm so sorry, Nate. I should've told you from the beginning. But I didn't think you'd believe me. Why should you? It's insane. I barely believe it myself. But it's happening."

Nate raised his head. His eyes peered into mine with a sharp clarity. "You say you remember everything about me that Annabel knew?" I nodded. "Then you know that I loved her." The words had an edge to them, and they were like a million shallow cuts to my gut. He leaned forward, so close our foreheads were inches apart. "Do you know how fucked up that is? That I loved the heart inside you, that the heart inside you loves me, and that somehow we're supposed to sort out our own feelings from this mess? How the hell are we supposed to do that?"

I pulled back and sat down on my butt across from him. The Catch was so loud inside me that its whispers set me shivering from head to toe. I was cold everywhere and I couldn't stop shaking.

"I know," I whispered. "I think it's me that loves you. Georgie. But I–I can't be sure."

Nate sank his hand into his hair and pulled. "God, Georgie. A day ago, I would've said I loved you, but now how can I know if it's you or the heart that I'm drawn to? I can't be in love with a dead girl. I can't be with someone I couldn't save."

"Then help me." I crawled forward. "Help me find out who killed her. If we do that, I know she'll let go, and we can figure out us on our own terms."

"But there's always going to be this between us." Nate tilted his head back against the fridge and stared up at the ceiling. "You're always going to have her heart. How can you be with me knowing I loved the old owner of it?"

"I don't know." I watched his face change, the shadows that clung to his eyes. "I only know that when I'm with you, everything is better. Everything makes more sense. I don't know if that's me or Annabel, and right now I don't really care."

"Well, I do. I care." He looked at me, the confusion in his eyes laid bare. "I don't know where you and I go from here. I really don't." He hauled himself to his feet and held out his hand to help me up.

Chills swept through me. I didn't want to have to travel the rest of this path without him. I took his hand, clinging to it as I got to my feet. I swayed when I stood, clutching at him to keep from falling.

"Are you okay?" Nate asked.

"Just dizzy," I murmured. "Stood up too fast, I guess." I swallowed hard, trying to get my equilibrium back.

"Sit down. I'll get you some water."

"I'm fine." I dropped onto the futon. Another wave of dizziness washed over me. I squeezed my eyes shut. When I opened them, Nate was in front of me with a glass of water. He watched me take a sip, his eyes narrowed, then pressed the back of his hand against my forehead.

"What the—" I jerked away but he kept his hand there.

"You know, you're really hot."

"Gee, thank you—"

"No, I mean you're burning up."

"I still feel like I'm freezing from being outside so long." As if to prove my words, a chill ripped through me. I shuddered from head to toe.

"Well, you feel like you have a fever." Nate disappeared into the bathroom. I heard him rummaging through the cabinet in there. I touched my own hand to my temple. Nate was right; my skin was on fire.

My mind swam through another wave of dizziness. I tightened my coat around myself. Dizziness. Chills. Fever. Nate appeared in the doorway of the bathroom with a thermometer in his hands, but I didn't need it to know what was going on.

Rejection.

CHAPTER TWENTY-TWO

I called Dr. Harrison first, who told me to *go directly to the hospital, do not pass Go*. Then I called Mom.

"What?" she screeched into the phone.

I repeated what I'd told her in a voice that I tried so hard to keep from shaking. *Meet me at the hospital. I'm having rejection symptoms. No, I'm not alone. I'm with Nate.*

"I'm going with you so shut up," he'd told me when I said I could get myself to the hospital. He kept his arm gingerly around my shoulders as the cab slid through the streets of Boston, but not even his presence could calm the fear that gripped me. Wet snow slapped against the windows. I closed my eyes and listened to the *whoosh* of tires on slush. It had been a month since my surgery; I'd thought I was safe. But I'd opened my heart to Nate and this was what wormed its way in.

The cab skidded to a stop in front of Mass General. Nate paid the driver and helped me inside. The woman at Admissions had already been alerted to my arrival and slapped a bracelet on me. As we turned away from her desk, Mom charged in through the sliding doors. Her coat was buttoned wrong.

"Georgie? Baby?" She snatched me away from Nate and

pressed her hands to my face. "You're going to be okay. Where's Dr. Harrison?"

"Cardiology," the Admissions clerk piped up.

"I've already been admitted," I said, holding up my braceleted wrist.

"Let's go." She sent a tight little smile in Nate's direction. "Thank you for bringing her."

"Oh. You're welcome." He turned to go.

"Wait," I said. "Can you stay? Please?"

Nate looked from me to my mother. "I don't think..."

"Georgie, come on." Mom tried to propel me toward the elevator but I stood firm.

"I want him to stay. Please."

Mom exhaled a hard breath. "Fine. If he wants to."

I met Nate's eyes. His gaze softened on my face. "Lead the way."

The elevator ride up to Cardiology was silent and tense. I clutched the rail against the wall as one wave of dizziness after another crashed over me. *It doesn't mean the transplant failed*, I told myself. An acute rejection episode was common. I'd read that in the post-op orders the hospital had given me after my surgery. But still...a rejection episode could also mean that the transplant *had* failed...

I squeezed my eyes shut for an instant. *Don't fail*, I begged Annabel. *Don't die twice.*

The elevator doors opened to reveal Dr. Harrison. "Well, we hoped we wouldn't see you back here," she said. She took my elbow gently and guided me down the hall. Mom stuck right by my side while Nate hung back. I knew he was uncomfortable, that everything was still so weird with us, but I needed him there. He was the only thing tethering my heart to my body, the only of-this-world link between Annabel's life and mine.

Dr. Harrison brought us into a room similar to the one where I'd spent all those days after my surgery. Fear vice-gripped my insides and I froze in the doorway. What if this was the last room I saw? What if my last vision in this world was of these pale beige walls?

"It's okay, baby." Mom brushed a lock of my hair behind my ear. "I'm right here."

"Don't leave," I whispered, but I was looking past her, over her shoulder to Nate. He gave me a small, gentle smile and slid into the chair beside the door.

Dr. Harrison cleared her throat. I backed into the room. The door swung shut but I could still see Nate through the little glass window cut into the heavy wood. He was still here. He was going to stay. Dr. Harrison stepped in front of me and drew the curtain. I tore my eyes away from the door.

"Change into the gown and get settled in," she told me. "We're going to start you on what's called triple therapy where we blast a combination of immunosuppressive drugs into your system. We'll keep you overnight and see where we are in the morning. If the rejection symptoms have reversed, we'll just adjust your daily meds and that should be that."

"A–and if the symptoms haven't reversed?" I asked. My throat was dry, my tongue like paper.

"We'll deal with that if we have to. It's a big if."

But it's still an if, I wanted to say. I bit my lip instead and slipped into the shapeless piece of fabric they called a gown. Maybe I didn't want Nate to stay. He might change his mind about me if he saw me in this thing.

Mom sat beside me while we waited for Dr. Harrison to come back with the IV. She brushed a lock of hair away from my eyes. "Where were you? I thought you were going out with Ella and Toni."

"I did. I went over to Nate's after." I leaned my head back on the stack of pillows.

"I'm not mad," Mom said quickly. I raised an eyebrow at her. What would she have to be mad about? Did I have to get permission for every step I took? "I was just…surprised to see him. That's all." She picked up my hand and held it against her cheek. "Everything's going to be okay, Georgie," she said, and for a moment, I was seven again and had just scraped my knee climbing a tree in Linden Park. "You're going to be just fine."

I swallowed the hard, hot lump in my throat. "I love him, Mom," I whispered. It felt good to tell my mother something true after all these weeks of lying.

She gave something between a laugh and a sob and half stood to kiss my forehead. The door opened and Dr. Harrison came in with Maureen, the nurse who'd looked after me before. "I remember you," Maureen said with a smile. "Hopefully you won't be staying too long this time around."

I smiled back at her, genuinely glad that she was the one putting in my IV. I'd been worried that Dr. Harrison had found out that Maureen told me about Jane Doe and that the nurse had gotten in trouble, but clearly that hadn't happened. I looked away as she eased the needle into my arm and adjusted the knob under the liquid bag. "This'll set you right in no time," she said.

Dr. Harrison left with the promise to be back in a couple of hours. Mom sat for another moment, stroking my hand, and then suddenly jumped to her feet. "Oh my God!" she exclaimed. "I haven't even called your father yet!" She grabbed her purse from the table by the bed. "I'll be just outside."

I pressed the button to raise the bed a little and looked at Maureen. "Can you arrange the pillows like you did when I was here before?" I asked. "I tried to re-create that at home, but apparently it's some magic skill you have."

She laughed. "Sure." I leaned forward and she slid the pillows around. "Does that lovely young man outside belong to you?"

"Oh." Heat came to my cheeks that had nothing to do with rejection. "Um, I'm not really sure yet."

"Well, he's not sitting out there for his health." She plumped one of the pillows. "Lucky girl."

I stared up at her. *Lucky girl?* I'd gotten a heart transplant from a dead prostitute who was stealing my memories in order to lead me to her killer. Oh yeah, I had *awesome* luck.

And yet…

If it hadn't been for Annabel, I would never have met Nate. If it hadn't been for Annabel, I would be dead.

I blinked. "Yes," I said slowly, "I guess I am."

She gave the pillows one final pat. "There you go."

"Thanks." She turned to go. "Can you—"

"Send him in? Sure, honey."

I eased back onto the pillows and closed my eyes for a moment before Nate came in. I tried to imagine the meds winding their way into my veins, healing me. *Let me live. Let me live. If you let me live, I'll solve your mystery.*

"Hey."

I opened my eyes. "Hey." I indicated the hospital gown. "Nice look, huh?"

Nate laughed. He waved a hand over the chair my mom had vacated. "Can I sit?"

"Sure."

He scooted the chair right up to the bed. "You're going to be okay."

"You don't know that." I wished my voice didn't quaver so much.

"Rejection episodes are really common. Most transplant recipients experience at least one in the first six weeks after their transplant." He held his phone up. "I did a little research while I was out there."

I looked into his eyes. The words of my real fear formed in my mouth, and I voiced them to the only person who would understand. "What if it's not medical? What if…it's Annabel? What if she's mad because…because she loved you, and she doesn't want us to be together?"

Nate leaned his elbow on the edge of the bed and rested his chin in his hand. "There was so much about Annabel that I never knew. Maybe that's part of the reason why I loved her, because she was a mystery. But the one thing I know for sure about her, without a doubt, is that she was not cruel. She wants you to live, Georgie."

Tears hung heavy on my eyelashes. I blinked fast and they fell to my cheeks. "Do you…believe me?"

He sighed. "I don't know what I believe." His blue eyes seemed to darken as they beamed into mine. "But I think you have to stop thinking of your body and heart as separate things. They're one now. No matter whose heart it is, or whatever's going on with your memories. It's all one. You're not made up of pieces. You're a whole being."

My mouth fell open. God, he was right. Ever since the surgery, even before I knew I was losing my memories, I'd thought of my heart as apart, as foreign, as *not mine*. And once I'd learned about Annabel, that seemed like proof that it wasn't mine.

But Nate was right. No matter what Annabel wanted or where she led me, her heart was mine. It was not my body that was rejecting it. It was my mind.

When I opened my eyes the next morning, Nate sat in the chair next to the bed, drinking from an enormous Dunkin' Donuts cup. "Isn't that like consorting with the enemy or something?" I said, sitting up.

He leaned forward, a finger to his lips. "Don't tell Howard Schultz, but I like Dunkin's coffee better."

"Your secret is safe with me." I ran my hand through my hair, trying to smooth down what I could only imagine was a rat's nest. "You haven't been here all night, have you?"

"They kicked me off the floor at ten. I spent the night in the lounge." He set his coffee on the floor and looked at me. "I had a lot of thinking to do."

"Nate..."

"Wait." He held up his hand. "Let me talk." He scooted to the edge of the chair and rested his elbows on his knees. "I realized that when you first told me you had Annabel's heart, part of me wasn't surprised. Because I see her spirit in you. Her goodness."

I closed my eyes. He was still in love with her. She was all he would ever see in me.

"But then," he said, and my eyes flew open, "I remembered that I had thought that about you long before I ever knew you had her heart. And you can't tell me you didn't have those qualities before the transplant. After all, she's not possessing you, is she?"

I shook my head.

"I think what I'm trying to say is this." Nate laid his hands, palms up, on the bed. "I know this is complicated. I know this is the most messed-up meet-cute ever. But I think that maybe now, with all our cards out on the table, we can make something good out of this. Something...beautiful."

My throat was hot. "Does that mean...you believe me?"

Nate nodded. His eyes were overbright, whether from lack of sleep or emotion, I didn't know. "I believe you, Georgie. And I want to help you solve this." His fingers twitched. "Because no matter whose heart is in there, I want to be with *you*."

A sob escaped me. I turned on my side, careful of the IV tube, and laid my hands on his, palm to palm. Nate's fingers curled around mine. He lowered his head and kissed my hands, his lips like rose petals on my skin. The Catch sighed inside me, and I suddenly knew that Annabel had led me to Nate for a reason. Her heart wasn't whole without him. He was another gift, just like the life she'd given me.

"I just want to be sure about one more thing," Nate murmured, his mouth warm on my knuckles. He looked up at me. "You remember everything that happened with me and Annabel, right?"

"Yes." I squeezed his hands. "I know nothing—physical—ever happened between you. That's what you were going to say, wasn't it?"

The side of his mouth curled up. "I loved her, but I couldn't cross that line. Not as long as she…belonged to Jules."

At the sound of his name, my stomach flip-flopped. "Jules—I think he killed her, Nate. I think she knew too much about the Warehouse."

"I don't get something." Nate sat up straight. "If she's giving you her memories, why don't you know who killed her?"

"I'm getting them in order," I told him. "The last one I got was of her squatting in that apartment. It's like she wants me to have the whole story before she tells me the end. It's *incredibly* infuriating."

Nate snorted. "That's so typically Annabel."

"I need to know what the Warehouse is," I said. "But I can't force the memories. They come when she wants me to have them. Or when they're provoked..." My voice trailed off. I lay back on the pillows. "I just don't know what would provoke this one."

Nate stood. He smoothed a few stray hairs away from my face. "Don't worry about it now. You need to rest."

I gripped his wrist. "Don't leave, okay?"

"I won't. But your family's outside. You should spend some time with them." He bent over and kissed me. I slid my hand to the back of his head to keep him there for a moment longer. When he drew back, the blue of his eyes had deepened. "I'll be right outside," he said softly. He picked up his coffee and headed for the door.

"By the way, it's really mean to wave that coffee around when I can't have any," I said. He grinned and sidled out into the hall.

I touched my forehead. My skin was warm but not hot, and I didn't feel chilled at all. I laid my hand on my heart. Its beat was strong and sure, even as the Catch rose up. As I listened, I realized that my heartbeat and the Catch were in harmony. They were like two musicians in a duet—remove one and the entire melody would fall apart. We were entwined now, forever. Maybe it was time to stop trying to figure out where she ended and I began and just accept the whole of who I was now.

Dr. Harrison confirmed what I already knew inside: the meds had worked and the transplant had not failed. She adjusted my daily medication and released me. Nate walked out with me and my parents. He gave my hand a squeeze before loading me into the car.

"I'll call you later," he said.

I smiled at him as he stood aside for Mom. Just before she got in the car, she hugged him. Nate's eyes widened so much that I almost laughed out loud. He patted her shoulder.

"Come for dinner soon," she said and ducked into the car.

I gave him a little shrug as we pulled away. He waved until we had turned the corner. Mom twisted in the front seat to look at me. "He's a nice young man, Georgie."

"Um, thanks?" I sank down in the seat, my cheeks burning. As we drove home, I looked out the window at the world on the other side of the glass. Dr. Harrison said I should rest for at least a few days, but I hoped my parents didn't keep me cloistered in the house for too long. My world was now on the other side of that glass, where Annabel's was.

CHAPTER TWENTY-THREE

My mother kept me housebound for five days. She canceled all my lessons with Blount. She did allow Joel to come by, because the Juilliard audition was right around the corner. I went out of my mind with restlessness. The only good thing was that I had endless hours to practice. By Day Two, I had mastered that tricky spot in the Poulenc. By Day Four, I sounded better than the recording. I played for hours every day just to drown out the Catch, which was louder than ever, trying to get me back on the case. By Day Five, I was dying to do just that.

"Mom," I whined at breakfast, "it's fifty degrees out today. I need fresh air."

"I don't know, honey. Dr. Harrison said—"

"Dr. Harrison said a *few* days. It's been five. I'm going to lose it!" I took a deep breath. "Please."

"Well…" Mom set her coffee cup down. "Where you thinking of going?"

"Um, Nate's?"

Her face brightened. "Oh, I guess that's okay." He'd stopped by a couple of times during my incarceration and had been so charming that Mom had had no choice but to join Team Nate.

I'm free! I texted Nate on my way upstairs after breakfast.

Finally! Meet me at All Saints after my shift.

That gave me enough time to practice. I closed my bedroom door and went straight to my music corner. I wanted to show Joel how much I'd improved at my next lesson. Juilliard was ten days away. I wanted my life back on track by then with all the plans I'd made still in place.

I played until my fingers ached. When I put the oboe away, I touched it gently, like there was a glass bubble around the instrument that I didn't want to break. That I didn't want Annabel and her world to break either.

The air outside tasted delicious when I left the house a little while later. Manny picked me up at the curb and drove me to All Saints. Nate wasn't there yet and the basement was practically empty so early in the afternoon. The only other person there was Tommy, who sat at the kitchen table doing her nails. She gave me a smile when I sat down. "You're welcome to it," she said, nodding towards the bottle of glittery purple nail polish.

I looked at my plain fingers, which I'd always thought were a little stubby. "I could use a little glam," I said and reached for the bottle.

"Couldn't we all?" Tommy lifted her hand and blew on her fingertips. "Have any more breakthroughs?"

I accidentally brushed my cuticle with the base coat. Tommy pushed a bottle of polish remover and a box of Q-tips across the table to me.

"What?" I asked.

"A breakthrough. You said you had one the last time I saw you here."

"Oh right." It seemed so long ago that I figured out Annabel had been a foster kid. I'd had so many revelations since that one. "Actually, yeah. Practically daily."

Tommy grinned. "You sound like me a year ago."

I finished with the base coat and waved my hands in the air to dry them. "What do you mean?"

"When I first started the program, I think I had an epiphany every other day." She gave a small shrug. "Eventually the epiphanies just become part of your life. Like, every day there's something new to learn."

"But—is that a good thing or a bad thing?" I wondered out loud. A pit weighed in my stomach. I learned something new every day too…but it was knowledge I didn't want.

Tommy scrunched her face up and thought about it for minute. "I don't know. I guess it just depends on what you do with the new information. You can choose to hate it or embrace it."

I thought about all the nights I'd lain awake, angry at Annabel for stealing my memories. Where had that anger gotten me the next morning? Nowhere. "Maybe you're right."

"Eh, what the hell do I know? I'm just trying to figure it out along with everyone else." She laughed at herself, a deep sound that came right from her gut.

I reached for the polish. "Hey, let me see your hands," Tommy said. Before I could say anything, she took my hands in her own. Instead of examining my nails, she peered at my palms.

"Huh." She traced one of her purple nails from the base of my knuckles to my wrist. It tickled; a giggle escaped me. She glanced up. "Sorry, hon. I've just never seen a heartline like yours."

My breath caught. "A what?"

"A heartline. See?" She held my palm up so I could see, and ran her finger along one of the grooves in my palm. "This is your heartline. Most people's come to about here." She jabbed her fingertip lightly into the middle of my palm. "But yours keeps going. Not only that, but you have a break in it."

I leaned in to see where she indicated. There was a tiny space near the top of my heartline, and then it continued on, all the way down to the base of my wrist. "What does that mean?"

"Major transformation," she said. "Like a rebirth."

A shiver ran through me.

"Anyway, I think that's what it is. I read a book about palmistry a few months ago, and ever since then, I can't stop looking at people's palms." Tommy gave my hands a little shake. "It's amazing how different everyone's are," she continued. "Like snowflakes."

"Have you ever seen someone with a really short heartline?" I asked.

Tommy froze and her fingers went cold against mine. She looked up at me from under her eyelashes, which had grown wet.

"Yes," she whispered. "Annabel's."

An icy chill swept over me. "I'm sorry," I said softly. "I shouldn't have asked."

Tommy shook her head. She blinked fast and a tear escaped down her cheek. She brushed it away and looked out the window for a long time. A quiet stillness stretched between us. I finished painting my nails in the silence. When I laid my palms flat on the table, she looked back at me, her eyes bright but dry.

I didn't want to upset her, but there were so few people I could talk to about Annabel. "Do you mind if I ask you something? About Annabel?"

"Are you *trying* to ruin my mascara?"

"It's okay. We don't have to talk about her."

"No." Tommy rested her chin in her hand, her nails brilliant against her skin. "Talking about people who've died keeps them alive. Besides, you need stuff for your article, right? Ask me anything."

Anything? There was so much… I remembered the story Nate had told me about Annabel the first time I'd come to All Saints on my own. Even though I knew that story from Annabel's memories, I still loved hearing it from Nate's point of view. "Tell me about the last time you saw her."

Tommy sat up straighter. "I remember it exactly. I think about it a lot. It was the middle of January. She came in here late, which was weird because she was usually out working at that time of night."

"Why do you think she wasn't that night?" My brain was whirring and clicking. Middle of January was close to the time she had been killed.

Tommy shook her head. "I don't know. We don't ask those kinds of questions, you know? But she was upset about something. And I guess I figured that's why she wasn't out working, and I didn't want to pry." Tommy's eyes looked sad. "I probably should've pried. But with Annabel, you just never knew how deep you could dig. She was touchy."

"How did you know she was upset?"

Tommy raised her forefinger to her mouth and was about to bite it when she spotted her fresh polish and snatched it away. "She had this really strange expression on her face. Like freaking *Sophie's Choice*."

"Like *what*?" In the files of Annabel's memories, this one was not there. I needed Tommy to remember it for me.

"You've never seen that movie?" I shook my head. "Oh, you really should. Meryl Streep won an Oscar for it. Anyway, the Nazis make Meryl—Sophie—choose which of her kids to send to the gas chamber. And she gets this look on her face. And that's the look Annabel had that night."

I wanted to shake, to shudder, but I was frozen. "Why? Why did she look like that?"

Tommy's deep eyes narrowed. "Because I think she did have a Sophie's Choice to make. She's looking at me like that for a long time, and I'm just quiet, waiting for her to talk. Finally she asks, 'What do you think is more important, your own life or the greater good?' And I said that depends. If you think you're gonna go on to do great things, then your own life. But if you think you're gonna spend the rest of your days turning tricks on the street, then the greater good." Shadows darkened Tommy's face. "That's why I think about it all time. That was a really mean thing to say, given what she did."

I reached across the table and touched her hand, careful of our fresh paint jobs. "Annabel didn't kill herself, Tommy. She was murdered."

She stared at me, her face streaked with shock. "What? How—who?"

"I don't know, but I'm going to find out." I narrowed my eyes at her. "Did she say anything else after that?"

Tommy shook her head. "I couldn't get another word out of her. But her face—that expression went away. Like she knew what she had to do and she was okay with it."

I swallowed, trying to digest this, trying to fit this piece with the parts of the puzzle I already had.

The basement door opened. Nate came in with a gust of wind behind him. "Hey," he said when he saw me and Tommy. "It's my two favorite girls."

"Oh stop it," Tommy said. She pointed a long purple-polished finger at me. "You've got yourself a good one there."

"Yeah, I know," I murmured, my cheeks warm. I got up and met Nate halfway across the room. He caught me in his arms, tilted my head back with his hand, and gave me a long kiss. Behind us, Tommy whistled. I smiled against Nate's mouth, wanting to draw out the moment before I had to pull away, before the real world intruded.

When he finally drew back, Nate asked, "Are you up for a little walk?"

"Sure." I tucked myself close to his side. "Where are we going?"

"Our strawberry friend hasn't shown up for the last few days," Nate said. "I think we should go looking for her."

"I think you're right," I said. "She's the only connection we know of to the Warehouse."

"We'll start at the halfway house I sent her to. It's not far from here. Bye, Tommy!" he called over his shoulder as we headed to the door.

I turned. "Thanks for the palm reading. And the conversation."

Tommy waved her hand. "Anytime. And don't mess up your manicure!" she called after me just before the door closed behind us.

Nate looked down at me as we walked across the lawn. I wished I could live in the softness of his gaze. "Any more lost memories?"

I hunched my shoulders. "If there are, I wouldn't know I'd lost them. Would I?"

"I guess not." He squeezed my hand. "We'll figure it out."

By his side, with his warmth emanating through me, I truly believed we would. We were an army of two, and we would win. How could we not?

After walking for about ten minutes, Nate nudged me to a halt. "This is it."

I looked up at the old Victorian. It had been painted a cheery yellow with red shutters. Nate and I climbed the steps and rang the bell. A middle-aged woman with long braids opened the door. "Nate! How nice to see you." She gave him a hug. "How are things at All Saints?"

"Fine," Nate said. "This is my friend, Georgie."

"Lovely to meet you." She hugged me too. She was all soft and squishy, like a well-loved teddy bear. "I'm Susan. Come on in."

"Susan's a hugger," Nate muttered to me as we followed her into the house. She jangled as she walked, and beneath her flowing skirt, I glimpsed ankle bracelets with little bells on them just above her clogs. She took us right back into the kitchen and poured two cups of dark tea without asking if we wanted any. When she handed me mine, I looked into it and sniffed.

"It's ginger root," Susan said. "I make it myself."

Of course she did. I took a sip. It tasted like a cozy cabin in wintertime, like the Christmas memory I had forgotten. I buried my face in its steam and took a long drink.

Susan smiled. "So. What brings you here?"

Nate set his mug down on the counter. "Wanted to know what happened to the girl I sent over here a couple of weeks ago. We haven't seen her since then."

"Yeah, she was here." Susan sighed. "A few days ago, I caught her shooting up in the bathroom."

"Shit." Nate gritted his teeth and leaned back against the counter. "Do you know where she went?"

Susan shook her head. I looked back and forth between her and Nate. "Wait—you just kicked her out? No second chance or anything?"

The corner of Susan's mouth turned up in a sad half-smile. "I had to. Our policy is one strike, you're out. I've learned that if you give second chances, addicts will take a third, fourth, fifth, and so on." Her eyes rested on my face. "I don't enable here. They have to *want* help. She didn't."

"But she could be in real trouble."

"It's not Susan's fault," Nate said to me. "She did what she could."

Except turn her out on the street again, I wanted to say, but I kept my mouth shut. It was obvious that Susan was a caring person and knew a lot more about this than I did. But this girl was our one lead to the Warehouse, and now we had no idea where she was.

"Why are you looking for her?"

Nate glanced at me. "We think her pimp might be involved in something big. Trying to figure out what that is."

Susan leaned her head back and took in a deep breath. "Nate, don't go poking around. Leave it to the authorities. If you know something, tell the police and let them handle it."

Nate grimaced. "The police are useless. Trust me, I know." He shot me a quick glance and I knew he was thinking of Sarah.

"Besides, I've already gone to them and nothing's been done," I added.

"It takes time," Susan insisted. She sighed. "Look, whatever you do, just be careful. Promise?"

"Promise," Nate said. We finished our tea and Susan walked us to the door. As we passed the living room, I saw a group of girls clustered around the coffee table, flipping through a magazine. They were laughing and jostling, calling each other names in playful, teasing voices. I looked back through the house. Whatever Susan's philosophy was, it was working for some of these girls.

As we stepped onto the porch, I turned back to Susan. "What's her name? She never told us."

Susan leaned against the door frame, hugging herself against the cold. "She said we should call her Kitty. Like Kitty Cat.

But I'm sure that wasn't her real name and she wasn't here long enough for me to get it." She gave us a last smile and shut the door softly behind us.

"How are we going to find her now?" I asked as we headed back to All Saints.

"I don't know." Nate ran his hand through his hair. "She could be anywhere."

"Hang on." I stopped and pressed my fingers to my temple, as if to keep the idea from leaping out of my head. "She used to stay with Annabel at 826 Emiline, didn't she? Maybe she'd go back there. We know there's no one living there yet."

Nate pointed at me. "You are brilliant. Do you know that?"

"Yeah, well. That fancy private school better be good for something."

We changed direction and headed for Emiline Way. Our footsteps thudded through my heart, each step drawing closer to the place where Annabel had breathed her last breath. Part of me didn't want to see it again, but part of me craved being in a place that still held so much of her. Graying snowdrifts lined the sidewalk that led up to the steps of number 826. I tilted my head back and looked up to the balcony, still identifiable by a lone piece of yellow police tape that snapped in the wind. "I think there's a light on."

Nate tried the door but it was locked, and there was no Harvey to let us in. A Post-it note that read "Out of order" was taped over the buzzer. "Great." I stepped back and looked up again. "Should we yell?"

When Nate didn't answer, I lowered my gaze and squinted at him. He was hunched over the door. I had to peer over his shoulder to see what he was doing. "Are you seriously picking that lock?"

"Sometimes it helps to have friends in low places." Nate fiddled with the lock until I heard the latch click. He tugged the handle and the door swung open. "Not something they teach at that fancy school, do they?"

"Definitely not."

We headed toward the stairs. The building felt more alive than it had when we'd been here with Harvey. I could smell food cooking and hear televisions humming behind closed doors. From somewhere deep inside the concrete walls, a baby cried.

At the top of the third landing, I rested against the wall to catch my breath. Nate shifted from foot to foot, glancing up at the rest of the stairs we had to climb. My chest eased and I pushed away from the wall. From down below, I heard the front door open and close a few moments later, as though more than one person had come in. I leaned over the rail and looked down.

Two black-coated figures were coming up, their footsteps heavy and fast. My throat went dry. The one in front, with the shiny pointy-toed boots...he raised his head, and for one frozen instant, our eyes met.

I launched away from the rail and grabbed Nate's hand. "Come on, come on," I panted. The footsteps below grew louder and faster. I pushed myself against my heart, ignoring the burn that seared through my ribs. "He—saw—us—"

"Who?"

"Jules."

At the name, Nate's hand tightened on mine, so hard I thought my fingers would break. He dragged me up the stairs. We didn't stop on Annabel's floor. Halfway up to the next landing, I tugged his arm. "Kitty—"

"We can't." Nate's face was white, his brow pinched. "Remember what Char said." He ran up to the next landing, pulling me behind him. Below, I heard the footsteps stop. I risked a glance over the rail and saw Jules looking up and down the corridor.

"We can't just leave her," I whispered into Nate's ear.

He swallowed hard. His face was half in shadow, but I could see that his insides were being torn in two by the expression on his face. He pulled me close to him. "But I can't let him hurt you either," he murmured.

I buried my face in his shoulder. Down below, I heard knocking. A door creaked open. Kitty's voice floated up, an undercurrent of fear running through it. "Hey, Jules."

"Hey, baby girl," Jules purred. "Got a special job for you."

"Okay." Her voice shook. "Just—just let me change."

"Sure. Let Marco help you." I heard footsteps shuffle and peeked over the rail. Marco slapped Kitty's ass and followed her into the apartment. The door clicked shut behind them. Opposite the apartment, a shadow crept up the stairs toward us. I didn't need to see his actual figure to know it was Jules.

"Move, move," I whispered and pushed Nate deeper into the darkened hallway. It was fortunate that Harvey was such a terrible landlord. The lights here had burned out, giving us cover.

Jules's boots clicked on the concrete steps as he ascended. Nate pulled me all the way to the end of the hall. In the same moment that we realized it was a dead end, Jules appeared at the other end of the hallway. Nate shoved me behind him as the three of us faced each other. I felt like a gunslinger in the old Wild West, only I'd forgotten my gun while the other guy had brought two.

"Hey!" Jules yelled, his voice bouncing off the walls. "I thought I told you what would happen if I saw you again."

"We just wanted to make sure Kitty was okay," Nate said. I stepped out from behind him, but Nate crossed one arm in front of me to keep me from going further. His arm was a strong, solid barrier. If he was afraid, he wasn't showing it.

"You think I don't take care of my girls?" Jules stepped forward, each footfall a warning. "Is that why you sent her to that halfway house?"

"She looked sick," Nate said. "I sent her there to make sure she got a decent meal or two."

"I'll say if she's sick or not. I'll be the one who feeds her." Another step toward us. "Not some hippie crackpot dishing her a bunch of lies about me. I'll be the one who says where she goes and where she doesn't." Step, step. "What you don't seem to understand—no matter how many times I tell you—is that Kitty is mine. Anything she does, she does because *I* tell her to."

I clutched Nate's arm, my fingers digging into the thick wool of his coat. "What about Annabel? Did you take care of her too?"

Jules shook his head, clucking his tongue. "Poor Annabel. It's a shame what happened to her."

"What you did to her, you mean," I said. Nate pushed back at me, a warning to keep my mouth shut.

"I did what I had to do." Jules shrugged. "It's really too bad. Annabel was one of my best. But you know"—he cocked his head—"in my line of business, girls come and girls go. They are all replaceable."

"Like slaves," I growled. "That's all they are to you, aren't they? Not human beings who deserve a better chance at life—"

"Georgie." This time the warning in Nate's voice was clear. Even Jules heard it and laughed.

"Listen to your boyfriend," he said. He smoothed the front of his cashmere coat. "You know, it's lucky for you that I make it a rule not to do my own dirty work, and my boy is busy downstairs with Kitty. Otherwise I'd take some pleasure in seeing him dirty up this hallway with you." He pointed his finger at us like a gun and mimed pulling the trigger once, twice. I shuddered. Jules laughed, a deep, cold sound that echoed off the walls.

One of the apartment doors swung open and a beefy guy with no neck stepped into the hallway. "Hey, some of us work the night shift," he snapped. "Take your little party someplace else." He slammed the door shut with a loud bang.

"Gladly." Jules eyed us. "How about you two leave first? Because if Marco sees you when he's done…well, I just can't be responsible for his actions."

Nate grabbed my arm and propelled me down the hall. But when we passed Jules, Nate ground to a halt and stared at him for a long breath. "You know," Nate said, his voice low, "one of these days, your empire is going to come crumbling down."

"And when it does," I said, "I'm going to dance in the ashes."

Jules leaned in close to my face. "I think you'll dance for me long before that," he whispered and kissed the tip of my nose.

I jerked back, a scream forming in the back of my throat, but Nate dragged me to the stairs before I could let it out. "Don't, don't," he muttered as we ran down each flight. My nose burned worse than the pain in my scar. I wanted to cut it off, get rid of anything that Jules had touched…

We burst out into the night. The sharpness of the air cut through me and I breathed in deeply. Nate pointed to the curb, where Jules's black SUV sat idling, and motioned for us to get around the side of the building.

"Call Manny," he said once we were out of sight of the car. "Tell him to pick us up around the corner."

"What? Why?"

Nate's jaw tightened. "Because I'd bet good money that Jules is taking Kitty to the Warehouse, and I want to follow them."

CHAPTER TWENTY-FOUR

Manny wound us through dark streets where the lights had long ago burned out, past deserted sidewalks and boarded-up buildings. Ahead of us, the taillights of the SUV shone red in the distance. "You have to keep two car lengths behind," Manny said.

"Not your first follow job, eh?" Nate said.

Manny snorted. "You'd be surprised how many wives don't trust their husbands. Usually with good reason."

I was quiet, my hand tucked tight into Nate's. The Catch reverberated in my chest, filling my ears with its strange *hiccup-hush* sound. Once again, I knew without a doubt that I was walking in Annabel's footsteps, that this was part of the road she'd traveled. I fixed my gaze out the front window and breathed deeply. My gut wrung itself out with dread and fear, twisting and turning…

The SUV turned a corner. Manny slowed, waited several beats, then turned after it. The images churned up to the surface. I gasped and doubled over. "Georgie!" Nate caught my shoulders but it was too late. I had already collapsed into the darkness of Annabel's memory.

It's pitch black, a room with no windows, and girls huddle together on the cold concrete wall. In that close dark, I smell fear. It fills my nostrils, chokes my throat, and worms its way down into my lungs. It's not just the other girls' fear. It's my own.

Every several minutes, the door opens and Jules takes another girl outside. One by one, the number of girls in the room dwindles. None of the girls who are left ask where the other ones went. They'll know soon enough.

I wrap my hands around my throat, trying to strangle the fear. I want out of here…but I have to know where the girls are being taken.

The door opens again and I have my chance. Just before it slams shut, I slide my shoe in. "Don't," warns one of the other girls, her voice shaky. "He'll kill you."

"He'll kill me anyway eventually," I mutter and peek out the door. A long, dimly lit hallway stretches on for miles. There are no windows. The air is muffled, as though a limited amount has been pumped into the space. It's a dungeon, the polar opposite of my kingdom by the sea…

I pick up my shoe and take the other one off. Holding them in my hands, I ease out into the hall, my back to the wall. Shadows zigzag from the floor to the ceiling. When I'm far enough away from the room, I break into a run.

My lungs burn, my breath heavy white puffs in the cold air. I reach the end of the hall and turn right. The labyrinth of hallways is shrouded in darkness. I'm blind as I race through, but it doesn't matter as long as I'm not in that room…

The floor slants upward and I'm rising, rising, rising. I come to a fork and stop, panting. My breath is so loud, it echoes off the walls.

Down to the right, the sound of raised voices, hoots and hollers, and loud rap music roils back to me. Whatever is going on with the girls, that's where it's happening. My feet stumble away from those sounds, my gut twisting in fear and revulsion. I want to know…and deep down I do know…but I force myself back.

I turn left and flee toward a pinprick of red light that shines from the end of the long corridor. The light grows and grows into an exit sign, like a lighthouse to a lost ship. I fling open the door and tumble onto the street. Light snow dusts the ground. I bend double, panting for the icy night air to fill my lungs…my side cramping… I straighten…

My eyes flew open. Nate's face peered into mine, his eyes a question. Manny said, "They've stopped."

I replied, "We're here."

CHAPTER TWENTY-FIVE

From the outside, it looked like nothing. An abandoned warehouse, windows with duct-taped cracks, and a dim light above the front door that flickered on and off. If I'd thought Annabel's old corner at the cemetery was the loneliest place I'd ever been, I was wrong. The Warehouse was far more desolate, a place whose gray brick walls told people to stay away.

Nate and I stood across the street, tucked into the corner, our eyes glued to the door with the flickering light. Even in its on-and-off dimness, I could make out a figure standing guard.

We went around the block and into the alley that ran behind the Warehouse. Darkness stretched the length of it, the only light from the pale moon. We picked our way down, skirting around broken crates and crushed boxes and piles of rotting wood. Every sound made us freeze, every movement deliberate and careful. Nate guided me around a tall stack of crates. As I passed them, my coat snagged on a loose splinter of wood. Without thinking, I tugged it free. The crates teetered and fell with a deafening clatter against the cobblestones.

We froze, Nate's hand so tight on mine that my bones crunched. He shoved me into the shadows against a slanted set of basement doors that rose up out of the concrete. We huddled into the little corner it provided, hidden from the side of the alley where the guarded door was, but if the guard walked down far enough, we would be seen.

A long beam of light swept over the alley, followed by footsteps. Closer and closer…the bright light fell on the toppled crates… I shrank into Nate, trying to make myself smaller.

Tires squealed on the street at the end of the alley, a heavy bass beat reverberating over the cobblestones. The guard swore and turned, and the light bobbed away from us as he jogged down to meet the car. I crawled on my hands and knees as far out as I dared. A silver Porsche idled at the curb. The guard opened the passenger side and three men in suits stepped out. They headed for the door, followed by the guard.

"Come on," Nate whispered and pulled me back to the basement doors. A rusted padlock held them together with a chain. Nate pulled out his little lockpick. It didn't take long for the padlock to give way. I fixed my gaze on the end of the alley as Nate bent over the doors and unlooped the rest of the chain with quick, sure fingers.

The doors groaned in protest as he pried them open wide enough for us to slip through. I activated the flashlight feature on my phone and pointed it down into the darkness below the door. A set of rickety stairs descended from the alley above. They shook when I placed my foot on the top step, so I crab-crawled down them on my hands and feet. Nate closed the door above our heads and followed me to the floor.

The flashlight gave off a small circle of light as I swept it around the room. Empty, dusty boxes were piled in the corners, and cobwebs hugged the rafters. Finally the flashlight illuminated another set of stairs on the other side of the basement. We headed up them. At the top, Nate cracked the door open an inch and peeked through.

"Clear," he whispered. We slid into the hallway.

My stomach bottomed out. It was exactly the same as Annabel's memory. Remembering it through her eyes felt so much safer. Now that I was here in the same place, standing where she had stood, the fear crept into my bones and lodged there. Eerie orange light glowed along the hall. I looked up and down the hall, trying to reconcile the reality with memory. In a breath-stopping moment, they synched up. I gripped Nate's hand.

"This way," I mouthed with a jerk of my head.

We tiptoed down one hallway, but when we turned the corner in the direction I knew we had to go, a guard stood at the opposite end. He faced away from us and I could see the dark outline of a gun tucked into the back of his pants. I backed up into Nate. His heart beat rapid-fire against my spine. We eased out of sight and back into the labyrinth of hallways. Two other corridors led us to dead ends. The third had another guard and we whipped away just before he turned.

I stopped in a pool of shadows and sank back inside Annabel's memory, where I heard the distant music pounding out a heavy beat from a room down the hall. My eyes flew open. I could hear it now, pulsating from the center of where the three guards stood. We had to get to the room with the music.

I pulled Nate back up the corridor. He tugged my arm, pointing to where the guard stood. I set my jaw and lifted one shoulder. He pressed his mouth into a thin line and followed me down the corridor.

At the end, the guard stood, looking out a set of double doors with paned glass windows. The music was so close that it shook the walls here. I squinted. Ten feet from us and ten feet behind the guard was another hallway. Streaks of light slanted onto the floor from that hall. The room was there.

I dropped to my hands and knees and crawled, hugging the wall where shadows lingered. Nate followed so close behind that his fingers brushed my legs. My eyes were fixed on the guard, the fear that he would turn around so thick inside me that I almost choked. When we got closer, I saw the white cord dangling from his ears. He was listening to an iPod. I tried to exhale but tension wrapped my body like a steel corset.

Music ripped through the air, screaming wails that didn't even sound like lyrics. The rhythm thumped into my rib cage, but my heart beat double time, tightening the corset, dripping steel into my veins until my blood was cold. We crept toward the room where the music blared and turned another corner so the guard was out of sight. Icy sweat trickled down my neck.

The room was a large square in the middle of the hallway and made entirely of floor-to-ceiling windows. Blinds were drawn down over the glass, but they were old and there was a peephole where they had bent. I brought my eye right up to the glass.

Strobe lights flashed inside so that the room looked fractured.

Images came to me in pieces, tiny fragments of the whole terrifying picture. Girls chained against the wall, men lining up to take their turn. *Flash.* Two girls in the center of the room, their bodies slick with sweat or oil or both, something long and thin connecting them as they thrust back and forth. *Flash.* A riot of men cheering them on, like a boxing match. *Flash.* My eyes didn't know where to look, didn't know how to stop looking, didn't know how to unsee what I was seeing. *Flash.* One of the girls in the center pulled away, cowering on all fours. *Flash.* Jules's steel-tipped boot smashed into her face. She scrambled back to the other girl, and they started fucking each other again. The men roared their approval.

Flash.

I sank against the glass, my eyes still fixed on the room, but the picture had come together now, one horrifying film that I couldn't look away from. Jules was running an underground sex club, a place where these men—these monsters—could see their sick fantasies brought to life. My vision swam around the room at the faces of the girls. God, they were my age or younger… They should be at home doing their homework and gossiping with their friends. Any of these girls could be my friend or classmate or neighbor…or me. The Warehouse was my own backyard.

Against the wall, one of the men finished with a chained girl. Just before another man took his place, the girl faced forward and her hair tumbled down around her shoulders. The light glinted off the red strands, and though her eyes slid in and out of focus—she was high on something—there was no mistaking her.

Kitty.

My body revolted. Nate felt me shudder and dragged me away from the window to a door on the opposite wall. He wrenched it open and pushed me inside. It was a closet filled with cleaning supplies. I twisted toward a bucket and vomited inside.

Nate closed the door, shutting us in darkness. His hands were gentle on my back and neck as I retched. "It's okay," he murmured. "You'll be okay."

But I wouldn't be, not ever. I would never be able to erase those images from my mind, no matter how long I lived. They would be with me forever. After a minute, I sat back on my knees, my breath ragged.

"How?" I panted. "How can those men do that?"

"As long as men can't get what they want legally, they'll pay for it."

I wiped my mouth with the back of my hand. "It's disgusting. No, it's beyond disgusting. There's not even a word for it." I leaned into Nate. When my breathing returned to normal, I pulled myself to my feet. "We have to get out of here. We have to go back to the police and get them here." I cracked open the door. The music and flashing light brought back a wave of nausea. I took a deep breath and shoved it down. Puking again wouldn't help us get out of this place.

We skirted around the room, past the guard on his iPod, and into a darkened hallway. As we turned toward the basement we'd come up through, I froze. "The girls," I whispered. "There might be other girls."

Nate took a deep breath and nodded. "Where?"

"Follow me." We fled down the long corridor that sloped downward, my eyes half-closed as I sank back into Annabel's memory. "This way," I panted, and we turned right. The doors on either side, the flickering fluorescent lights… I skidded to a stop in front of the room that I knew held the girls. The knob was locked. Nate jimmied it open with his pick.

As soon as the door swung open, that thick smell of fear washed over me. I coughed, clinging to the wall to stay upright. The dim light from the hall bled into the dark room, but it took a moment for my eyes to adjust.

"What the hell are *you* doing here?"

I blinked. Char stood in the middle of the room. Her hands were planted on her hips, but I could see the whites of her eyes. Only one other girl occupied the room, cowering in the corner. Her wide eyes were like jewels set into her pale face, and her gaze was fixed on the hallway behind us as though the devil himself would appear there any moment. Which he would.

I stepped into the room. "You have to come with us. *Now.*"

The other girl scrabbled to her feet but Char didn't move. "If you stay here, you will be taken to another room and gang-raped," I said. "Or you can come with us. Your choice." I turned to go. I could feel Char's resistance behind me, but we had no time. I grabbed Nate's hand and raced up the hallway. When I glanced back, both girls were just behind me, carrying their stiletto shoes in their hands.

I led them up, up, up the endless hallway as we traced our path back to the basement. The bass line of the music throbbed, following us, tracking us. My heart pounded in answer but nothing was loud enough to drown out the images I'd seen in that room.

We skidded around a corner, but halfway down the hall, I slid to a stop. "Wrong way, wrong way," I muttered. Everything looked the same. I pressed my hand to my heart, trying to see again the path that Annabel had taken out. My mind blurred, a mess of pictures and thoughts. I pointed in the direction I thought was right. But as soon as we'd turned another corner, I knew I was wrong.

A guard stood at the end of the hall, playing a game on his phone. He looked up as the four of us froze in plain view. "Hey!" he shouted and plunged his hand into his holster.

My scar seared as we fled back the way we came. This time, we took the right turn toward the basement. Footsteps pounded on the floors, filled my ears… They were right on top of us…they had to be… I risked a glance over my shoulder. The hall behind us was empty except for the shouts and sounds spilling into it from elsewhere in the labyrinth.

We pressed forward as the shouts grew louder behind us. Pain ached across my chest… My ribs were about to crack open… We slammed around another corner. At the end of the long hallway, the metal door that led to the basement shimmered, a beacon across a deadly sea. The guards' shouts bounced off the walls all around us; it was impossible to tell how close or far away they were.

Nate shoved me in front of him as we ran full-out toward the door. He fumbled with the knob, trying to grasp the slippery metal. "Hurry, hurry," I whispered, whirling to face the long hall behind us. The guards' voices were getting closer…their footfalls faster… As I spun back to Nate, something red gleamed on the wall next to the door. Like it was meant for me to find, I pulled the fire alarm tab.

Bells clanged out in every direction, ear-splitting, shattering the distant music into a thousand pieces. Nate flung open the door just as the ceiling opened up and water rained down. He propelled me into the basement. I stumbled into the darkness, followed by the two girls. Nate shut and bolted the door. His hair dripping, he crept up the stairs to the doors that led to the street. The girls and I huddled at the bottom of the steps, a steady *plip-plop-plop* falling from our soaked clothes onto the floor. Nate creaked the door open an inch and froze. Even from the sliver of space, I could hear the voices just outside in the alley.

Char pushed past me. I grabbed her arm and pointed to the street and the voices that rolled back to us. She wrenched out of my grasp and stalked up the stairs. Nate turned and blocked her, his eyes furious. She backed down to my level. I faced her, my jaw tight. A sliver of light fell across her face and I swallowed. It was not defiance that filled her; it was terror. I reached out and touched her arm. She flinched and hunched herself next to the other girl.

The voices from outside slithered in through the door. I crawled up the stairs next to Nate and listened.

"—asswipe pulled the fire alarm." Jules's voice was jittery and annoyed, his smooth confidence shredded apart. "Let's make this quick."

"Quicker the better." A deeper, quieter voice. "People have been sniffing around. If anyone finds out—"

Something about the voice was familiar, but whether it was from Annabel's mind or my own, I wasn't sure.

"No one will." The sound of paper, rustling and crackling. "This oughta make up for it."

I eased away from Nate and peeked through the slice of open door. They were right next to us, separated by half the doorway. I was at such an angle that I couldn't see their faces; all I could see were their hands. Jules's manicured nails were unmistakable as he handed the other man a thick envelope. I caught a glimpse of the thick wad of bills at one corner where the envelope wasn't fully closed.

The other man took the envelope and tucked the money in his pocket. "Nice doing business with you." As he shook Jules's hand, a flash of silver winked. A claddagh ring set with a green stone inside the center heart. *A Christmas gift from his daughter…*

Lowell.

CHAPTER TWENTY-SIX

Detective Curt Lowell, whom my father had clapped on the back, who had been eating cupcakes at our house just days ago, who had toasted me along with the rest of our friends. I doubled over, panting, my whole body aching. Michelle's father. I didn't like her...but I didn't want her to have a monster for a father either. *Why, why, why?* The question tumbled around my brain as I fought for breath. Had Annabel reported Jules to him? Had he warned Jules to clean the place before the police got there? And had he then eliminated the threat?

I straightened. It all made sense. Detective Lowell...had killed Annabel.

"Georgie. Georgie? Are you okay?"

I straightened. No, I was not okay. Our beloved neighborhood cop, a man my family had been friends with for years, was helping Jules. He was protecting an illegal sex club that exploited underage girls. He might as well have been inside, raping them himself. I gripped Nate's arm. "We have to get out of here."

Nate raised the door another inch. From the other side of the basement, the sound of the sprinklers stopped. "They're gone. Let's go," Nate said. I pushed the girls ahead of me and followed them up the stairs. The cold slapped me when I emerged onto the sidewalk behind Char, freezing my skin.

The silver Porsche still idled at the end of the alley. We pressed ourselves against the wall and inched down the opposite way. My breath stuck in my throat. This was the way Jules and Lowell had gone. I swallowed, bile stuck to the back of my throat. Every time I thought of Lowell, a fresh wave of nausea passed over me.

Nate peered around the corner and darted back. "He's out there."

"Who?"

"Jules." But it wasn't Nate that spoke. It was Char. Her body shook against me, her face a grotesque mask of fear. "He's everywhere," she breathed.

Nate took off his coat and put it around Char's bare shoulders. I peeked around the corner. Lowell was nowhere to be seen, but Jules was halfway down the block, talking on his cell. Far enough that he couldn't hear us, but close enough that if we tried to make a break for it, he would definitely see us. I glanced at the other end of the alley. The Porsche was still there and, presumably, so was the guard at that door. I leaned back against the wall, the bricks pricking me through my damp sweater, and pulled out my phone.

The dispatcher made me repeat my request three times. Whether it was because I was talking so low or because she couldn't believe where I was, I wasn't sure. But ten minutes later, a gleam of headlights swept over the desolate street and turned into the alley.

"What the fuck?" Jules's voice shattered the quiet. I shoved the girls into the cab as his footsteps came running. Nate and I dove in at the same time and slammed the doors.

"He's gonna kill us!" the other girl shrieked.

"Where the hell am I going?" Manny yelled.

"Just *go!*" Nate shouted and pulled the girl close to him to calm her down. The tires squealed as Manny peeled away. He swerved around the Porsche as the other guard darted toward us, but we were already barreling down the street before he could stop us.

I scrambled upright in the seat and watched through the rear windshield as Jules emerged from the alley, his face twisted with rage as he kept running after us. A street lamp lit up the window with a bright yellow glow. I only had time to see Jules's eyes widen before Manny stepped on the gas and we were out of sight.

I twisted forward and slid down the seat.

"It's okay," Nate said. "We're okay."

I closed my eyes and tried to breathe. "No, we're not. He saw me."

We took the girls to Susan's halfway house. As we climbed the steps to the door, my phone buzzed. "Where are you?" my mom demanded.

Good thing she hadn't called me fifteen minutes before. "I'm out with Nate," I told her.

"Georgie—"

"I'll be home by eleven." I cut her off and barely had time to hear her reluctant acquiescence before I hung up. When Nate and I were back in the cab, I turned to him. "It was Lowell."

"Who?"

"Lowell. The cop who was at our Valentine's Day party. He's the one Jules was paying off."

Nate's eyes widened. "How do you—"

"His ring. I saw his ring. He had it on at the party…said it was a Christmas present from his daughter…" I bent over. "God, I'm going to be sick again."

Manny jerked around but Nate waved him off. "She's fine. You're fine," he told me. "Just breathe. Are you sure?"

"Yes. I recognized his voice too." I straightened. "Jesus, Nate, I went right to him. I told him I thought Annabel had been murdered, and he's probably the one who killed her."

"We don't know that. It could've been Jules." The cab slowed at a red light.

"How long before he and Jules put two and two together and come after me?"

Nate hugged me close to him. "We don't know that they will. But…" He didn't have to finish the sentence; I knew how it ended. *Not long.*

I curled into him, breathing in his warm, safe scent. "I want to come home with you."

Nate closed his eyes. "Georgie…" His voice was hoarse, low. "You know I want that," he muttered into my hair. "God, how

I want that." He kissed my forehead. "But you should go home. You'll be safer there."

I didn't feel safe anywhere, except the circle of his arms. He held me tighter as the car trudged up the hill toward my house. We stopped at the curb and Nate walked me to the front door. "Stay put until you hear from me," he said as we climbed the stoop. "I mean it, Georgie. Don't go anywhere tomorrow until I come get you."

I tilted my head up to him. "Are you seriously telling me what to do? What are we, married in the fifties?"

"Geor—gie." Nate drew my name out with a sigh. "I just want you to be safe."

"I can't sit around and do nothing."

Nate pulled me hard against him, buried his face in my hair. "And I can't lose your heart. Not twice."

I turned my head so that my lips met the side of his neck. I covered his face with kisses until he cupped my cheeks in his hands and brought my mouth to his. All the fear and tension balled up inside me flowed away, as though its only cure was Nate. I clung to him, more alive in his arms than I'd ever felt in my life. His hands on me were strong and sweetly possessive. I could read the same thing I had in me, that it could so easily have been me in that room, that as long as these monsters roamed free, no girl was safe, that we could've died in the Warehouse tonight. But we didn't. We were here, alive…and together.

With a groan, Nate drew back. "You should go inside. It's cold and your hair is still damp." He ran his hand over my head, down the side of my throat.

"I could never be cold with you," I whispered. His eyes deepened until they were the darkest of blues, and he kissed me for a long moment that still ended too soon.

"I'll call you in the morning," he said as I unlocked the door. "Get some sleep."

I smiled at him and watched as he jogged back to the cab. My smile faded as they drove away. There was no way I would get any sleep tonight.

Mom sat in the living room, waiting up for me with an open book in her lap. "Did you have a good time tonight?"

I slid to a stop in the hallway and stared at her. "What?"

"With Nate. Did you two have a good time?"

"Oh. Um, yes." I backed up a couple of steps. "I'm tired, though. Good night."

Upstairs, I stood in the middle of my darkened room, my fingers itching for action, for time to pass quicker, for a resolution to this story that I had been written into against my will. Without Nate, I felt rudderless, unmoored. The air felt close and tight; with one small gust, it would drown me.

I crossed to the window and pushed it open. Cold tumbled in, and the distant salt sea tinged my nose. Another snowfall sat right on the edge of the night, waiting. The brass music stand against the wall gleamed orange as a streak of street light fell on it. I did have a tether, an anchor, one that had sustained me long before I ever met Nate. I grabbed my oboe and curled up on my window seat, cradling the three pieces of the instrument in my arms. What I had seen tonight had filled me with a chill that I wasn't sure would ever leave me, and my oboe was the only thing besides Nate that could keep me warm.

About two in the morning, the snow finally spilled from the sky. I watched it pile up around the tree trunks and fire hydrants and mailboxes. The light from the street lamp grew dim as the veil of snow thickened around it. My vision blurred, but it was hard to know whether it was my own eyes or the snow was smudging the world. For a moment, my eyelids shuttered…and when I blinked them open again, the scene before me was not the street outside my house.

Snow covers the wrought-iron balcony, the metal slippery beneath my feet… Hands grope at me, pushing me against the bars over and over… I try to fight them off, but they counter every blow. They come at me faster and harder…a voice repeating "Youcan'tyoucan'tyoucan't" over and over… The iron creaks, the rusted bars soft beneath my body weight. I cling to the rail, fingers grappling to hang on, to stay alive, but it gives way and then there is nothing but cold air against my face, nothing but my own scream in my ears…

I jerked upright. The cold, snowy night before me was my own. But Annabel's memory blurred with my own, the edges of our boundaries so frayed and overlapped by now that I didn't know where hers ended and mine began. What I did know was that I'd just seen the night of her death.

I pressed the pieces of my oboe to my chest, and the smooth rosewood calmed my heart. Why was the memory so frustratingly vague? All the other ones had been so vivid, so clear. This one was fuzzy, like a faded photograph. Was it because it was the last? Was Annabel reluctant to relinquish her hold on me, her last tenuous thread to life?

Wind gusted in through the window and blew a stack of papers off my desk. I set my oboe down with gentle tenderness and slid off the window seat. Pages torn from notebooks and articles clipped from newspapers for my current events class danced in the air. I circled the room after them, the papers as busy as my brain. What more did Annabel want from me? What did I need to do to get her final memory?

I settled all the papers back on the desk. Before I could weigh them down, one escaped. It fluttered to the floor and landed at my foot. I stepped on it to keep it still. In the slanted light from street lamps, Kitty's face smiled up at me. My blood froze. I picked the paper up and held it in front of my face. On one side was the article I had cut out, but I had never noticed what was on the reverse side—a quarter-page notice that jumped off the page.

Have you seen this girl?

Katherine Phelps

Missing since August 10, 2013

Anyone with any information, please call 1-800-Missing

Below it was the picture of Kitty. Her eyes bored into me. She looked younger, fatter, healthier…happier. Before she'd met Jules. Before she'd met Annabel. As I stared at the notice, the image of Kitty chained to the wall in the Warehouse slowly fed itself into my vision, blacking out the paper.

This had been Annabel's choice, the one that had haunted her the night she'd seen Tommy at All Saints. Knowing that girls like Kitty were being bought and sold on the street, could she live her life with blinders on and not do anything about it? Or could she take the blinders off and help the girls, even if that meant risking her life?

I knew what Annabel's answer had been, because it had cost her her life. She'd escaped the Warehouse with the knowledge of what went on there, and she'd been killed for it.

But who had killed her? Was it Jules, or someone else? Why wouldn't she give me the missing piece?

The answer came as a swift punch to my gut. I dropped to the floor, the paper gripped in my hand. How could I not have known this? How could I have felt everything else in her heart except this?

Annabel didn't care about justice for herself. Figuring out who killed her wasn't what she wanted me to do. She wanted me to stop what was happening in the Warehouse. She wanted me to finish what she'd started.

God, even dead, she was a better person than me.

All I cared about was getting my life back. And all Annabel cared about was getting back someone else's life, a life she would never have.

CHAPTER TWENTY-SEVEN

I didn't wait for Nate to call me. I didn't wait for my parents to wake up. As soon as the sun was up, I was at the curb, waiting for Manny to pick me up. I told him I was sorry that he'd become my personal chauffeur, sort of. He said it was okay because if it was his own daughter who kept going on these crazy escapades, he'd want her to have someone like him looking after her. I sank low in the backseat and stared out the window. My brain had stopped working, stopped weighing each choice and each step. I was moving on instinct now, following the heart, guided by what I knew Annabel needed me to do.

Save the girls. And to do that, I had to recover the memory of her death.

Something deep inside me knew what that would cost me, but I couldn't face that. I had to believe that she would accept something else as my sacrifice. I had to believe that she wasn't cruel, like Nate said, and that once I did what she asked, she would reward me.

Manny said nothing when we rolled to a stop outside 826 Emiline Way once again. He just raised an eyebrow. I patted his shoulder. "Wait for me."

"You got it, sweetheart."

The front door gaped open. I took that as a sign and slipped inside. Snow drifted into the entryway behind me. I needed to be on the balcony again. I had recovered all the memories leading up to this; surely being in the place where she died would give me the last one. My footsteps echoed in the dark stairwell. When I finally got to Annabel's apartment, I pushed the door open. The darkness inside the apartment was tangible. I could still feel her in here, the air thick with her presence. She was no longer an echo. She had become a ghost.

Bits of police tape still stuck out from the snow on the balcony. The metal creaked with my weight. The fearlessness that I'd felt the last time I'd been out here was gone. In its place was terror, but whether it was mine or hers, I didn't know.

My knees buckled and I sank down, the cold, snowy iron bleeding through my jeans. I could feel her struggle in my heart, how she had fought for her life here, how in those last moments she had wanted—*so much*—to live. In those moments, nothing else mattered. It wrapped me like a cloak, her fierce will to survive. That will was all that had kept her alive during those long hours of lying in the snow on the ground so far below. Long enough for someone to find her so that she could give me her heart.

I pulled my gloves off and pressed my bare hands to my chest. No matter how messed up everything else was, at the root of it all was the fact that she had given me her life. She had died so I could live. I lowered my head until it touched my knees. The truth shuddered through me. She had sacrificed everything. All she was asking for was an even trade.

"No," I whispered, hugging myself tight. "Anything but that. It's not fair."

But it is, the Catch answered, threading through my veins. Tears froze on my cheeks. "Just tell me," I begged. "Just tell me, and I'll finish it. But don't take *that* from me. Please."

Wind whipped over the balcony. A spare bit of police tape broke away and spiraled into the air, drifting down to the ground below, to where Annabel had lain for hours, her life draining away. "If you take this from me, I'll die too," I told her. The Catch crescendoed, louder than a symphony. "Fine," I said, getting to my feet. "Forget it. I'm done. I'm not giving that up, and you can't make me."

Snow drifted down from the floor above, dappling my shoulders. I paused at the door back into the apartment. Why wasn't she making me? Why wasn't she just giving me the memory and taking what she wanted in return? Why was this one different?

As if in answer, the image of Tommy flooded into my mind. I clutched the flimsy door frame. Of course. She had made a choice too, her Sophie's Choice. And that was what she was asking of me. She wanted me to choose, to want this, to know what was right in my heart and give myself up willingly. I sagged back down to the balcony. What the hell kind of choice was this, though? Keep the most important part of myself, and let Annabel's killer go free. Let the Warehouse keep running. Let the girls be forever enslaved to Jules.

Or sacrifice that part of me that kept me Georgie, and it would all come to an end.

Well, fuck.

I almost laughed out loud. It was absurd. Only a complete asshole would choose the former. And yet…I put my fist to my mouth. A month ago, before all this had happened, I probably would've made that choice. I'd lived my life with blinders on, Juilliard or bust, safe inside my Brookline bubble. Having Annabel's heart had removed those blinders and opened my eyes to the world around me.

Yes, there was ugliness, but there was also beauty. There was giving a bag of food to the homeless woman on the corner, even though you were starving yourself. There was sharing your precious strawberries with a lonely, lost girl who had nothing else to look forward to. There was being friends with another survivor like you who told it to you like it was. *If you think you're gonna go on to do great things, then your own life,* Tommy had said. *But if you think you're gonna spend the rest of your days turning tricks on the street, then the greater good.*

And there was Nate.

Playing for the New York Phil wasn't exactly turning tricks on the street, but I'd realized there was good that was greater than that dream. I straightened, my back pressed up against the door frame. I wanted to make a different mark on the world now. Something that reverberated through many people, not just me.

I got to my feet again, this time sure and steady, and went back into the apartment. "Okay," I said to the empty room. "Okay, I'm ready."

My body shook; I wasn't ready, not really, to lose that part of myself. What would my life look like without it? What would tether me to myself in its absence? I took one deep breath, two, three, four, trying to make myself willing. "It's okay," I said to Annabel, for I could feel her inside me and all around in the air in the room. "I accept it."

But still the memory of who killed her did not come.

I put my hands flat over my heart and moved them in slow circles. *Sukha*. Sweetness. With each breath, I called up Annabel's memories, in reverse order. The balcony. *Breathe*. The Warehouse. *Breathe*. The Sutton house. *Breathe*. Strawberry shortcake… My jaw clenched, the breath caught in my teeth. All the other memories were signposts along the path to find her killer. What the hell did strawberries have to do with anything?

And with one devastating click, the very first piece of the puzzle that I'd gotten fell into place.

-^v-

I made Manny drop me off around the corner from Nate's. I didn't want him to be responsible if anything happened in his cab, and I didn't want Nate to see me pull up. I paid Manny and sent him on his way.

I rang Nate's buzzer and listened to his footsteps in the hall. When he opened the door, his face crumpled with relief. "Jesus, where have you been? Why do you have a phone if you don't answer it?"

My heart twisted. I was about to make him a thousand times

more worried, but there was nothing I could do about it. His brows scrunched together at the empty container I held up in front of him. I hadn't cheaped out. If I was going down, I was going whole hog. Organic strawberries from Whole Foods, imported from California, $8.99 for a pint. God, they were good. In seventeen years, I'd never known what I was missing. It was like summer on my tongue, like endless days at the beach and long nights spent gazing up at the stars.

In my other hand, I held up the EpiPen I always carried in my backpack.

"Straight into my thigh and push hard," I told Nate just before my throat started to close up.

CHAPTER TWENTY-EIGHT

Every year for as long as I could remember, my father brought me to his office on Take Your Daughter to Work Day. When I was little, he'd let me color or read or do puzzles on his office floor. As I got older, though, he'd let me audit classes, listening to lectures on great literature, Renaissance painters, or neurology.

A couple of years ago, he'd taken me to the lecture of a visiting philosopher who had opened the dialogue with one simple question. "When are you happiest?"

Later, after the lecture, over lobsters at Legal Seafood, my dad had asked me the same question. "When are you happiest, Georgie?"

And I answered without hesitation. "Any time I'm holding my oboe."

The moment the adrenaline shot through my veins, I knew my happiest was gone. I didn't need to be reminded that I'd forgotten it. I knew, to the marrow of my bones and the bottom of my soul, that it was lost. If you were to place an oboe in my hands at that very moment, I would not remember how to play it.

—∿—

"Georgie. Georgie!"

I swam to the surface, pulled by Nate's voice. It was the only lifeline I had left. My eyelids fluttered open. "I know—"

"How could you do that?"

Nate's face came into sharp focus. His eyes flashed, his skin mottled red and white. He cradled me in his arms, but I could feel the tension in his body. I breathed deeply and slowly as the adrenaline worked its way through me. Somewhere inside me, a deep well of grief for what I had just lost threatened to bubble over. I shoved it down; I didn't have time to mourn.

Nate reached into his pocket. "I'm calling an ambulance."

"No."

"The instructions say seek immediate medical attention. I'm calling—"

"No," I managed again. The effort of talking ached. "I had to."

"You had to? You *had* to put your life in danger?" Now that things were clearer, I saw pinpricks of tears at the corner of his eyes. "What the hell were you thinking?"

"It was…a trigger." I struggled to sit up. Nate didn't help. His breath was very short, in and out of his nostrils. "She needed me…to be…close to death…like she was…that night."

"No." Nate pulled himself away from me and sat straight-backed against the stairs. It was only then that I realized we were in his hallway, just outside his apartment. The light from the chandelier winked above us. "She did not need you to do anything. You did not need to put your life at risk."

"How is this…any different than…the Warehouse?"

"You didn't know what we would find in the Warehouse," Nate snapped. "This is completely different. You willingly ate something you knew could kill you." His lips were so white that they almost disappeared into the rest of his face. "Do you have any idea what that was like? Holding your life in my hands?"

"I'm so sorry… I–I didn't think of that." I reached out to touch him but he swatted my hand away, hard.

"You should have!" His voice bounced off the walls. "This isn't just about you, Georgie! I'm involved too!"

"I know that—"

"No, I don't think you do." He dropped his volume, low but razor sharp. "You think you're the only one affected by this. You think you're the only one whose life is on the line. Well, you're not." He shifted up a stair and pressed his hands over his face. "Every girl I have ever loved has been broken by this world. Sarah. Annabel." He peered at me through his fingers. "*You.*"

"I have not been broken—"

"Georgie, I was holding you in my arms and you weren't breathing and I couldn't get a pulse—"

"That was the memory, not the allergy," I cried. "I was in Annabel's memory…unconscious…"

"But I didn't know that!" Nate yelled. "All I knew was that you were dead in my arms and I was responsible!"

"You weren't—"

"And all I could think," Nate said over me, "was *God*, I've failed this heart twice."

I looked at the floor. "I'm sorry. But I had to. I thought—"

"You *didn't think*, period!"

He was right, of course. I'd stopped thinking that morning, letting the heart move me from point to point to point. I lifted my gaze to him, but he wouldn't look at me. He stared at the wall over my head, his chest heaving. I knew he had every right to be mad, but I couldn't wait for forgiveness. "I need my phone," I said, looking around. "Where's my bag?"

Finally, he looked at me. Without taking his eyes off me, he reached behind him and pulled my bag into his lap. I held my hand out for it. He dug into the front pocket and drew out my phone. I scrambled up to my knees to grab it. He stood up so fast that I fell forward onto my elbows.

"Don't call an ambulance!" But by the time I got to him, he had already dialed.

"Liv? Hi, it's Nate." I breathed out. It was just my mom he'd called. "Yes, she's with me." He climbed higher and higher up the staircase. My legs quivered, betraying me as I tried to catch him. "Georgie had an allergic reaction. She's fine. I used her EpiPen. I'm sending her home in a cab. If she's not there in fifteen minutes, call me." He gave my mother his number and hung up.

"Why the hell did you do that?" I shouted. I grabbed the railing and hauled myself upright. "We do not have time for this!"

He threw the phone at my feet. It bounced off the thick carpet and landed a few stairs below. "You're done. I'll take it from here. You're done risking your life for this."

"I don't have a choice!" I climbed up to the step just below him and hit him hard in the chest. He flinched but didn't move.

"Do you have any idea how much I've lost?" My voice cracked as I thought of my oboe, sitting forlornly in its corner at home. "What I need to get back? I thought you understood that!"

Nate leveled his gaze at me. "I do. But I can't lose this heart again. I thought *you* understood *that*."

He pushed past me on the stairs and picked up my phone. I listened to him call Manny to pick me up. At least he wasn't calling an ambulance. My body was still shaking, but whether it was from the allergy or the adrenaline or the memory, I didn't know. It could've been all three, jumbled up inside me. We didn't speak as we waited for the cab or as he put me into it once it pulled up to the curb. "Are you coming with me?"

"I'm too mad to even look at you right now," he snapped. "Take her home," he told Manny and slammed the door.

I watched him walk back to the house, his shoulders slumping more and more with each step he took. I knew the toll this was taking on him, because I was paying the same toll.

But as Manny turned the corner, I tore myself away from the window. My body might be jumbled, but my mind was not. "Change of plans," I said.

In the rearview mirror, Manny raised his eyebrow. I tightened my jaw. Nate was wrong. I wasn't done. And he couldn't take it from here because I knew something he didn't.

The identity of Annabel's killer.

CHAPTER TWENTY-NINE

As the cab careened through winding streets, I dug into my bag and pulled out the little card I'd shoved into the front pocket all those days ago. My fingers shook as I dialed. There was a gaping hole in my heart for what I had just lost, and I didn't know which was worse, the oboe or Nate. I now had nothing to anchor me. I closed my eyes and took a deep breath. That wasn't true.

I had myself.

The phone on the other end rang and rang. *Please be there*, I begged silently. At last, on the sixth ring, she answered. "Detective Russell."

"It's Georgie Kendrick," I said. "I have more information for you." I told her everything I knew and where to meet me.

"We're on our way. Stay in the car, Georgie," she warned me. "These people are dangerous."

"Okay," I said, knowing as the word left my mouth that it was a lie. There was only one person who could finish this, and that was me. No one else had the stake in this that I did.

I hung up with Detective Russell just as Manny screeched to a halt in front of the graceful brownstone. I rocketed out of the backseat. The cops would be here soon, but it was just me and Annabel now, the way it had started.

At the top of the stoop, I saw that the front door stood wide open, almost like Annabel's killer was waiting for me. My heart ricocheted off my ribs, and I pushed up the stairs. By the second landing, pain wrapped my chest but I pressed upward one more flight. I slammed to a halt in front of apartment number three and knocked.

The lock clicked. The knob turned. The door swung open. I stared into the last face Annabel had ever seen. "It...was...you," I gasped.

Michelle's eyes widened. She tried to slam the door, but I caught it against my palm and forced my way in. "What...are you doing here, Georgie?" she asked, her voice high and forced.

"You killed her. You killed Anna Isabel Leeland."

Michelle froze. Late-morning light lengthened her shadow across the floor, elongating her figure. "How—how do you know her name?" she whispered.

"You tried to make her a Jane Doe," I said, "but she didn't stay dead."

"She was going to turn my father in." Michelle's voice tremored like a million little earthquakes. "She was going to take him away from me."

"Do you have any idea what your father is doing?" I stepped further into the apartment and Michelle backed up. I saw her glance at a desk behind her. "Do you know how many lives he's ruined?"

"What about my life?" Michelle edged backward. "My dad is all I have. He's struggled my whole life to give me anything I wanted. That's all he was doing. He did it to pay my tuition…so I could go to school and have a future."

"And all Anna wanted was to help those girls," I said. We were dancing a strange waltz, me stepping forward and her stepping back. "She didn't mean for you to get hurt."

"She didn't care!" Michelle yelled. "She kept saying that I was collateral damage, that there were thousands of girls who would be saved." Her face was hard. "What good is that to me? If my dad goes to jail, I'll have nothing. I'll have no one."

And no one understood that better than Annabel. I felt her pain in my heart, a deep ache of understanding. She knew better than anyone what it was to be alone in the world.

"I couldn't let her," Michelle said. "I couldn't let her take him away from me." She took another step back. "And I can't let you either." She was right up against the desk now. Her hands fumbled with the drawer.

My heart registered the black steel in her hands before my eyes did. I stilled, the barrel of the gun the center of my universe. Nothing else existed. "Michelle. The police are on their way here. I've already told them everything." My lips moved but it sounded like someone else's voice. "If you hurt me, you'll have a lot more to answer for."

Michelle's hands were rock solid, holding the gun steady at my head. "You have no idea what I'm capable of, Georgie."

I felt Annabel's memory again, her desperation to live, her struggle to fend Michelle off. But Michelle's desperation was stronger, her need greater, her hands pushing pushing pushing until Annabel was gone… "I do, actually," I said. "I know exactly what you're capable of."

"How can you possibly?" Down the endless barrel of the gun, Michelle's eyes were pointed and sharp. "You've never had to fight for anything in your whole life, Georgie. You've always had everything handed to you. I've had to claw my way to where I am, over the trust fund babies at Hillcoate—"

"And that gives you an excuse to kill?" Anger bubbled over my fear. "God, you knew, didn't you? You knew what your dad was doing and you let it go because you think you're better than those girls. Who cares if some fourteen-year-old gets raped, as long as you get your tuition paid, right?"

"Shut up!" The gun wavered, just a fraction. I stepped back but she followed, the gun still level with my face. "I didn't know. Not until she made the report. I was at the station, dropping something off for my dad. We overheard her…and I could tell from his face that she was telling the truth…"

"And he went off to warn Jules," I murmured. "And you went after her, to Emiline Way."

"I didn't go there to kill her." Michelle swallowed hard. I shifted oh-so-slowly so that my back was to the front door. Where the hell were the cops? How long ago had I called them? Ten minutes? An hour? Time had ceased to exist.

"I just went there to talk to her," Michelle went on. "To stop her. But she wouldn't give in… I pushed her and she fought back and…and…she went over the balcony." Her eyes slid between sharp and soft. "It happened so fast. I didn't know what to do so

I called my dad and he told me to leave her, to take her identification and make her a Jane Doe..." She snapped her gaze back to me. "If she'd just given in...if she hadn't fought back..."

"She was fighting for her life." The Catch flowed through me, and every emotion that Annabel had felt in those last moments flooded my veins. "She had just as much right to live as you did." I breathed short and shallow. "You treated her exactly the way you think you've been treated by me. You treated her as less-than."

"She *was* less-than!" Michelle's face contorted into an ugly mask. She tilted her head and leveled the gun at my nose. "Why do you—"

She broke off. We heard it in the same moment, footsteps in the hall, pounding up the stairs. Michelle narrowed her eyes at me. I leaped backward and collided with the door frame at the same moment that she lunged forward. The gun fired, a deafening, ear-splitting blast that made us both shriek. The bullet ricocheted off the opposite wall. I flung my arms over my head and crouched down. Michelle stood over me, her eyes wild, the gun still clutched in her white-knuckled grasp.

The footsteps came closer. I peeked through my arms. My heart knew who it was before he appeared. "It's over," Nate said when he reached the landing. Michelle whirled around to face him. "I saw the cops coming down the street when I got here."

I pushed myself up the wall to my feet. "Michelle, don't make it worse for yourself. Just give me the gun. I know it was an accident, that you didn't mean to kill Anna." Nate's intake of breath was audible from where I stood. I'd forgotten that he didn't have the whole story. Michelle and I were the only ones who knew what had happened on the balcony that night. I stretched my hand out to Michelle. "Give yourself up now and it will be easier."

She looked back and forth between me and Nate, the gun moving with her body as she turned. It was so close to my face that the acrid smoke from the shot singed my nostrils.

"What about my dad?" Michelle found my eyes with hers, and the fire in them almost burned me. "Do you really think they'll go easy on him?" I couldn't see anything but her forefinger, resting against the trigger. "He did it all for me." Her voice rose into a keen. "I won't betray him."

"He's already betrayed you by making you a part of this," Nate said.

"No." She shook her head. Her cheeks were splotchy with tears and sweat. "No. I won't let this happen. Not because of some fucking whore that no one gives a shit about."

The Catch slowed my heartbeat. In one instant, I thought of all the people who did care about Annabel, all the people whose lives she had touched. Tommy. Kitty. The homeless woman around the corner from All Saints. Nate. *Me.* "I do. I give a shit about her."

She turned and faced me fully. The hallway, Nate, the world all dropped away. "Why? Why the hell do you care about some dead hooker?"

I reached out and grasped the gun, my hand over hers. I pulled her to me so that the barrel pressed right into my chest, right against my heart. "Because she saved my life," I said. "Because if you hadn't killed her, I would've died."

I only had time to see Michelle's eyes spill over, and then she was on the floor, crumpled in a heap. The gun dropped from her fingers. I kicked it away and knelt beside her. "So in a way," I said, low so that only she could hear, "I owe you my life too."

Michelle stared at me, her face a question. I wanted to tell her that part of me understood, that what she'd done had been out of love for her father, that there were no winners here. But I couldn't make myself say the words, because in the end what she had done was unforgivable.

From three floors below, doors banged open and voices filled the hall. Police officers swarmed up the stairs, led by Detective Russell. She walked over to Michelle and squatted down beside us. "Your dad's in custody," she said, gentle and low like she was comforting a scared kitten. "He tried to protect you, but we knew what had really happened." She put her hand on Michelle's shoulder. Michelle flinched and curled into herself. "You need to come with us now."

One of the officers came over and helped Michelle to her feet before handcuffing her. He walked her downstairs, reading her rights as they descended. I watched them go, the air thick around me. When Russell touched my arm, I jumped.

"I thought I told you to stay in the car," she said, her deep brown eyes flashing at me. "You could've gotten hurt."

"I'm sorry," I said. "But I had to—see it through myself."

She pressed her lips together and nodded. "I get that," she said. "I'd been tracking Detective Lowell ever since that girl—Anna—made that report," she said. "But I'd been doing it on the sly because I knew I wouldn't get approval from the force. It wasn't until you called me this morning that I had solid evidence—and a witness—against him." She glanced at Nate and back at me. "We went to the place you called the Warehouse. We found Jules there, along with enough evidence to bring down his whole operation."

"The girls," I said. "What about the girls?"

She smiled. "They're safe. Thanks to you."

Something inside me broke open. I bent over, shaking with sobs, tears streaming down my face. I would have collapsed, but I felt strong arms come around me and hold me up. Nate. I twisted into him and buried my face in his neck. His hands stroked my hair, my back, my arms, his breath soft on my cheek.

"It's over now," he whispered. "She can rest in peace."

And I knew he was right, and that the thing I'd felt breaking inside me was Annabel, finally letting go of my heart. I'd done what she needed me to do, finished what she had started. I clung to Nate, my raft, my lifeboat, my anchor in this storm… my lifeline.

Russell led me to the living room couch. Another detective took Nate into Michelle's bedroom, and they wrote down our separate statements of what had happened. As I talked, I felt my body settle into itself, everything in its proper place. I hadn't been this comfortable in my own skin since before my surgery. When at last Russell had enough, I was breathing calmly.

Nate emerged from the other room and I stood up. "I'll be in touch," Russell said to me.

"Anything you need," I told her.

"Next time you leave this to the professionals," she added.

"I hope there won't be a next time," I said, and she smiled warmly at me. I followed Nate out of the apartment and down the stairs. More officers swept in with boxes and bags and other evidence-gathering equipment. When we reached the front stoop, a forensic team was on their way in. I watched them disappear into the building and dropped to the top step. The stone was cold beneath me but somehow it felt good. Real. Alive.

Nate sat down next to me. I knocked his knee with my own. "How did you know where I went?"

"Please. Like I trusted you to actually go home," he said, knocking me back. "I got in a cab a minute after you left and followed you." He swallowed. "I never even thought of Michelle."

"Neither did I." I hunched my shoulders. "But I guess people are capable of anything when they're backed into a corner."

Another squad car pulled up to the curb. The passenger door popped open and an officer got out, waving over her shoulder at the driver. As the car rolled away, I saw a familiar figure in the backseat.

It was Jules.

He looked out the window at the same moment I recognized him. Our eyes met. He stared at me and I could almost see the wheels turning in his brain, a furious understanding that I was responsible for him being handcuffed in the backseat of a cop car. I lifted my chin and smiled at him. He turned away and slid down the seat, out of sight, a silent acknowledgment that Nate had been right, and his empire had crumbled. I exhaled long and slow. *The girls were safe.*

The officer jogged up the stairs. Nate and I squished into each other to let her pass. I stayed pressed into Nate even after the officer was out of sight. Nate took my hand and traced his thumb across my palm. "What did you lose to get the memory of her death?" he asked softly.

I looked at our entwined fingers. "I don't know how to play the oboe anymore."

Nate shifted so that he faced me fully. "Oh, Georgie." He squeezed my hand into both of his. "You'll get it back. We solved her murder. Everything should reset, right?"

I had to believe that. I didn't know what my world without the oboe looked like. "I thought it would, but I don't remember anything that I've…forgotten."

"Maybe it's not like a dam," Nate said. "Maybe it's like a small trickle, and you'll remember things little by little."

I leaned into him and rested my head on his shoulder. "I think, maybe, memories become imprinted in our DNA. Like how Annabel's were in her heart. And if that's true, then maybe my memories will come back when they're provoked, like how Annabel's came to me."

Nate raised my hand to his lips and kissed each knuckle. I breathed in the deep, woodsy scent of him. "Besides," I said, "I have a whole lifetime to make new memories."

We stared at each other for a long moment, just drinking each other in. An officer ran down the stairs to grab something from the squad car at the curb but we barely noticed him. Nate took my face in his hands. "I love you, Georgie. I swear I will spend the rest of my life making sure you know that." His breath was sweet and warm on my skin. "Just please don't do anything stupid like eating strawberries ever again."

I laughed and leaned in until our foreheads touched. "I am *so* sorry about that." His lips met mine for a moment, but I pulled away a fraction of a breath. "And I swear I will spend the rest of my life helping you find Sarah."

A choked sound escaped his throat before he dragged me to him and covered my mouth and face and neck with kisses. For a moment, the world fell away; the cops jogging up and down the steps and the cars whizzing by on the streets all disappeared, and it was just us.

Finally, we broke apart and sat in comfortable silence. Nate reached into his pocket and pulled out a brightly colored square something. He handed it to me. "I saw this in Michelle's room," he said. "The detective said I could show it to you before they took it for evidence." It was a coin purse, made of woven cloth in every different color. I looked up at him, my brow creased. "It's Annabel's," he said.

I turned it around and around in my hands. No memory came to me, no flash of insight. I breathed out slowly. I had finished her work, and she had left me to live my life. The heart was well and truly mine now.

I unzipped the purse. Inside were a handful of coins, a five-dollar bill...and an ID card. I drew the card out. It was a state identification card.

People usually looked like zombies in their DMV pictures, but Anna was radiant. She was a completely different person in this picture than the one who haunted her foster-care file. She was laughing, as though someone off-camera had told a joke and snapped the picture the moment she understood the punch line. Her blond hair tumbled over her shoulders, and a rebellious streak of blue decorated a thick swath near her face.

My eyes moved over her name and address and fixed on the little red circle just beneath it. I knew that Nate had seen the red circle too, because his hand tightened on mine and his breath caught.

I gazed up into his face. We smiled at each other through our tears.

Anna Isabel Leeland was an organ donor.

AUTHOR'S NOTE

Trafficked children are hiding in plain sight.

That was the message on the billboard I passed every day while I was writing this novel. Many people think that sex trafficking is something that happens overseas, but sadly it is just as common here in the United States.

The organizations mentioned in this novel are real and making huge strides to help trafficked women get off the streets and get their lives back. FAIR Girls—which stands for Free, Aware, Inspired, Restored—has a chapter in nearly every major metropolitan area. You can get involved at any level, from becoming a sponsor to buying jewelry made by recovering girls. Visit them online at www.fairgirls.org. They also have a crisis hotline at 1-855-900-3247.

The Coalition Against Trafficking in Women is an international organization that seeks to empower women across the planet, from redefining prostitution laws to ending the demand for trafficked women and girls. Find out how you can take action at www.catwinternational.org.

If you are aware of trafficking in your area or are in crisis yourself, call the National Trafficking Hotline at 1-888-373-7888.

Because everyone deserves the chance for a better life.

ACKNOWLEDGMENTS

Although this story explores some dark places, I wrote *The Forgetting* in a state of complete joy, and that is because of the encouragement, love, and generosity of many people.

To my agent, Irene Goodman, who gently pushed me into letting go of the past and moving on to something new. For emailing me over a holiday weekend to tell me that the ending had made her cry, and for believing in this story from day one.

To my original acquiring editor, Leah Hultenschmidt, for giving this book a chance. A huge heap of thanks to my current editor, Aubrey Poole, for taking the book on with such enthusiasm and aplomb and for her good-naturedness in the face of my neuroses. To Eileen Carey and Adrienne Krogh for my phenomenal cover. To Kate Prosswimmer, Becca Sage, Rachel Gilmer, Amelia Narigon, and the entire Sourcebooks team for their dedication to this book and to me as an author.

To Becky Ousley at LifeSource for educating me about the organ donation process. To Cynthia Thaik, MD, and her wonderful staff for vetting my research and taking care of my own heart.

To Laura Baker, whose Fearless Writer and Laws of Motion classes were absolutely instrumental in the creation of this novel.

It was in her classes that I grew immensely as a writer and truly learned to trust my instincts.

To Alexandra Billings, a great teacher of art and life, for inspiring the character of Tommy.

To Barb Wexler for always being there for me, both as a writer and a friend. To Linda Gerber, Ginger Calem, and Julie O'Connell for helping me climb out of the pit of despair that preceded this book. Much, much gratitude to Lizzie Andrews, Anne Van, and Will Frank for their constant encouragement and dedication to helping me tell this story. Special thanks to Jen Klein, whose astute notes were essential in getting this book finished. And deep, eternal gratitude to Romina Garber, without whose love and friendship I would be one very sad panda.

To the incredible kid-lit community in Los Angeles and to the Class of 2k14 for surrounding me with so much support.

To the wonderful people of the Republic of Pie in North Hollywood for keeping me fueled with caffeine and sugar, and for creating such a wonderful environment for writers to work in.

To my sister and brother-in-law, Tanya Maggi and David Russell, for believing in me, making me laugh, and telling me all about the hidden quirks of Boston. To my parents, Joe and Dot, for being proud of me even if I hadn't written a book.

To Chris and Emilia. You are my heartlines.

ABOUT THE AUTHOR

Nicole Maggi was born in the suburbs of upstate New York and began writing poems about unicorns and rainbows at a very early age. She detoured into acting, earned a BFA from Emerson College, and moved to NYC where she performed lots of off-off-off-Broadway Shakespeare. After a decade of schlepping groceries on the subway, she and her husband hightailed it to sunny Los Angeles, where they now reside surrounded by fruit trees with their young daughter and two oddball cats. She is also the author of the *Twin Willows Trilogy* (Medallion Press). Visit her at www.nicolemaggi.com.

WATCHED

C.J. Lyons

He can't run, and he can't hide.

Jesse is terrified. For four years a twisted hacker named King has hijacked his computer webcam, collecting incriminating photos and videos that he uses to blackmail Jesse. So far, Jesse's given in to King's ruthless demands in order to protect his family. But now King wants something that's too horrible to contemplate—and if he doesn't get it, he'll kill Jesse's little sister.

Jesse is trapped. King's always watching. There is no escape.

Then hope arrives in a plain manila envelope. Inside is a cell phone and a note: *I can help.*

GONE TOO FAR

Natalie D. Richards

Send me a name. Make someone pay.

Piper Woods can't wait to graduate. To leave high school—and all the annoying cliques—behind. But when she finds a mysterious notebook filled with the sins of her fellow students, Piper's suddenly drowning in their secrets.

And she's not the only one watching...

An anonymous text invites Piper to choose: the cheater, the bully, the shoplifter. The popular kids with their dirty little secrets. And with one text, Piper can make them pay.

But the truth can be dangerous...